CITY OF

Kevin Barry's story collection, *There Are Little Kingdoms*, won the Rooney Prize in 2007. His short fiction has appeared widely on both sides of the Atlantic, most recently in the *New Yorker*. *City of Bohane* is his first novel.

ALSO BY KEVIN BARRY

There Are Little Kingdoms

CITY OF BOHANE

Kevin Barry

JONATHAN CAPE
LONDON

Published by Jonathan Cape 2011

4 6 8 10 9 7 5

The author acknowledges the support of the Arts Council of Ireland

First published in Great Britain in 2011 by
Jonathan Cape
Random House, 20 Vauxhall Bridge Road,
London SW1V 2SA

www.randomhouse.co.uk

Addresses for companies within The Random House Group Limited
can be found at: www.randomhouse.co.uk/offices.htm

The Random House Group Limited Reg. No. 954009

A CIP catalogue record for this book is available from the British Library

ISBN 9780224090575

The Random House Group Limited supports The Forest Stewardship Council
(FSC®), the leading international forest certification organisation. Our books
carrying the FSC label are printed on FSC® certified paper. FSC is the only
forest certification scheme endorsed by the leading environmental organisations,
including Greenpeace. Our paper procurement policy can be found at
www.randomhouse.co.uk/environment

Typeset in Dante MT by Palimpsest Book Production Ltd,
Falkirk, Stirlingshire

Printed and bound in Great Britain by
CPI Group (UK) Ltd, Croydon, CR0 4YY

for Olivia Smith

I
OCTOBER

1

The Nature of the Disturbance

Whatever's wrong with us is coming in off that river. No
argument: the taint of badness on the city's air is a taint off
that river. This is the Bohane river we're talking about. A
blackwater surge, malevolent, it roars in off the Big Nothin'
wastes and the city was spawned by it and was named for
it: city of Bohane.

He walked the docks and breathed in the sweet badness
of the river. It was past midnight on the Bohane front. There
was an evenness to his footfall, a slow calm rhythm of leather
on stone, and the dockside lamps burned in the night-time
a green haze, the light of a sad dream. The water's roar for
Hartnett was as the rushing of his own blood and as he
passed the merchant yards the guard dogs strung out a
sequence of howls all along the front. See the dogs: their
hackles heaped, their yellow eyes livid. We could tell he was
coming by the howling of the dogs.

Polis watched him but from a distance – a pair of hoss
polis watering their piebalds at a trough 'cross in Smoketown.
Polis were fresh from the site of a reefing.

'Ya lampin' him over?' said one. 'Albino motherfucker.'

'Set yer clock by him,' said the other.

Albino, some called him, others knew him as the Long
Fella: he ran the Hartnett Fancy.

He cut off from the dockside and walked on into the Back

Trace, the infamous Bohane Trace, a most evil labyrinth, an unknowable web of streets. He had that Back Trace look to him: a dapper buck in a natty-boy Crombie, the Crombie draped all casual-like over the shoulders of a pale grey Eyetie suit, mohair. Mouth of teeth on him like a vandalised grave-yard but we all have our crosses. It was a pair of hand-stitched Portuguese boots that slapped his footfall, and the stress that fell, the emphasis, was money.

Hard-got the riches – oh the stories that we told out in Bohane about Logan Hartnett.

Dank little squares of the Trace opened out suddenly, like gasps, and Logan passed through. All sorts of quarehawks lingered Trace-deep in the small hours. They looked down as he passed, they examined their toes and their sacks of tawny wine – you wouldn't make eye contact with the Long Fella if you could help it. Strange, but we had a fear of him and a pride in him, both. He had a fine hold of himself, as we say in Bohane. He was graceful and erect and he looked neither left nor right but straight out ahead always, with the shoulders thrown back, like a general. He walked the Arab tangle of alleyways and wynds that make up the Trace and there was the slap, the lift, the slap, the lift of Portuguese leather on the backstreet stones.

Yes and Logan was in his element as he made progress through the labyrinth. He feared not the shadows, he knew the fibres of the place, he knew every last twist and lilt of it.

Jenni Ching waited beneath the maytree in the 98er Square.

He approached the girl, and his step was enough: she needn't look up to make the reck. He smiled for her all the same, and it was a wry and long-suffering smile – as though to say: More of it, Jenni? – and he sat on the bench beside. He laid a hand on hers that was tiny, delicate, murderous.

The bench had dead seasons of lovers' names scratched into it.

'Well, girleen?' he said.

'Cunt what been reefed in Smoketown was a Cusack off the Rises,' she said.

'Did he have it coming, Jen?'

'Don't they always, Cusacks?'

Logan shaped his lips thinly in agreement.

'The Cusacks have always been crooked, girl.'

Jenni was seventeen that year but wise beyond it. Careful, she was, and a saucy little ticket in her lowriders and wedge heels, her streaked hair pineappled in a high bun. She took the butt of a stogie from the tit pocket of her white vinyl zip-up, and lit it.

'Get enough on me fuckin' plate now 'cross the foot-bridge, Mr H.'

'I know that.'

'Cusacks gonna sulk up a welt o' vengeance by 'n' by and if yer askin' me, like? A rake o' them tossers bullin' down off the Rises is the las' thing Smoketown need.'

'Cusacks are always great for the old talk, Jenni.'

'More'n talk's what I gots a fear on, H. Is said they gots three flatblocks marked Cusack 'bove on the Rises this las' while an' that's three flatblocks fulla headjobs with a grá on 'em for rowin', y'check me?'

'All too well, Jenni.'

It is fond tradition in Bohane that families from the Northside Rises will butt heads against families from the Back Trace. Logan ran the Trace, he was Back Trace blood-and-bone, and his was the most ferocious power in the city that

5

year. But here were the Cusacks building strength and gumption on the Rises.

'What's the swerve we gonna throw, Logan?'

There was a canniness to Jenni. It was bred into her – the Chings were old Smoketown stock. Smoketown was hoors, herb, fetish parlours, grog pits, needle alleys, dream salons and Chinese restaurants. Smoketown was the other side of the footbridge from the Back Trace, yonder across the Bohane river, and it was the Hartnett Fancy had the runnings of Smoketown also. But the Cusacks were shaping for it.

'I'd say we keep things moving quite swiftly against them, Jenni-sweet.'

'Coz they gonna come on down anyways, like?'

'Oh there's no doubt to it, girl. They're going to come down barkin'. May as well force them to a quick move.'

She considered the tactic.

'Afore they's full prepped for a gack off us, y'mean? Play on they pride, like. What the Fancy's yelpin'? Ya gonna take an eye for an eye, Cuse, or y'any bit o' spunk at all, like?'

Logan smiled.

'You're an exceptional child, Jenni Ching.'

She winced at the compliment.

'Pretty to say so, H. O' course the Cusacks shouldn't be causin' the likes a us no grief in the first place, y'check? Just a bunch o' Rises scuts is all they is an' they gettin' so brave an' lippy, like? Sendin' runners into S'town? Why's it they's gettin' so brave all of a sudden is what we should be askin'.'

'Meaning precisely what, Jenni?'

'Meanin' is they smellin' a weakness, like? They reckonin' you got your mind off the Fancy's dealins?'

'And what else might I have my mind on?'

She turned her cool look to him, Jenni, and let it lock.

'That ain't for my say, Mr Hartnett, sir.'

He rose from the bench, smiling. Not a lick of warmth had entered the girl's hand as long as his had lain on it.

'Y'wan' more Cusacks hurted so?' she said.

He looked back at her but briefly – the look was his word.

'Y'sure 'bout that, H? 'nother winter a blood in Bohane, like?'

A smile, and it was as grey as he could will it.

'Ah sure it'll make the long old nights fly past.'

Logan Hartnett was minded to keep the Ching girl close. In a small city so homicidal you needed to watch out on all sides. He moved on through the gloom of the Back Trace. The streets of old tenements are tight, steep-sided, ill-lit, and the high bluffs of the city give the Trace a closed-in feel. Our city is built along a run of these bluffs that bank and canyon the Bohane river. The streets tumble down to the river, it is a black and swift-moving rush at the base of almost every street, as black as the bog waters that feed it, and a couple of miles downstream the river rounds the last of the bluffs and there enters the murmurous ocean. The ocean is not directly seen from the city, but at all times there is the ozone rumour of its proximity, a rasp on the air, like a hoarseness. It is all of it as bleak as only the West of Ireland can be.

The Fancy boss Hartnett turned down a particular alleyway, flicked the cut of a glance over his shoulder – so careful – then slipped into a particular doorway. He pressed three times on a brass bell, paused, and pressed on it twice more. He noted a spider abseil from the top of the door's frame, enjoyed its measured, shelving fall, thought it was late enough in the year for that fella, being October, the city all brown-mooded. There was a scurry of movement within,

7

the peephole's cover was slid and filled with the bead of a pupil, the brief startle of it, the lock clacked, unclicked, and the red metal door was slid creaking – *kaaarrrink!* – along its runners. They'd want greasing, thought Logan, as Tommie the Keep was revealed: a wee hairy-chested turnip of a man. He bowed once and whispered his reverence.

'Thought it'd be yourself, Mr Hartnett. Goin' be the hour, like.'

'They say routine is a next-door neighbour of madness, Tommie.'

'They say lots o' things, Mr Hartnett.'

He lit his pale smile for the Keep. He stepped inside, pushed the door firmly back along its runners, it clacked shut behind – *kraaank!* – and the men trailed down a narrow passageway; its vivid red walls sweated like disco walls, and the building was indeed once just that but had long since been converted.

Long gone in Bohane the days of the discos.

'And how's your lady wife keepin', Mr H?'

'She's extremely well, Tommie, and why shouldn't she be?'

A tautness at once had gripped the 'bino's smile and terrified the Keep. Made him wonder, too.

'I was only askin', Mr H.'

'Well, thank you so much for asking, Tommie. I'll be sure to remember you to her.'

Odd, distorted, the glaze that descended for a moment over his eyes, and the passage hooked, turned, and opened to a dimly lit den woozy with low night-time voices.

This was Tommie's Supper Room.

This was the Bohane power haunt.

The edges of the room were lined with red velvet

banquettes. The banquettes seated heavy, jowled lads who were thankful for the low lights of the place. These were the merchants of the city, men with a taste for hair lacquer, hard booze and saturated fats.

'Inebriates and hoor-lickers to a man,' said Logan, and it was loud enough for those who might want to hear.

Across the fine parquet waited an elegant brass-railed bar. Princely Logan marched towards it, and the obsessive polishing of the floor's French blocks was evident in the hump of Tommie the Keep's back as he raced ahead and ducked under his bar hatch. He took his cloth and hurried a fresh shine into the section of the counter where Logan each night sat.

'You've grooves worn into it, Tommie.'

Logan shucked loose from the sleeves of his Crombie and he hung it on a peg set beneath the bar's rail. The handle of his shkelper was visible to all – a mother-of-pearl with markings of Naples blue – and it was tucked into his belt just so, with his jacket hitched on the blade the better for its display. He smoothed down the mohair of the Eyetie suit. He picked at a loose thread. Ran dreamily the tip of a thumb along a superstar cheekbone.

'So is there e'er a bit strange, Tommie?'

There was a startle in the Keep for sure.

'Strange, Mr H?'

Logan with a feint of innocence smiled.

'I said is there e'er a bit of goss around the place, Tommie, no?'

'Ah, just the usual aul' talk, Mr Hartnett.'

'Oh?'

'Who's out for who. Who's fleadhin' who. Who's got what comin'.'

9

Logan leaned across the counter and dropped his voice a note.

'And is there any old talk from outside on Big Nothin', Tommie?'

The Keep knew well what Logan spoke of – the word already was abroad.

'I s'pose you know 'bout that aul' talk?'

'What talk, Tommie, precisely?'

''Bout a certain . . . someone what been seen out there.'

'Say the name, Tommie.'

'Is just talk, Mr Hartnett.'

'Say it.'

'Is just a name, Mr Hartnett.'

'Say it, Tom.'

Keep swivelled a look around the room; his nerves were ripped.

'The Gant Broderick,' he said.

Logan trembled, girlishly, to mock the name, and he drummed his fingertips a fast-snare beat on the countertop.

'First the Cusacks, now the Gant,' he said. 'I must have done something seriously fucking foul in a past life, Tom?'

Tommie the Keep smiled as he sighed.

'Maybe even in this one, Mr H?'

'Oh brave, Tommie. Well done.'

The Keep lightened it as best as he could.

'Is the aul' fear up in yuh, sir?'

'Oh the fear's up in me alright, Tommie.'

The Keep hung his bar cloth on its nail. He whistled a poor attempt at nonchalance. Tommie could not hide from his face the feeling that was current in the room, the leanings and nuance of the talk that swirled there. Logan used him always as a gauge for the city's mood. Bohane could be a tricky read. It has the name of an insular and contrary place, and certainly, we are given to bouts of rage and hilarity, which makes us unpredictable. The Keep tip-tapped on the parquet a nervy set of toes, and he played it jaunty.

'What'd take the cares off yuh, Mr Hartnett?'

Logan considered a moment. He let his eyes ascend to the stoically turning ceiling fan as it chopped the blue smoke of the room.

'Send me out a dozen of your oysters,' he said, 'and an honest measure of the John Jameson.'

The Keep nodded his approval as he set to.

'There ain't no point livin' it small, Mr Hartnett.'

'No, Tommie. We might as well elevate ourselves from the beasts of the fields.'

2

The Gant's Return

That hot defiant screech was the Bohane El train as it took
the last turn onto De Valera Street. The El ran the snakebend
of the street, its boxcar windows a blurring yellow on the
downtown charge. The main drag was deserted this wind-
less a.m. and it was quiet also in the car the Gant was sat
in. There was just a pair of weeping hoors across the aisle
– Norrie girls, by the feline cut of their cheekbones – and
a drunk in greasy Authority overalls down the way. The El
train was customarily sad in this last stretch before dawn –
that much had not changed. The screech of it was a soul's
screech. If you were lying there in the bed, lonesome, and
succumbed to poetical thoughts, that screech would go
through you. It happens that we are often just so in Bohane.
No better men for the poetical thoughts.

The Gant took a slick of sweat off his brow with the back
of a big hand. He had a pair of hands on him the size of
Belfast sinks. The sweat was after coming out on him sudden.
It was hot on the El train – its elderly heaters juddered like
halfwits beneath the slat benches – and the flush of heat
brought to him a charge of feeling, also; the Gant was in a
fever spell this season. The tang of stolen youth seeped up
in his throat with the rasping burn of nausea and on the El
train in yellow light the Gant trembled. But the familiar
streets rushed past as the El train charged, and the pain of

memory without warning gave way to joy – he was back! – and the Gant beamed then, ecstatically, as he sucked at the clammy air, and he listened to the hoors.

'Fuckin' loved dat blatherin' cun' big time!' wailed one.

'Fucker was filth, girl, s'the bone truth of it,' consoled the other. 'Fucker was castin' off all o'er the town, y'check me? Took ya for a gommie lackeen.'

He was back among the city's voices, and it was the rhythm of them that slowed the rush of his thoughts. He had walked in off Big Nothin' through the bogside dark. He had been glad to hop the El train up on the Rises and take the weight off his bones. The Gant was living out on Nothin' again. The Gant was back at last in the Bohane creation.

Down along the boxcar, he saw the Authority man mouth a sadness through his sozzled half-sleep, most likely a woman's name – was she as green and lazy-eyed as the Gant's lost love? – and the city unpeeled, image by image, as the El train screeched along De Valera: a shuttered store, a war hero's plinth, an advert for a gout cure, a gull so ghostly on a lamp post.

Morning was rising against the dim of the street lights and the lights cut just as the El screeched into its dockside terminus. The train locked onto its berth – the rubber jolt of the stoppers meant you were downtown, meant you were in Bohane proper – and the El's diesel tang settled, and died.

He let the hoors and the drunk off ahead of him. The Gant as he disembarked was fleshy and hot-faced but there was no little grace to his big-man stride. A nice roll to his movement – ye sketchin'? The Gant had old-time style.

The station is named Bohane St Francis Xavier, officially, but everyone knows it as the Yella Hall. The Gant sniffed at the evil, undying air of the place as he walked through. Even at a little after six in the morning, the concourse was rudely alive and the throb of its noise was by the moment thickening. Amputee walnut sellers croaked their prices from tragic blankets on the scarred tile floors, their stumps so artfully displayed. The Bohane accent sounded everywhere: flat and harsh along the consonants, sing-song and soupy on the vowels, betimes vaguely Caribbean. An old man bothered a melodeon as he stood on an upturned orange crate and sang a lament for youth's distant love. The crate was stamped Tangier – a route that was open yet – and the old dude had belters of lungs on him, was the Gant's opinion, though he was teetering clearly on Eternity's maw.

Choked back another tear did the Gant: he was big but soft, hard yet gentle.

The early edition of the *Bohane Vindicator* was in but the bundles had as yet to be unwrapped by the kiosk man, who listened, with his eyes closed, to an eerie sonata played on a transistor wireless – at this hour, on Bohane Free Radio, the selector tended towards the classical end of things, and towards melancholy. Nodded his head softly, the kiosk man, as the violins caught.

Oh we'd get medals for soulfulness out the tip end of the peninsula.

The Gant settled into the blur of faces as he passed through. The faces, the voices, the movement – all the signals were coming in clear. They told that he was home again; it was at once painful and beautiful. He looked for her in every woman he passed, in every girl. He bought a package of tabs off a lady of great vintage wrapped in green oilskins: Annie, a perpetual of the scene.

'Three bob . . . tuppence?' she said.

14

There seemed to be that question in it, for sure, as if she recognised him back there beyond the dead years.

'Keep the change for me, darlin',' he said.

A hoarseness to his voice, emotional, and his accent was still quietly of the peninsula even after the long years away. Years of sadness, years of blood – this Gant had his intimate agonies. A snatch of a lost-time song came to him, and beneath his breath he shaped the words:

> 'I was thinkin' today of that beaut-i-ful land,
> That I'll see when the su-un goeth down . . .'

The hoors who had wept on the train were ahead of him now on the concourse. They had gathered themselves. They were painting on bravery from snap-clasp compacts as they walked. The hoors would be bound, he knew, for Smoketown, and its early-morning trade. The Gant watched as they went through the Yella Hall. Ah, look: the quick switching of their bony buttocks beneath the thin silk fabric of their rah-rah skirts, and the way their calves were so finely toned from half their young lives spent on six-inch spike heels. The sight of the girls made him sentimental. He had run stables of hoors himself as a young man. There was a day when it was the Gant had the runnings of Smoketown, a day when the Gant had the runnings of the city entire.

Was said in Bohane the Gant had run it clean.

He stopped for a shot of tarry joe by the main portal of the Yella Hall. It was served expertly by a midget from the back of a licensed joe wagon. He watched, rapt, as the midget tamped the grounds, twisted a fix on the old Gaggia, arranged a tiny white cup to catch the pour. The midget also was familiar – a squashed little brow, a boxer's nose, oddly sensuous lips. Same midget's father, the Gant would have sworn, had the licence on that chrome wagon before him. The generations tag so in Bohane. He drank the joe in one, and shivered. He thanked the midget, and paid him, and he let the coffee's bitter kick arch his eyebrows as he looked out to the first of an October morning. The gulls were going loolah on the dockside stones.

Of course those gulls were never right. That is often said. The sheer derangement in their eyes, and the untranslatable evil of their cawing as they dive-bomb the streets. The gulls of Bohane are one ignorant pack of fuckers. He had missed them terribly. He laughed out loud as the gusts of morning wind flung the birds about the sky but he drew no looks – sure the Yella Hall would be crawling with wall-bangers at the best of times.

The Gant set out towards the Smoketown footbridge. He took a scrap of paper from his pocket and opened it. He read a hand that had not changed with the years – still those big, nervous, childish letters – and its scrawl spelt out these words:

Ho Pee Ching Oh-Kay Koffee Shoppe.

The Gant had a wee girl to meet at this place. It was a good time for such a meeting – he could be lost among the crowd. Smoketown, he knew, would be black at this hour of the morning. The late shifts from the slaughterhouses and the breweries were only now clocking off. Bohane builds sausages and Bohane builds beer. We exist in the high fifties of latitude, after all, the winters are fierce, and we need the inner fire that comes from a meat diet and voluminous drinking. The plants worked all angles of the clock, and after the night shift, it was the custom to make for S'town

16

and a brief revel. In the dawn haze, the brewery lads were dreamy-eyed from hopsfume, while the slaughterhouse boys had been all the silver and shade of night up to their oxters in the corpses of beasts, filling the wagons for the butchers' slabs at the arcade market in the Trace, and the wagons rolled out now across the greasy cobbles, and it was a gorey cargo they hauled:

See the peeled heads of sheep, and the veined fleshy haunches of pigs, and the glistening trays of livers and spleens, skirts and kidneys, lungs and tongues – carnivorous to a fault, we'd ate the whole lot for you out in Bohane.

The Gant hunched his big shoulders against the morning chill. The lowing of condemned beasts sounded in bass tones on the air – our stockyards are laid out along the wharfs. The Gant stepped over a gutter that ran torrentially with fresh blood.

How, he wondered, was a man expected to think civilised thoughts in a city the likes of it?

He kept his head down as he walked. He would try not to romance the place – he had work to do. His was a face where the age receded as often as it surfaced. Sometimes the boy was seen in him; sometimes he might have been a very old man. The Gant's humours were in a rum condition – he was about fit for a bleed of leeches. His moods were too swift on the turn. He was watchful of them. He had a sack of tawny wine on him. He untwisted its cap and took a pull on it for the spurt of life – medicinal. There was pikey blood in the Gant, of course – the name, even, was an old pikey handle – but then there's pikey blood in most of us around this city. Have a sconce at the old gaatch of us – the slope-shouldered carry, the belligerence of the stride, the smoky hazel of our eyes; officer material we are not.

Of course if you were going by the reckoning of pikey bones the Gant was old bones now for certain. He was fifty years to paradise.

And life tumbled on, regardless.

All the red-faced lads went in chortling twos and happy threes in the direction of the footbridge. These gentlemen of Bohane tend to be low-sized and butty: the kind who would be hard to knock over. Smoketown is their bleak heaven. And there is an expression here to describe a man in moral decline:

There is a fella, we say, who's set for the S'town footbridge.

It is a humpback bridge of Big Nothin' limestone. The Gant walked it and reached its high point, above the black river, about the nauseous rush of the Bohane river, and he descended into Smoketown. Each of our districts has a particular feeling, a signature melody, and he felt the dip in the stomach, the swooning of the soul, the off-note, that entrance to this neighbourhood brings.

Smoketown laid out its grogshops, its noodle joints, its tickle-foot parlours. Its dank shebeens and fetish studios. Its shooting galleries, hoor stables, bookmakers. All crowded in on each other in the lean-to streets. The tottering old chimneys were stacked in great deranged happiness against the morning sky. The streets in dawn light thronged with familiar faces. The Gant felt at once as if he had never been gone. He might get a twist yet on the combinations of the place. Maybe the Ching girl would give instruction.

The Gant threw a swift look over the shoulder – in his condition, he was intuitive – and he spotted that the Authority man from the El was on his trail now, and apparently had sobered. His movement, then, was already noted – the Gant scolded himself for being so taken. High innocence! But to be followed was in some ways a relief. It told that his name meant something yet. He stopped on his way and rested against a grogshop wall. He saw the Authority man stop also and peer casually at a stack of mucky postcards.

To throw him off, the Gant entered a hoorshop, and he found there that most familiar of S'town fragrances – the age-old blend of rash-calming ointment, Big Nothin' bush-weed, and penny-ha'penny scent.

He paid the tax to a scowling hoor-ma'am, and he ascended to the upstairs slots, and there on the rush matting he spent time with a Norrie girl, and there was little enough but time spent.

'Are you lonely?' she said to him.

'I'm so lonely I could claw my fuckin' brains out,' he said, and she laughed, and she lit a coochie for him.

'Dinky little number, ain't ya?' he said, dragging deep.

'You wanna have another try off it?' she said.

Later, when he emerged to the street again, the Authority man was no longer to be seen, and the Gant moved on towards the Ho Pee. Now the city shimmered in the new morning's light, its skyline loomed in shadow, but it was what was out and beyond again, the Gant knew, that was the cause and curse of us.

Beyond was Big Nothin'.

3

A Marriage

The Hartnett seat was a Beauvista Gothical, a gaunt and lumbering old pile, all elbows and chimneys. Its thin, tall windows were leaded and reproachful, its gable ivied, the brickwork sharply pointed and with a honeyish tone that emerged fully now against the blue of late morning in October. It sat plumb on a line of po-faced old manses that made a leafy avenue up top of the Beauvista bluff. The Bohane Dacency had built their Beauvista residences to face away from the city – though the money that built them had been bled from it – but Logan Hartnett and his wife were Trace-born, the pair of them, and they kept a rooftop garden on a terrace shaded by the chimney stacks, and it was oriented to look back across the great bowl of the city, as though in nostalgia for it. They spent a whole heap of time up there.

Catch them in the morning light – so elegant and childless.

Logan sat at the wrought-iron table. He wore ox-blood boots laced high, a pair of smoke-grey, pre-creased strides, and thin leather braces worn over a light blue shirt. He was tentative in his private domain. He warmed his hands on a bowl of tea and he regarded his wife.

'You knocking along the town, girl?'

'Why'd you ask?'

'It's a simple question, Macu.'

'You want every minute of my fuckin' day, don't you?'

Macu, from Immaculata, her sidelong glance hot with Iberian flare. Her father was a Portuguese off a fishing boat who got beached up in the creation. He married Trace, and Macu was dark-complected and thin, with a graceful carry of herself, and a sadness bred into her. One of her eyes was halfways turned in to meet the other, but attractively so.

'All I'm asking is are you going to town?'

'Hard to keep away,' she said.

'Who are you seeing in town?'

She wore a sleeveless fox-fur jerkin against the chill of the morning. She worked a pair of secateurs along the wall-creeping rose bushes. She ignored the question. Sometimes, she could knife the very thought of him. Right there between the shoulder blades – feel the sweet bite and settle of an eight-inch Bohane shkelp. But the slyness in him could soften her still.

He winced at the sour herbal bite of the tea. She went to the table and poured a fill for herself. She had let it stew till it was brown as old boots.

'Nettles,' she said.

'Surprise me,' he said. 'Ne'er a chance of a mug of joe in this place, no?'

'Good for the kidneys,' she said.

'Nice to know,' he said.

By the look of him, he had hardly slept but that was not new. An hour or two, no more, and Logan Hartnett was awake to the city again. The black shadows beneath his eyes made for a gauntness but this, he maintained, merely added to his air of wasted elegance. She'd gainsay him but halfways believe it.

'Got to head down soon myself,' he said.

'All fall apart without you,' she said.

Bohane was seasonably calm down there. Always there are these pet days in October, when the impression of peace – at least – lies briefly on the place. Church bells sounded and did not pierce so much as emphasise the drowsiness of the morning.

'Got the fiends to talk to, ain't I?' he said.

'Ain't you always,' she said. 'The Fancy, the Fancy . . .'

It was the last morning there would be heat enough in the sun to sit outside. He sipped at his tea. There was a fresh worry in him, a sliver, from somewhere, and she enjoyed that, and she knew not to try and coax it. It would come soon enough.

'You seein' Girly?'

He sighed.

'Oh, I'll look in, I suppose.'

Girly Hartnett, the mother, was eighty-nine years of age, and in riotous good health. Girly was the greatest rip that ever had walked the Trace but she resided now in a top-floor suite at the Bohane Arms Hotel. The curtains hadn't been drawn back in decades.

'Kisses from me,' she said.

'She'll be waiting on those.'

It was satisfaction to lay a hand on the flatness of her belly. Holding well, she felt, all things considered. Logan, he always said she could crack walnuts between those thighs. He squinted as he watched her. His skin was almost translucent in the morning light. She saw now he was ready to reveal the bother.

'Well,' she said.

He smiled at the read she had of him.

'It's probably just old talk.'

'S'what the place is made of, Logan. What's it particular?'

'They're saying the Gant's back.'

She was not prepared for this.

'Gant Broderick?'

'You know any other Gants?'

She tried to keep an evenness to her voice.

'Who's sayin' this?'

'Word all over. Word in the shebeens. Word on the wynds. Word is, he's back on Nothin'.'

'Shitetalk,' she said.

'In all probability,' he said.

When it was the Gant had the Bohane runnings, it was Macu had been by his side.

Her father had been taken by Bohane – the place has a way; visit just once and you will forever be homesick for it. He opened a bar on De Valera Street. He called it the Café Aliados after a square of his home town. He married, and the girl was born, and she gave a measure of youth back to him, a late radiance in his life. The Aliados became a haunt of the Back Trace Fancy as the years passed. Hard for a Fancy boy not to notice the looker working the joe machine, capping the beer, laying out the saucers of pumpkin seeds. A lick of the tarbrush, surely, but she was Bohane to her bones, Bohane in the sharpness of her glance and the quickness of her tongue.

The Bohane taint was stronger than blood.

'Y'worried?'

He looked at her, open-faced. He shrugged and turned again to the morning sun.

'If there was truth in it,' he said, 'the timing wouldn't be so hot.'

'Why so?'

'Cusacks are playing up and all, girl. Could have random assaults coming at me from all fucking sides.'

'S'the fun o' the life you picked, Logan.'

'That *we* picked. I hear you.'

He would not ask her directly how she felt about the Gant's return. There are areas too tender for even the longest marriage. Twenty-five years the Gant had been gone out of Bohane.

It was the morning when she would bring in the pot plants from the rooftop terrace – the hardwind would soon be up for real. She set to the task as though she had no other cares but she kept her eyes down and hidden from him.

Her mind raced, her heart ached.

The dim greens and blues of her pitcher plants murmured to her in the morning sun.

4

A Powwow on the Rises

Directly across the bowl of the city from Beauvista was the rude expanse of the Northside Rises. The aborigines of Bohane had over the years bred themselves too plentiful for the narrow wynds of the Back Trace – long winters, dark nights, romantic natures – and flatblocks were built on the Rises to house the overflow. Trace and Rises families are almost all blood-related, if you go way back, and this perhaps explains the depth of the bitterness between them.

The Rises is a bleak, forlorn place, and violently windy. Too little has been said, actually, about living in windy places. When a wind blows in such ferocious gusts as the Big Nothin' hardwind, and when it blows forty-nine weeks out of the year, the effect is not physical only but . . . philosophical. It is difficult to keep a firm hold of one's consciousness in such a wind. The mind is walloped from its train of thought by the constant assaults of wind. The result is a skittish, temperamental people with a tendency towards odd turns of logic. Such were (and are) the people of the Northside Rises.

This particular noon, however, as Ol' Boy Mannion loped stylishly along the wasted avenues of the Norrie terrain, an October lull still governed. On either side of the avenues, the flatblocks were arranged in desolate crescent circles, and the odd child leapt from a dead pylon, and dogs roamed in skittish packs, but mostly it was quiet, for the Rises is by its nature a night-time kind of place.

Tipping seventy, Ol' Boy dressed much younger. He wore low-rider strides, high-top boots with the heels clicker'd, a velveteen waistcoat and an old-style yard hat set at a frisky, pimpish angle. Ol' Boy had connections all over the city – he was the Bohane go-between. He was as comfortable sitting for a powwow in the drawing room of a Beauvista manse as he was making a rendezvous at a Rises flatblock. Divil a bit stirred in the Trace that he didn't know about, nor across the Smoketown footbridge. He was on jivey, fist-bumping terms with the suits of the business district – those blithe and lardy boys who worked Endeavour Avenue down in the Bohane New Town – and he could chew the fat equally with the most ignorant of Big Nothin' spud-aters. The Mannion voicebox was an instrument of wonder. It mimicked precisely the tones and cadence of whoever he was speaking to, while retaining always a warm and reassuring note. Hear him on Endeavour and you'd swear he had shares in the Bohane First Commercial; hear him out on Nothin' and you'd swear he was carved from the very bog turf.

Ol' Boy, bluntly, was political.

He approached now a flatblock circle of the Cusack mob. A gent name of Eyes Cusack waited for him on the diseased green space out front of the blocks. He leaned back, brooding, against a burned-out generator shed. He smoked. He acknowledged Ol' Boy by dropping his tab and stomping it, and the men embraced, mannishly and briefly.

'Things with you?' enquired Ol' Boy.

Eyes was named so for good reason. He saw the city through tiny smoking holes set deep in a broad, porridgy face.

'Lad o' mine wearin' an eight-incher of a reef 'cross his chest,' he said. 'Smoketown.'

'Heard there was an incident alright,' said Ol' Boy. 'Will he pull through for you, Eyes?'

'Well, he ain't gonna be botherin' no dancehalls for a time. An' this is a nephew o' mine, Mr Mannion. This a lad o' me brud's, like? I said blood? Me brud's gone loolah on accoun' and his missus gobbin' hoss trankillisers like they's penny fuckin' sweets, y'check me?'

He was bald and stout, Eyes Cusack. He was in a vest top, trackies and boxer boots – the standard uniform of a Rises hardchaw this particular season – and he wore an unfortunate calypso-style moustache.

'I'd say hold off on things for a breath or two, Eyes, if you can at all.'

The Mannion tone was pitched low as a calming strategy but it was no use – Eyes had a want on for vengeance.

'Long Fella ain't had none o' his lads reefed, Mr Mannion. Long Fella wanna know this ain't gonna play out pretty, like.'

Ol' Boy nodded his understanding. He leaned back with Eyes Cusack against the generator shed and together they looked out over the sighing city.

'There's a Calm has held for a good stretch in Bohane,' said Ol' Boy. 'Be a hoor if it went the road, like.'

'I ain't the one been wieldin' a shkelp.'

'Arra, you know it's Hartnett has the Smoketown trade.'

'Sweet Baba Jay pass down the rights, he did?'

Ol' Boy raised his eyes.

'Let's not bring the Sweet Baba into things just yet,' he said.

Eyes pushed off from the shed with a bitter little jolt of the shoulder blades and he turned to face Ol' Boy square.

27

'I wan' word got to him and got to him flashy, y'hear?'

'Go on.'

'Wan' word to him that I got the flatblocks stacked behind me. Got people in every circle. Got the MacNiece, the Kavanagh, the Heaney. Wan' word got to him that reparations need makin'. An innocent lad reefed, like?'

'Ah, Eyes, there ain't gonna be no –'

'Reparations, Mannion! S'my word, like. Tell him a fair shake o' the Smoketown trade'd work for me.'

'And what's he gonna say to me, Eyes?'

'Tell.'

'He's gonna say Eyes Cusack is sending aggravators into Smoketown by design. He's makin' a martyr for the uptown so as to get a hold o' leverage, plain as. He's gonna say you're spoilin' to smash the Calm.'

'Gonna say all that, he is?'

He turned to go, Cusack. Made as though he had a royal hump on. Ol' Boy tried again.

'Eyes? Y'ain't been asked to turn over no face, check? You just got to say your lad was rogue. That he was messin' where he shouldn't have been messin'.'

'That's a lad o' me brud's, Mannion. Me brud in bits an' his missus all drooly an' spooked off the hoss –'

'Ah let it go, Eyes, would you? Let the Calm hold an' we can all get on with our business.'

'Get word to him that I'm willin' to sit and talk a Smoketown divvy.'

'A divvy I would very much doubt, Eyes.'

A hard jab of a forefinger from Cusack, then:

'If he wanna keep the Trace under Hartnett colours? Wanna keep slurpin' his oysters below in Tommie's and keep playin' footsie with his mad fuckin' cross-eyed missus –'

'Leave a man's wife out of it.'

'He wanna keep suckin' the wind? Then he'll sit an' he'll talk a fuckin' divvy on fuckin' Smoketown!'

Ol' Boy shut his eyes – the worst of it was when they got brave.

'So you want me to go down to the 'bino with an out-and-out threat, like?'

A smile from Eyes Cusack the likes of which you wouldn't get off a stoat in a ditch.

'Tell him I got the flatblocks stacked.'

'Don't do this, Eyes.'

'Fella gets back what he gives out, Ol' Boy.'

'That's said, yes.'

'An' maybe he got old stuff comin' back 'n' all, y'sketchin'? Hear tell of a certain man pass this way in the bleaky hour . . .'

'This mornin' gone?'

'Same one. A man what hop an El for the downtown.'

'Who are we talkin' about, Eyes?'

'That's a man the Long Fella wanna watch 'n' all.'

'I said who're we talkin' about, Eyes?'

'Long Fella know him well enough. His missus know him 'n' all.'

Ol' Boy raised softly a palm in warning.

'Plenty o' folk have thought before Hartnett was weakening. Same folk feedin' maggots down the boneyard now.'

'Just get the word out for me, Mannion.'

He nodded, and he let Cusack move along. He watched the old scut hoick a gobber and tug the trackies from the crack of his arse. Shook his head, Ol' Boy – they had no fucking class up on the Northside Rises.

A winter's bother was brewing then. Blood would flow

and soon. But there was the possibility, Ol' Boy realised, that too long and persistent a Calm might be no good for the city.

A place should never for too long go against its nature.

5

The Mendicants at the Aliados

Above De Valera Street the sun climbed and caught on each of the street's high windows and each whited out and was blinded by the glare; each became a brilliant, unseeing eye. The light seemed to atomise the very air of the place. The air was rich, maritime, nutritious. It was as if you could reach up and grab a handful of the stuff. The evil-eyed gulls were antic on the air as they cawed and quarrelled and the street beneath them was thick with afternoon life.

Yes and here they came, all the big-armed women and all the low-sized butty fellas. Here came the sullen Polacks and the Back Trace crones. Here came the natty Africans and the big lunks of bog-spawn polis. Here came the pikey blow-ins and the washed-up Madagascars. Here came the women of the Rises down the 98 Steps to buy tabs and tights and mackerel – of such combinations was life in the flatblock circles sustained. Here came the Endeavour Avenue suits for a sconce at ruder life. The Smoketown tushies were between trick-cycles and had crossed the foot-bridge to take joe and cake in their gossiping covens. The Fancy-boy wannabes swanned about in their finery and tip-tapped a rhythm with their clicker'd heels. De Valera Street was where all converged, was where all trails tangled and knotted, and yes, here came Logan Hartnett in the afternoon swell. He was . . .

Gubernatorial.

Like a searchlight he turned his cold smile as he walked. He picked out all the De Valera Street familiars. He spotted a haggard old dear from the Trace. With one arm she pushed a dog in a pram, with the other she cradled a cauliflower, and he leaned into her as he passed.

'Howya, Maggie, you're breaking hearts, you are?'

Logan in the afternoon was almost sentimental – it was the taint that set him so. When he whispered to his old familiars, it was as if he hadn't seen them for years.

By Henderson the Apotechary:

'How-we-now, Denis? Any news on the quare fella?'

By Meehan's Fish 'n' Game:

'Is that lung giving you any relief, Mrs Kelly?'

By the Auld Triangle:

'When do the bandages come off, Terence?'

His smoke-grey suit, finely cut, set off nicely his dead-house pallor. The walk of him, y'sketch? Regal, yes, quite so, and he made grand progress towards the Café Aliados.

De Valera Street runs its snakebend roll from the base of the Northside Rises all the way down to the river. It separates the Back Trace from the New Town. Its leases are kept cheap and easy – buckshee enterprises appear overnight and fold as quick. There are soothsayers. There are purveyors of goat's blood cures for marital difficulties. There are dark caverns of record stores specialising in ancient calypso 78s – oh we have an old wiggle to the hip in Bohane, if you get us going at all. There are palmists. There are knackers selling combination socket wrench sets. Discount threads are flogged from suitcases mounted on bakers' pallets, there are cages of live poultry, and trinket stores devoted gaudily to the worship of the Sweet Baba

Jay. There are herbalists, and veg stalls, and poolhalls. Such is the life of De Valera Street, and Logan Hartnett at this time had the power over it.

He approached the Aliados. The crowd walked a perceptible curve around its front entrance in due respect. The Aliados opened onto Dev Street from the front and to the Back Trace from a laneway door. It was still, after all these years, the afternoon haunt of the Hartnett Fancy. He ducked down the laneway so as to come in, as always, by the side door – a creature of ritual and set habits. A scatter of his boys lounged inside at the low zinc tables. They smoked, and they drank tiny white cups of joe, and they ate sesame seeds and pumpkin seeds from saucers of thin china delft, and they sighed, languidly, as they leafed through the fashion magazines. The Aliados was no longer in the hands of Macu's people, her father had long since passed, but somehow it had an air of wistfulness for the old country yet: a lingering *saudade*.

Logan took his usual table down back of the long, low-lit cafe. He had a clear view to both doorways from here – he was careful. He hung his jacket on a peg set for the purpose in the wall behind. The wall held photographs, faded, of ancient football teams. These were from the long-gone days when Bohane would have won All-Irelands. The girl – who was as homely as he could reasonably hire, not wanting his boys overly distracted – brought him his joe and a saucer of seeds and he smiled for her sweetly in thanks. The murmuring of talk among the Fancy boys was lower since Logan had entered the place. He smiled now for all of them. He turned the smile around the room; it was a masterpiece of priestly benevolence. Nobody was fooled by it for a minute – Logan's smile was packed with nuance.

Before its arc had fully swung the cafe, its message – its news – had changed many times, just a half-degree of a turn here, a half-degree there, adjusting minutely as it settled on the various parties of the room.

You would be in no doubt whatsoever as to your current standing within the ranks of the Hartnett Fancy.

Logan flicked his coffee cup with a fingernail. It *tinked*, pleasingly. He sighed then in long suffering. Examined his nails – a manicure was overdue. He allowed a particular glaze to settle over his fine-boned features. It was as though to emphasise the extent of a martyr's devotion to the city; his devotion.

Now the custom at the Aliados, afternoons, was that mendicants would take a high stool at the bar and there they would wait precisely in turn for their brief audience with Logan. That an audience could begin was signalled by the slightest raising of the pale Hartnett eyebrows. This afternoon was a quiet one – just a couple of men waited. Logan signalled that the first of them might now approach, and it was the whippet-thin butcher Ger Reid who came dolefully across the tiled floor.

Wary always, Logan would be, of a thin butcher.

Reid was allowed a seat at the table beside him. He sat on the seat's edge, and he had the look, close up, of a man lately a stranger to peace. Logan took his hand, gently, and held it.

'You're not well, butcher?'

'I ain't so hot at all, Mr Hartnett.'

'Ah my poor man.'

The butcher raised his eyes as though the mystery of his misfortune might be read up there on the Aliados's smoke-cured ceiling.

'I've a . . . situation, sir.'

'I know that, Ger.'

'What's goin' on, Mr H, is . . .'

'I know, Ger.'

He held the butcher's hand yet and he stroked it most tenderly. Eye-locked the poor fucker.

'It's your wife, Ger. It's Eileen. She's been getting familiar with Deccie Cantillon, hasn't she?'

Reid scrunched his face against the threat of tears. That his situation was known made the humiliation complete.

'With your own cuz, Ger?'

Reid burped hard on deep, ragged sobs. Logan placed a forearm along the butcher's spindly shoulders. Noted the way the shoulders jerked and fell with the sobs, and he enjoyed the feeling of that.

'S'what I'm dealin' with now, sir!'

'Oh my poor child of the Sweet Baba . . . Oh Deccie Deccie Deccie . . . Deccie's . . . below in the fish market, isn't he? . . . Ah . . . You can never trust a fishmonger, Gerard. That is what I'd always say. That would be my advice to you. It's the way they'd be looking down all day at those dead glistening little eyes. How're they going to come out of that right?'

'I only know of it the last week, Mr Hartnett . . . I haven't slept.'

'Only know of it myself the past fortnight, Gerard.'

A dart of animal pain went through the man. Logan smiled as his forearm felt the shock of the words jolting the butcher's slight frame.

'Oh I have dark fuckin' thoughts, Mr Hartnett!'

'I'd well imagine, Ger. Sure he's lappin' her out an' all, I'd say.'

The butcher now openly wept.

35

'Would you say, Mr Hartnett?'

'He's like a little cat at a saucer of milk, I'd say.'

The butcher stood and bunched his wee, gnarled fists but Logan pulled him gently into the seat again.

'Oh I have dark fuckin' thoughts, sir! Dark!'

Logan placed a finger to his lips and softly blew. Brought his lips then to the butcher's ear.

'Gerard? You're going to stow those thoughts for me. Hear? I'm going to look after this for you, Ger.'

'Are you, Mr H?'

'Yes, Gerard. I'll look after the fishmonger. And you can look after the adulterous cunt you married.'

His pale skin caught the low light of the Aliados – the skeleton of him was palpable, there greyly beneath the skin, the bone machine that was Logan Hartnett – and he smiled his reassurance; it had weight to it in Bohane.

'But we need be very careful, Ger. You hear what I'm saying to you?'

'I do.'

'Think on. If anything unpleasant were to befall a particular cuz, who'd those fat polis fucks come lookin' for?'

'You mean everyone knows, Mr Hartnett?'

'The dogs on the streets, Gerard.'

'Ah Mr Hartnett . . .'

The butcher's head dipped, and tears raced down his cheeks, and they fell towards the zinc top of the table, but Logan one by one caught them as they fell.

'So where'd the polis be sticking the old beak, eh?'

'I hear what you're sayin' to me, Mr Hartnett.'

'It'll be taken care of, Gerard. You can trust me on that. Now go back to your work and put this out of your mind like a good man, d'you hear?'

'It's hard, Mr Hartnett.'

'I know it's hard, Gerard. Or I can imagine so.'

'Thanks, Mr H.'

The butcher rose to go.

'Of course, Ger, you know that I'll be back to you in due course?'

'I know that.'

'Favour done's a favour answered, Gerard.'

'Yes, Mr Hartnett, sir.'

In such a way in the city was a man's fate decided. Logan Hartnett yawned, stretched, and stirred a half-spoonful of demerara into his joe. The Aliados eased through its slow, afternoon moments. The Fancy boys talked lazily of bloodshed, and tush, and new lines in kecks. They combed each other's hair and tried out new partings. Logan brooded a while, and went into his own smoky depths, and then he signalled again with a raising of his eyebrows. No surprise at all the next man to shuffle from a high stool. It was Dominick Gleeson, aka Big Dom, editor of the city's only newspaper, the *Bohane Vindicator*. Of course, it was in no small part thanks to Logan Hartnett that the *Vindicator* remained the city's only paper. Its masthead slogan: 'Truth or Vengeance', as inked above a motif of two quarrelling ravens.

The Dom was a busy-faced lardarse who walked a soft-shoe shuffle, and as he came padding across to the Long Fella's table, already he was muttering sadly, as if the machinations of life in the city had become too much for him. Dom fed on an all-meat diet and he had the high colour of it. He carried with him a small glass of moscato wine and the following morning's proposed editorial comment. He laid the copy before Logan, took a seat, removed grandly a silken handkerchief from inside his three-quarter-length autumn coat, and mopped his bone-dry brow.

'Oh my angina,' he sorrowfully wheezed.

Impatiently, the copy was brushed aside.

'Summarise for me, Dominick.'

The fat newsman leaned forward and allowed on his features a moist, hammy scowl.

'I'm after comin' out bullin' against the plan for a Beauvista tram, Mr H.'

He sipped at his moscato and winked broadly. Tiptoed his fingers across the tabletop and onto the saucer of pumpkin seeds – Logan swiped the fingers away, and Dom winced, blew on them, and adopted a look of brutalised innocence. Logan couldn't but grin.

'Your rationale, Dom?'

'I'm sayin' the las' place that need a tram is Nob Hill, sir.'

Beauvista was always referred to thus in the *Vindicator*'s common-touch argot.

'I'm sayin' the Bohane Authority would be far better off spendin' the bucks on improving the El train and serving the dacent ordinary people . . .'

With chubby fingertips Big Dom mimicked a tiny violin.

'. . . of the Northside Rises.'

'Good man, Dom. We want the Rises kept well buttered.'

'Of course, we just got to be seen to be sayin', like. There ain't no fear the Authority will pay the slightest bit o' notice, Logan. The Beauvista tram?'

He fisted a soft palm happily.

'She's a lock, sir.'

'Happy news, Dominick. We won't have to lug our old bones up that bastard of a hill.'

The newsman was also established, naturally, in a Nob Hill manse, and he shuddered his relief.

'Lungs are like broken stout bottles in me on account of it, Logan.'

'Oh you suffer, Dominick.'

'Don't be talkin' to me, sir. The latest is I'm after gettin' a class of a shake in the mitt, are you watchin'?'

Dominick held up his left mitt and quivered it dramatically.

'Could it be an excess of self-abuse, Dom?'

The newsman's eyes popped in outrage.

'If I threw ya tuppence, would ya lower the tone?'

Big Dom sat back then, and he sighed as he let his piggy little eyes swivel about the cafe. In the sigh, there was his blunt opinion of things: that this place would be the end of him yet.

'What I wanted to ask you, Mr H . . .'

'Yes, Dom?'

'Is regardin' the Cusack situation.'

'Oh? Is there a Cusack situation, Dominick?'

The Dom chuckled.

'What we're wondering, Logan, is there any hope at all that, ah . . . that . . . *things* might hold off for a stretch yet?'

'Who the *we*, Dom?'

Gleeson glared indignantly.

'I'm speakin' on behalf o' the Bohane people, Mr Hartnett!'

Logan leaned forward for a low-voiced confide:

'I ain't the one sending martyrs of young fellas across the footbridge, Dominick. I ain't the one rousing the flatblocks.'

The Dom showed his palms. He moaned, softly, and he let his eyes roll up in his head until all that could be seen was the whites – this to signify the delicate politics the city required, and the weariness such work exacted from an honest soul.

'I know they're wall-bangers to a man, H, an' feckin' uppity with it. But all we're sayin' . . .'

'The *we* again, Dom?'

'Okay, Mr Hartnett. Truth be told, I'm carryin' representations from the Authority.'

'Ah, I see now.'

'Bohane Authority is at a critical stage in negotiations with the NB, Mr Hartnett.'

NB, in Bohane cant: the Nation Beyond.

'So I believe.'

'NB tight enough with the aul' tit this year, H.'

'I understand it's the way.'

'So the last thing we need is one half o' the town tryin' to ate the other half. This place got a bad enough name as things stand, Logan.'

'You're saying that the Authority wishes for the Calm to persist, Dom, until such a time as the NB tit has been successfully massaged?'

'That's very nicely put, Mr Hartnett.'

Logan knit his elegant fingers beneath his chin.

'I'm reasonable, Dom. I wouldn't be fouling the air still if I wasn't. Our only problem is we got a loolah up on the Rises and he has a horn on him for a massive fucking ruck. And I can't be seen to back off.'

'I'm knowin' this all too well, Logan.'

'And! I've got a fucking maniac outside on Big Nothin' and he's working his own plan.'

'You're talkin' about the Gant Broderick.'

'I am indeed, Dominick. So here's what I'd say to you. If

40

ye want the Calm to stretch for a while, I'll play my part but on a particular condition.'

'Name it, sir.'

'Get me a bead on the Gant.'

The fat newsman soul-wrestled for the cheap seats.

'Ah, Logan . . . The Gant's a man with a quare stretch o' history to his name outside on Nothin' . . .'

'You've contacts out there, Dom.'

'I have, but . . .'

'I'm sending my boys out. And your very best contact is to meet with them. And they better be given the Gant's precise whereabouts, Dom. Whatever fucking rock he's hiding under, we need to know it.'

Dom trembled his jowls.

'Mr Hartnett? Peoples got long memories in Bohane. If the Gant got hurted . . .'

'I want a bead drawn on the big unit, Dom. Do you hear me clearly?'

'Cathedral bells, Mr Hartnett.'

'Good. Have we any other business?'

They smiled, and they shook, and the newsman took his leave. Logan reached for his jacket, removed from its breast pocket a red handkerchief, and wiped his hands. He ate seeds, then, and he drank joe, and he examined the reach of his manipulation. He smiled for the young gents of the Fancy. They watched him with the usual regard, awe, puzzlement.

The day they could snag a read on him would be the day he would lose them.

6

Big Nothin' Rendezvous

Was the day following a pair of hombres by the name of Wolfie Stanners and Fucker Burke took to the High Boreen. The Boreen is the main passage across the Big Nothin' wastes – a double-width cindertrack passable in most weathers. Smaller tracks lead from it into the hills and onto the bog and down briary laneways peopled by haggard souls in cottages that sag with damp, and loss, and sadness. The rain fell hard as the boys grimly walked, and rain was no surprise to the place. A low bank of cloud had moved in from the Atlantic and broke up when it hit the foothills of the Nothin' massif. The bog was livened and opened its maw hungrily for the rain. The boys squelched along and eyed with disgust the effect of the mud on their high-top boots. The rain ran in fresh silver freely down the gullies of the hills and fed the patient lakes and the poppy fields also were sated. Even in the midst of the rain, sunlight flashed from behind the cloud-bank – it peeped out for a few seconds at a time, skittish as a young thing, and showed the colours of the rain. The yellow of the high-summer broom had faded in memory of that summer. There was a thick silence from the direction of the pikey reservation – 'the rez', as it is known in the Bohane cant – a most sinister silence, and the boys were watchful of the pikey lands, easterly. Never know what could come flyin' at you from that direction.

'I'm tryin' to get this straight in me noggin,' said Fucker.

'Here we go,' said Wolfie.

'The fuck how we gonna find the big unit, Wolf?'

'We're gonna have a bead drawn, Fucker.'

'Hey but Wolf? We don't know fuckin' Nothin' from fuckin' no place, y'heed me?'

'Shut up, Fucker.'

These boys were the roaming lieutenants of the Hartnett Fancy. The mood was not good.

'But seriously, Wolfie? I mean there's a whole heap o' Big fuckin' Nothin' out here, y'sketchin'?'

Indeed, it was a rude expanse. The reeds that fringed the wee lakes swayed but barely in a light breeze. Big Nothin' is a place of thorn and stone and sudden devouring swampholes. It has an infinity of small wet fields. The fields are broken up by rough and ill-formed drystone walls that tend to give out altogether about two-thirds of the way across a field. A lazy job, the walls. It wasn't Presbyterians put up those walls.

'What we know about the big unit?' said Fucker.

'The Gant Broderick,' said Wolfie. 'Halfways pikey, halfways whiteman. Been gone outta the creation since back in the day. Was the dude used to have the runnins before the Long Fella. Use' t'do a line with the Long Fella's missus an' all, y'check?'

Fucker's jaw lolloped.

'Say she was a proper lash in her day, like?'

'She ain't too bad now, Fuck.'

'Ain't, like.'

'Wouldn't kick her outta bed for atein' anchovies, like.'

'No way, Wolf. The way the eye be class o' turned in on her, like? Bit tasty.'

On a stone wall Wolfie and Fucker paused to rest a while. They smoked, and they savoured a spectacle. In the near distance, a scraggle of country lads cantered around a small field. Polis trials were coming up, and to get a start in the Bohane polis, a lad is expected to be able to lep over a six-bar farm gate of the type made by the sand-pikeys who live on the dunes oceanside of the city. The lads jogged in a staggered line around the irregular perimeter of the field and in sequence one of them would break off from the stagger, take a sprint for the field's gate and have a lep at it. Knees, elbows and chins were taking punishment down there. The Bohane polis was spud-ater to a man.

'Smart-lookin' crop,' said Wolfie Stanners.

'World-beaters,' said Fucker Burke.

Wolfie and Fucker were by their nature city boys. They were not built for the wilds. If he had his way, Fucker would have been sat on a bollard of the Bohane front, with a pipeload of herb on the draw and a dangerous glare trained on the river traffic. If he had his way, Wolfie would have been patrolling the Trace and S'town in the Fancy's cause – with *concrete* under his feet – and bustin' the heads of Norrie scuts.

'Got the fuckin' spooks up in me, Wolf.'

'Well, that's Big fuckin' Nothin' for ya, ain't it, Fucker?'

The boys bitterly climbed to their feet and hit again along the High Boreen. Went deeper into the Nothin' wastes. They came to a particular turn and took it and it led to a ridge path that skirted a granite knoll. Made a harlequin spectacle out on the bog plain, these boys.

Fucker wore:

Silver high-top boots, drainpipe strides in a natty-boy mottle, a low-slung dirk belt and a three-quarter jacket of saffron-dyed sheepskin. He was tall and straggly as an invasive weed. He was astonishingly sentimental, and as violent again. His belligerent green eyes were strange flowers indeed. He was seventeen years of age and he read magical significance into occurrences of the number nine. He had ambition deep inside but could hardly even name it. His true love: an unpredictable Alsatian bitch name of Angelina.

Wolfie wore:

Black patent high-tops, tight bleached denims with a matcher of a waistcoat, a high dirk belt, and a navy Crombie with a black velvet collar. Wolfie was low-sized, compact, ginger, and he thrummed with dense energies. He had a blackbird's poppy-eyed stare, thyroidal, and if his brow was no more than an inch deep, it was packed with an alley rat's cunning. He was seventeen, also, and betrayed, sometimes, by odd sentiments under moonlight. He wanted to own entirely the city of Bohane. His all-new, all-true love: Miss Jenni Ching of the Hartnett Fancy and the Ho Pee Ching Oh-Kay Koffee Shoppe.

'Get 'round the far side o' that hill,' said Wolfie, 'an' we should see the place, yeah?'

'Like I know the fuckin' bogs from fuckology,' said Fucker.

They were headed for a low tavern out at Eight Mile Bridge. A tout was to be met there. They walked on through the damp air.

'If yer askin' me?' said Fucker.

'Well, I ain't,' said Wolfie.

'If yer askin' me,' said Fucker, 'Logan H, he gone seriously fuckin' para, like.'

'Logan H, he always *been* para, Fucker. You don't land the

45

runnins o' Bohane without bein' seriously on the fuckin'
para side, y'check me? S'how y'keep suckin' wind.'

Fucker waggled his beanie head in puzzlement.

'But what's this old Gant cunt gonna go and do on him?
Who got the juju over Logan, like? He's well protected, the
Long Fella.'

'Ours ain't to reason why, Fucker. We's oney the boys,
like. Yet.'

They came upon the Bohane river. Feeding directly off
the bog, it was a tarry run of blackwater, and it burbled its
inanities. Fucker listened as they walked, and was antsy, and
he ran the tip of his tongue across his cracked, nervous lips.
He let free a nagging worry.

'You an' the Jenni-chick gone kinda serious lately, Wolf?'

'We's a lock, Fucker.'

'Knew I ain't been seein' you around the place so much
of an evenin'.'

'Missin' me, Fucker?'

'Aw she's a wee lash an' all, like. I wouldn't blame you, kid.'

'Breed a bairn off her quick as you'd look at me.'

'You would? A Chinkee gettin' bred off a ginge? Weird-
lookin' fuckin' baba, no?'

'Stow it, Fucker.'

The river ran, and the Nothin' massif loomed in a grey
haze, and swaying briars scraped at the boys' noggins, and
Eight Mile Bridge was at last reached.

'Spud-ater Central,' said Wolfie Stanners.

A scatter of inebriates hung out beneath the great stone
arches of the bridge. They sucked at their sacks of tawny
wine. Misfortunate souls in beanie hats, ragged-arsed trews,
ancient geansais. The boys eyeballed them hard as they passed.

'Awful to see fellas let themselves go,' said Fucker.

'No self-respec' is the prob,' said Wolfie.

They went down a short fall of carved stone steps to the old tavern: the Eight Mile Inn. The inn was set low on the river's bank to dodge the hardwind's assaults. It was lit only by turf fires and the boys squinted in the gloom as they entered.

Door creaked shut behind, and slammed, and wisps of steam like spectral maggots rose from their damp coats in the inn's fuggy heat.

Their eyes adjusted. They picked out their man at a far corner. As was arranged, he read a copy of the *Vindicator*. Gestured with it as the boys entered. He was a nervy-looking old-timer with milk-bottle shoulders. Mug of brandy before him. A few old bogside quaffers in flat caps were slung about the dim corners but they kept their eyes down. Wolfie and Fucker crossed the room and slid onto the high stools either side of the tout. Wolfie called a pair of amber halves off the fat-armed Big Nothin' wench behind the counter. She served them, and was all slow and lazy-eyed about it – a lass, no doubt, with notions of being carted off to the city some day. The boys pointedly ignored her. At length, Wolfie addressed the tout in a sidelong whisper.

'Understand,' he said, 'that the man from the paper put word to you?'

'Mr Gleeson, he did.'

'Know why we're here so?' said Fucker.

'It's about a bead wants drawin'.'

'You the man to draw it for us, cove?'

'The man ye're lookin' for been seen awrigh', like.'

'Seen when and where?'

'Would it mean somethin' t'ye if I said, like? Ye know Big Nothin', ye do?'

'Said when and where?'

'He oney comes out on night walks.'

'Comes out where, cove?'

'Comes out. Walks abroad.'

Fucker snapped.

'Fuck's walks a-fuckin-broad mean, fuckface?'

'He walks Nothin'.'

'There's a whole wealth,' said Wolfie, 'o' Big fuckin' Nothin' out here, in't there?'

'Where's it he's kippin', cove?'

'That ain't known.'

The boys threw their hands up. Consulted each other quietly. They were tempted already towards a spilling of blood but wary of the report that needed making to Logan Hartnett. The spud-ater knew this well. Spud-aters – they can be as cute as shithouse slugs.

Fucker sat on his hands and bit his bottom lip. Wolfie, more the diplomat of the pair, changed tack.

'You'd be a fella who'd take a turn 'round Smoketown the odd time, sir?'

'Now,' said the spud-ater, 'we are talkin' decen' cuts o' turkey.'

'An' what'd have an interest for you 'cross the footbridge, sir?'

The old-timer's eyes sparkled.

'I'd lick a dream off the belly of a skinny hoor as quick as you'd look at me.'

Wolfie nodded soberly, as though appreciative of the spud-ater's delicate tastes.

'Draw a bead and you'll have your pick o' the skinnies,' he said. 'Could have a season o' picks.'

'A season?'

'Cozy aul' winter for ya,' said Fucker. 'Buried to the maker's name in skinnies and far gone off the suck of a dream-pipe, y'check me?'

The old tout sighed as temptation hovered.

'Oh man an' boy I been a martyr to the poppy dream . . .'

'An' soon as you done with the dream-pipe,' Fucker teased some more, 'there'd be as much herb as you can lung an' ale to folly.'

'All dependin',' said Wolfie, 'on you drawin' a bead on the man's berth for us, check?'

Spud-ater considered the dregs of his brandy.

Swirled it.

Drained it.

Wolfie nodded for the bar wench to bring him another. She did so. The spud-ater swallowed a fresh nip and savoured it and wrinkled with some delicacy his nostrils. Said:

'That man we're talkin' about? That's a man with a wealth o' respect behind him out here on Nothin'. Lot o' friends here still.'

'Hear ya, cove.'

'A man like that? A man that go waaaay the fuck back on Big Nothin'? Man like that get a bead drawn on him for a pair o' Fancy headjobs . . . I mean no offence.'

Wolfie held up a forgiving palm.

'None taken, sir.'

'All I'm sayin'? It mightn't auger so well for the fella that draws a bead on Gant Broderick, y'get me?'

'Don't say the name,' said Wolfie.

The tout massaged then slowly with one the other his Judas palms. Niggled at the decision.

'You gonna draw the fuckin' bead for us?' said Fucker. 'Or we passin' the time o' fuckin' day, like?'

49

The old-timer put his face in his hands. Looked sadly at the boys then, nodded, and bit down hard on his lip. Jerked a thumb outside.

'Meet me under that bridge a week t'moro,' he said. 'Three bells in the a.m. An' boys? It's gonna be moonless.'

7

The Lost-Time: A Romance

Quick as a switchblade's flick the years had passed and she was forty-three years old. She walked each evening in the Bohane New Town, as if every step might bring her further from the life she had made. But always she circled towards home again.

Macu wore:

A silk wrap, in a rich plum tone, with her dark hair stacked high and shellacked, and her bearing was regal, and a jewelled collar-belt was clasped about her throat; the dullness of its gleam was in the evening light a soft green burn.

By custom, this was the hour of the paseo for the Bohane Dacency – the hour when a parade of the New Town was decorously made. Here was Macu among the delicate ladies as they gently wafted along the pretty greystone crescents.

The paseo whirl:

One might trouble one's dainty snout with a whiff of the taleggio displayed in an artisanal cheese shop, or run one's nails along the grain of a silvery hose shipped in from Old Lisbon (if the route was open), or take a saucer of jasmine tea and a knuckle of fennel-scented snuff at a counter of buffed Big Nothin' granite.

But there was a want in these ladies yet, and it was for the rude life of youth. These old girls had Rises blood in them or they had Back Trace bones, one or the other. Most of the money in Bohane was new money, and it was a question merely of a lady's luck if she was to be headed for a Beauvista manse or for the Smoketown footbridge.

Macu in the reminiscent evening walked the New Town and she traced a mapline to her lost-time.

It was one of those summers you're nostalgic for even before it passes. Pale, bled skies. Thunderstorms in the night. Sour-smelling dawns. It brought temptation, and yearning, and ache – these are the summer things. And sweet calypso sounded always from the Back Trace shebeens. Fancy boys sucked on herb-pipes in the laneway outside the Café Aliados. Aggravators were on the prowl from the flatblock circles of the Rises and the ozone of danger was a sexy tang on the air.

Skirmishes.

Blood spilling.

Hormones raging.

And the Trace Fancy had the Gant Broderick's name to it then. That would have been the day in Bohane – she smiled now as she recalled it – a Fancy boy would wear clicker'd clogs with crimson sox pulled to the top of the calf and worn beneath three-quarter-length trackie cut-offs, with a tweed cap set back to front, a stevedore donkey jacket with hi-viz piping, the hair greased back and quiffed – oh we must have looked like proper fucking rodericks – and a little silver herb-pipe on a leather lace around the neck.

Her mother was gone by then and her father was weakening. There was a greenish tint to his skin in the low light of the Aliados. Always wincing, always reaching for his lower back. Macu was taking on the upkeep of the caff, and she was quick-tongued with the Fancy boys who lounged there.

They hung off the Aliados's tapped-brass counter and were dreamy-eyed for her. She was skinny and seventeen and working it on wedge heels. A darting glance from under the lashes that'd slice a boy's soul open. A bullwhip lash of the tongue and they'd whimper, swoon, let their eyes roll. Macu was the first-prize squaw that summer back deep in the Bohane lost-time.

The Gant was a slugger of a young dude and smart as a hatful of snakes. Sentimental, also. He had washed in off the Big Nothin' wastes, the Gant, and it was known in Bohane there was a good mix of pikey juice in him. A rez boy – campfire blood.

See him back there:

A big unit with deep-set eyes and a squared-off chin. Dark-haired, and sallow, and wry. The kind of kid who wore his bruises nicely. A cow lick that fell onto his high forehead.

Her father warned her off – pikeys is differen', he said – and the warning lent its own spice; fathers never learn.

The Gant jawed a mouthful o' baccy barside of the Aliados one night, and he winked at her, and he said what's it they call yez anyway, girl-chil'? Macu, s'it?

'Back off, pike,' she said. 'Y'foulin' me air, sketch?'

The Gant down the Aliados vibed it like he was an older dude. Summer nights in Bohane, with tempers coming untamped, and tangles in the wynds, and he was losing some of his boys to the dirks of the uptown aggravators. That put its heaviness on him.

He loaded the sad glare on Macu.

She turned it straight back to him.

Oh these were good-looking young people, in a hard town by the sea, and the days bled into the sweet nights, and it was as if the summer would never end.

'Macu, you get time off ever, girl?'

A shyness on him she could hardly believe. The runnings of the town under his shkelp belt already and he was blushing for her.

'Me aul' dude ain't the hottest.'

'I see that, girl.'

'Busy, yunno . . .'

'Get to get an aul' walk in sometime, though? A turn down the river, Macu?'

He showed no front when he talked to her. She liked the rez spiel that came from him. She liked those spun-out Big Nothin' yarns. Of the old weirds who roamed out there and of the paths that opened to the Bohane underworld. Of the cures and the curses. Of the messages writ in starsign on the night sky. The Gant had the weight of Nothin' in his step. It felt grown-up to walk the Bohane Trace with the Gant by her side. They took it slowly.

'I ain't lookin' for no easy lackeen,' he said.

'Y'ain't found one,' she said.

He spoke of the taint that was on the town. He spoke often of premonition. He said it came to him as a cold quiver at the base of the spine. He said that it came in the hour before dawn. He said if he stayed in the creation, he'd come to a bad end sure enough. He said there was no gainsaying that. He said he had the feeling – he said it was in the blood.

'Sounds to me like a rez boy gettin' spooked,' she said, and she traced the tips of her fingers along the creases of his hunched neck.

'I got a feel for these things,' he said.

The Bohane river blackly ran. They fell into its spell. It became official in the Trace that summer that Macu from the Aliados was the Gant Broderick's clutch. He told her that he loved her and that his love caused the fear inside to amplify.

'Before was like I ain't had so much to lose,' he said.

'Y'breakin' me fuckin' heart, pike,' she said.

'Don't want to miss seein' what you turn into,' he said.

He said that already they were conspiring against him in the Fancy. He said he was watchful of more than one.

'Like who?'

'Like the skinny boy. You know who.'

He talked about leaving the peninsula behind. He asked her to come with him.

'But go *where*, G?'

'Maybe . . . Go across over?'

'That fuckin' scudhole?'

'I won't go without you, girl.'

'I dunno, G . . .'

'I could set us up, girl. You could follow me over . . .'

In the New Town, at the hour of the paseo, she looked carefully over her shoulder – sketch? – and it was clear: she had not been followed by a Fancy scout today. She turned into the quietest of the Endeavour Avenue cafes. Ol' Boy Mannion waited for her there on a high stool. He smiled but she did not answer the smile.

'What's this about, Ol' Boy?'

'I'd say you know or you wouldn't be here.'

'I won't see him, Ol' Boy.'

He passed across the letter.

'Just read what he's written to you, Macu.'

8

Night on Nothin'

Midnight.

Big Nothin'.

A trailer home.

And Jenni Ching was butt-naked on the sofa bed.

The trailer was a double-wide aluminium, twenty-two-foot long, and it contained the fold-out bed, a pot-belly stove, an odour of intense sadness, a set of creaking floorboards, and the Gant Broderick. The Gant also was naked, and he was straining, with his eyes tightly shut, to recall the darkest of all his dark times – this so as not to come.

Hardwind was up, and it raged across the bog outside, and it made speeches in the stove's flue; threats, it sounded like, in a spooky, hollowed-out voice: an eerie song for the Gant as he grimly thrusted.

Jenni Ching was on her hands and knees, with her slender rump in the air, and a brass herb-pipe clamped in her gob. She cast over her shoulder a bored glance at the Gant. He looked as if his heart might at any moment explode. His face was purpled, blotched, sweaty.

'If y'wanna take five,' she said, 'jus' holler.'

The mocking tone was too much for him, was too delicious, and the Gant spent himself. He fell onto his back and was ashamed then. His heart was a rabid pit bull loose inside his chest.

Jenni Ching consulted the wall clock.

'Three minutes even,' she said. 'You're comin' on, kid.'

She turned and sat back against the sofa bed's headrest. She drew her legs up about her. She relit her herb-pipe, sucked on it deep, and blew a greenish smoke. The Gant risked an eye at her. She smiled at him, so feline.

'This what it feel like?' she said.

'What?'

'Love.'

'Sarky for your age, girl.'

She placed her tiny feet on his wheezing chest. He laid his hand across her feet and it covered them entirely. She wriggled her toes, the ten, taunting tips of them. Sighed.

'So what's the script with Ganty-boy?' she said. 'An' no more bollick-talk about settlin' in the countryside an' growin' cabbages.'

'Why shouldn't I settle, Jenni? Rest me old bones.'

She drew a hard suck on the pipe, held the smoke, and then reached and pulled his face to hers, laid her mouth on his, and sent with a sharp hiss the blowback.

He glazed.

Coughed.

'Don't always agree with me,' he said, his chest heaving, his humours all twisted.

She reached again and held with her tiny iron hand his chin. Locked a glance.

'An' you'd be doin' the fuck what out here, Gant, 'xactly?'

'I'm supposed to be askin' the questions, Jenni.'

'You havin' an' aul' chat with the stoats, G? Goin' fishin'?'

'You doin' a little fishin' yourself, Jenni?'

'All I'm doin' is talkin' to ya. All I'm doin' is passin' the lonesome aul' night, y'check me?'

'You got the gift for talk, girleen.'

She was tiny. She lifted her feet from his chest. She swung her legs from the sofa bed. She padded to the door of the trailer and unclasped the catch and pushed out the door agin the hardwind. She looked out to the night. A swirl of stars made cheap glamour of the sky above the bog plain.

Without looking at him:

'Y'plannin' damage for the 'bino, Gant?'

'Would I confide as much?'

'The 'bino's had wall-bangers come lookin' for him before, Gant. Same boyos down the boneyard since. An' it's a spooky aul' spill o' moonlight y'gets down that place, y'sketchin'?'

The Gant with a cheeky grin:

'Time does he come along S'town in the evenings, Jenni? Usually?'

She spat the same grin back over her shoulder.

'This look like a tout's can to you?' she said.

'Are you fuckin' him, Jenni?'

'You jealous, G?'

'Or does he mess with the Fancy tush at all?'

'Happens that the Long Fella don't mess with no tush.'

'Oh?'

'Looked after in his marriage is Mr H. He's takin' about as much as he can handle up Beauvista way off the skaw-eye bint.'

A sly one. Knew where to aim; knew where to bite.

'Oh? Happy, are they? The Hartnetts?'

She shook her head, and shaped a curious snarl and somehow he read truth here.

'Happy? Who's happy in fuckin' Bohane? Ya'd be a long time scoutin' for happy in this place.'

She gathered up her clothes and began to dress in the oily candlelight of the trailer. The girl was close to unreadable in the Gant's view. She had told him nothing about the Fancy, nor about the S'town operations, nor about the movements of Logan Hartnett. Even so, she was keeping close, she was calling on him, and consenting to his bed. It was said this Ching girl had a count to her name already and the Gant was inclined to believe it from the taste of her.

'You can't stay a while?'

She didn't dignify that with an answer.

And it was a moody Gant she left on the sofa bed as she took off into the night again. Cat's eyes on her. As easy in her stride out on Nothin' as she was in S'town or the Back Trace.

Watch her close, Gant.

But he relished her, despite himself, and he asked then for forgiveness as the trailer's siding creaked ominously in the night. Awful thing to still have a taste for young 'un and you up to the view from fifty.

He lay among the stew of his thoughts a while. Now that was a murky old soup. He rose wearily after a time and dressed. He felt bone-ache and sad bliss. He went outside for a taste of the wind. His mind for a brief stretch ran clear. He closed his eyes and tried to bring himself to the lost-time, but it could never be regained. He would never take back the true taste. He had known it just once and it was Macu's.

The Gant walked a keen edge always across the territories of the mind. At any moment he might trip to either side and fall into the blackness. Of course, it is a husky race of people we're talking about outside in the Bohane creation, generally. Cursed and blessed with hot feeling.

Images from the lost-time now came to him in quick assault. When she was eighteen. When she walked with him. The way that she spoke to him. The way that her lips shaped to form his name.

He walked on into the night and he shook his great, bearish head against memory, and he briefly wept, and he chortled at himself then for the weeping. Oh this is a nice package you're presenting, Gant. Oh this is a nice game you've got yourself involved with. And nice people to play it with.

Careful, Gant.

He walked the Nothin' plain. The hardwind by 'n' by walloped a little sense into him. A feral goat watched from a high vantage, its eyes a glaring yellow. The Gant willed himself to straight thinking. He felt the tread of their shared past underfoot. Your step there, he thought, and my step here. That's your step there, and my step here, on the days that we walked out, Macu, in the noonday of the lost-time.

Nostalgia, on the peninsula, was a many-hooked lure.

The Gant had come back early in August. At once, he had fallen victim to our native reminiscence. In the Bohane creation, time comes loose, there is a curious fluidity, the past seeps into the future, and the moment itself as it passes is the hardest to grasp. The Gant came back with a couple of hundred in his pocket and a pair of busted boots on his feet and a reefed shoulder gone halfways septic – that was as much as he had to show for twenty-five years gone. A hot summer day with the bare lick of a breeze to it and the breeze among the long grasses whispered the old Nothin' mysteries. The bog was dried out and above it a shifting black gauze of midge-clouds palpitated and the turloughs

60

had drained off and there was that strange air of peace in the hills: never-changing, sea-tanged, western. The horizon wavered in hard sun over the poppy fields as the workers toiled in silhouette at the crop. Bleached light on the plain of Nothin' and a fado lament wailed distant from somewhere on the pikey rez. His feet were blistered.

The breath came hard and jaggedly in him as he made it to Ol' Boy Mannion's longhouse. It was set in a valley's dip, and as he quietly came on the place, he saw that its door was open. This was as expected – Ol' Boy in the summer was by long habit to be found at his Nothin' residence. The Gant stuck his head inside the door. He leaned against the jamb to slow his breath.

'Benni,' he said.

Ol' Boy looked up from a settle in the dank and fly-thick shade, and he showed not a flicker of surprise.

'You been settin' the world on fire, Gant?'

The Gant raised his eyes. Ol' Boy stood and shook his head woefully.

'So who's responsible for this masterpiece?' he said.

'By mine own fair hand,' the Gant said.

'Ah, come in out of it, would you? Before you frighten the fuckin' ducks.'

The Gant sat in the shade of the longhouse and at length he took his breath back. Ol' Boy asked no questions. Just waited it out.

'E'er a notion where a fella could lay his achin' bones, Benni?'

'You'll have to let me see about that.'

Ol' Boy busied himself. On the stove he mixed up a bowl of pinhead oatmeal and he added a measure of Jameson to the pour of cream. He made a place at the table for the Gant and watched as he came slowly across the flagstones.

'S'either yer gone rickety before yer time or there's a story worth gobbin', G?'

The Gant grimaced.

'Y'lie down with dogs,' he said.

As the Gant ate, Ol' Boy examined the shoulder wound. He took a bottle of evil-smelling fluid from the high shelf and dabbed it on a wedge of cotton and applied the cotton to the wound.

'Landed just a lucky stretch shy of a lung, Gant,' he said. 'And it have the look of a cratur who's came at ya with a rusty blade, boy?'

'Y'get off the peninsula,' said the Gant, 'and you find they got no class.'

Ol' Boy salved the wound as best he could and shook another measure of the fluid onto it, for badness' sake, and the Gant hissed a startle of pain. Ol' Boy blew on the wound.

'Trust me,' he said, 'I'm a nurse.'

He dressed the wound neatly. He was dainty about his work. He'd patched up more than a few go-boys in his day.

'An' you're back here why, Gant Broderick, precisely? What bizarre fucking notion has weaselled itself into that sorry noggin o' yours?'

He rapped his knuckles on the Gant's head. The Gant laid down his spoon and thought a moment.

'You'd find there's a quare aul' draw to Big Nothin',' he said.

'An' what about to Bohane city?'

'Maybe we need to talk about that an' all, Mr Mannion.'

Ol' Boy's opinion, which he transmitted in a single, sharp

glance, was that Bohane wasn't the same place it had been twenty-five years back.

'S'pose it'll be interestin' whatever happens,' he said.

The Gant agreed that it would be.

'I need a place out here, Benni. Gather me thoughts, you know?'

So it was that Mannion had set him up with the trailer home. Told him to lie low a while and keep his snout to the wind: see how she blew.

Trailer was a hard find even to an aborigine like the Gant. It was located in the lee of an old quarry's wall and it had that shelter at least from the evil of the hardwind. The trailer sat across an expanse of bog from a small lake. You'd barely drown a child in it, as they say of such a lake out on Nothin'. The lake's waters were dark and cloudy and thatched at the verges with an accumulation of broken reeds. The Gant had settled to this place, and he watched the summer fade into autumn, and heard the hardwind rise, and he knew that winter was on the soon-come.

He walked the October night its length through. He came into a white space of mind and it was restful. He circled the plain. Towards dawn, he walked across the splintered boards of an old jetty by the small lake – the boards gave and groaned as he walked, the boards sang – and he crouched there, and he felt the looming presence of the Nothin' hills beyond. Dark shadow of mountain against the waking sky. He felt a presence; he felt it as a great tenderness. And then he heard its voice.

'Oh Baba?' the Gant pleaded. 'Oh Sweet B?'

9

Girly

Girly Hartnett lay in bed at the Bohane Arms Hotel. Eighty-nine she was, and bored. The boredom she sung with a frequent sighing. Her top-floor suite's black velvet drapes were as always drawn – Girly had seen more than enough of Bohane city to last her a frigging lifetime. She was on a diet of hard booze and fat pills against the pain of her long existence. She was regally arranged on the plump pillows of a honey-mooners' bed. Girly's days were slow, and they ran headlong into her nights, and she lay awake most of the nights, and yet she could never quite place the nights once they'd passed. Could never quite get a fix on the fuckers. As often as the hotel had juice enough to run a projector, she watched old movies on a pull-down screen. Girly liked old movies and menthol ciggies and plotting the city's continued derange-ment. The Hartnett Fancy held the runnings of Bohane, and there were those who'd swear the steer was Girly's yet as much as Logan's. She could identify every knock on her door and she cried an answer now to her son's.

'Get in to me!'

The worry in him she read before he had his long bones folded in the bedside chair.

'How we now?' he said.

She raised a brittle hand to her throat, Girly, and let its fingers fraily rest there.

'Not long for the stations, boy.'

'So you been saying.'

They did not kiss nor lay a hand to each other. The Hartnetts were not touchy-touchy people. The Hartnetts were Back Trace: blood and bone.

'Time you callin' this anyhow?'

'It's gone seven alright.'

'Was goin' to get onto the morgue,' she said. 'See if they'd ta'en in any long pale-lookin' fuckers.'

'Been busy, Girly.'

'Busy gowlin' around,' she said. 'Bring me flicks, y'did?'

'Did, Girly.'

He passed over the reels and she examined them.

'Y'got me nothin' with Tab Hunter an' Natalie Wood, nah?'

'They didn't have anything.'

'Arra Jay.'

'I tried, Girly.'

'Tab and Natalie made some beautiful pictures.'

'You been saying.'

'Word was they were doin' a line.'

'Go 'way?'

'There'd be photos at premieres.'

'We got uptown aggravators working a caper, Girly.'

'Natalie in a class of an ermine wrap. Tab in peg pants and a knit shirt. *Beige!*'

'Cusack says he got the flatblocks stacked, Girly.'

'Course the wan o' the Woodses was hangin' offa everythin' in kecks. Man-crazy.'

'I said Eyes Cusack, Girly. Word I have? He has families behind him. He has the McGroartys, the Lenanes, the Sullivans . . .'

65

'They said filth about Tab, of course. I never believed a word o' what they said about Tab.'

'It's good word, Girly. We're talking three families at least weighing in with the Cuse. And that's a wealth of fucking headjobs, no?'

'Ferocious the muck they threw at Tab.'

'I think he's about to throw a shape, Girly.'

'You know I wouldn't repeat what they said about Tab? Wouldn't soil the roof o' me mouth with it.'

'What way should I play it?'

Girly reached for the bedside bottle of John Jameson and poured a decent measure to her tumbler. She offered him the bottle. He shook his head, closed his eyes, and massaged with bunched fingertips the space between them. He swung his booted feet onto the bed. Soon as they landed she batted them away.

'Watch me fuckin' eiderdown,' she said.

She tasted and savoured the whiskey. Colour rose up in her – a purplish rush to chase the greyness.

'Yunno I'd a dream there a while ago,' she sighed, 'and who arrives into it only Fernando Lamas above on a horse?'

'Girly, listen to me! Eyes Cusack is about to make a move down the 98 Steps.'

'Of course in my mother's day? In Peggy's time? There would have been sixteen picturehouses in Bohane at that time. Is there just the one now still?'

'Just the one.'

'And all it's showin' is maggots lickin' the melt off each other.'

'Girly?'

'Shut up, I'm thinkin'.'

She closed her eyes. She was an unspeakable age as Bohane lives go. She blinked hard.

'Cusacks been hustlin' in the Trace?'

'Not in the Trace but in Smoketown. And making plenty of noise up on the Rises, up in the shebeens. Putting new skins on their lambeg drums, is the word, and they got their chanters tuning up.'

'Norrie fuckin' nonsense!'

'But how'll I go at it, Mam?'

She shook her head to dismiss his fear.

'Catnip to Wolfie and the boys,' she said.

He nodded.

'That's the way I'm hoping. But if we hadn't enough of a head count . . .'

'Who've we to call in, child?'

He regarded her dolefully.

'Most of the bridges are fairly well burned at this stage.'

'Who're you tellin. But we've no one at all?'

'Unless I hit out the dunes and try talk to –'

'Arra fuckin' Jay!'

They let the matter quieten before them. Both teased through it in the silence. No decision was ever made quickly or rashly by a Hartnett. At length, Girly spoke up.

'D'ya find me anythin' with a young Yul Brynner, nah? From the days o' the hair?'

'No, Girly. I found you *The Wanderers* alright?'

He raised the case to her.

'I see that,' she said.

These evening times together were brief but an unbreakable custom. Each of them eased in the company of the other. She eyed him carefully, and he drew back just a fraction from the examination – this was evident in a slight tensing of the shoulders, which she noted. Also, the way he had taken up the reel cases from the eiderdown, and the way he turned them nervously in his hands.

'That's a quare weight you're carryin',' she said, 'on account of a few Norrie wall-bangers?'

Girly let that sit a moment, then:

'So how's herself keepin'?'

Logan allowed his feint, yellow smile.

'Marvellously,' he said.

Girly nodded, as though greatly satisfied.

'From what I'm hearin',' she said, 'the Gant Broderick is still a han'some cut of a man.'

He flung the reel cases onto her bed and rose to go.

'Here,' he said. 'Go watch your aul' films.'

She snorted a laugh as he went. She listened carefully for the precise heft of the slam he gave the door, and she laughed again when it loudly came. Served the pale fucker right for marryin' boat trash.

De Valera Street down below thrummed with the slow build of night: its rude energies were gathering. Yes and October was ending, the last of it falling from our diseased civic trees, and there was Trouble with a Big T on the Bohane soon-come.

Girly in the vast bed wriggled with delight.

10

In a Smoketown Patois

Dark came on Smoketown. Was a hell of a place in the black night – a sad-dream world across the footbridge. On the skinny streets the old town houses leaned in to each other: how-we-now? As though the old houses they was holding one another up, like. This Smoketown you take one brick from the pile and the whole heap'd come tumbledown. Smoketown it don't even make a square mile in size: a tight, small, squashed-up place, hard-pressed its airways, its troubled lungs, and the air had an oily feel in the night. Smoketown generators chugged like good things. Mark this: if there was juice nowhere in Bohane, there'd be a bit left all the same for the S'town operations.

The madwoman of Smoketown paraded in her white cowgirl suit, sequins aglitter, and directed the sky traffic of angry gulls.

A toothless she-man hoor with painted-on eyebrows tossed shouts to the sky from the footbridge.

A violently unpredictable Alsatian bitch name of Angelina dragged along on a leash the Fancy lieutenant Fucker Burke.

Fucker and Angie were in and out of the Chalk 'n' Cue.
Fucker and Angie were in and out of the Land o' Baize.
Fucker and Angie were in and out of the 147.

The fuck was Wolfie was what Fucker and Angie wanted to know.

Chiefly spud-aters on the S'town streets at this hour – they'd be in need of a knee-trembler and the suck of a dream-pipe before hitting the Boreen and dragging their woeful souls across the Nothin' wastes.

Edmund 'The Gypo' Lenihan came 'cross the footbridge with a honey-blonde sixteen-year-old in tow – fresh tush recruited off the Rises, with a big brazen puss on: there'd be no fear of her.

Low throb of the grindbars as they was gearing up – sinuous basslines rumbled as the early-shift gals shinned the bars and spun there, and slid again, their dead eyes lurid.

Fish wagons (Hartnett-owned) unloaded to the Chinkee troughs – fins and spines and bones for the chowder, oh it is some quare-lookin' craturs you get swimming the Bohane river.

A blur of booze-pasted faces moved along the streets.

Chinkee dives, hopper bars, dream salons.

And here at last came Wolfie Stanners out of the Ho Pee Ching Oh-Kay Koffee Shoppe – five foot two inches of pure man in a velveteen puffa and a pair of stormtrooper lace-ups.

His ginger bonce swivelled and searched as he marched the Smoketown streets.

He fell in with Fucker Burke and Angelina outside the Land o' Baize.

Narky look off the Wolfie-boy, Fucker reckoned, and rightly.

'Was lookin' for ya, Wolf.'

'I been lookin' for Jenni, ain't I? You seen fuckin' Jenni, yuh?'

'Ain't, Wolf.'

'Said y'seen Jenni anywhere about, Fuck?'

Mad eyes swivellin' in the Wolfie-boy puss.

'Said I ain't seen her, Wolf.'

'Fuck she at 'n' all, like?'

Taint of badness on the Bohane air had its various strands and jealousy was not the least among them.

'Dunno, Wolf. Ain't seen –'

Wolfie turned and without breaking stride took a flying kick at the door of a dream salon, and issued a raspin' grunt, and the effort seemed to calm him some, and he set to the S'town prowl and the night's business.

'Word off the 'bino?'

'Word is – Cantillon.'

'Tonight?'

'Word.'

'Let's do it then. There any sign o' the fishmonger, Fuck?'

Oh and indeed the unfortunate Deccie Cantillon had chosen the wrong evening for an S'town crawl. Not bad enough he was doing jigger with the missus of his own cuz – misfortunate Ger Reid, master butcher – but he was bothering Smoketown tush too.

'On a fanny crawl, is he?' Wolfie said.

'He be at the pay-for tush an' all,' Fucker confirmed.

Angelina dragged on the leash, and the boys followed, and soon enough Cantillon was made out in the S'town haze.

A whippety cratur, Cantillon, with mackerel scales all over his hands, in his forties, sharp-featured, a card player, looked after hissel', a sculpted Frenchie-looking nose just built for a tush-chaser, the thick hair slathered back with a pawload of perfumed gunk, top five buttons of a purple dress shirt

71

open to the night even though it was deep end of October in Bohane, the west's evil winter looming.

Deccie followed his pecker around the narrow streets.

Angelina and the boys followed Deccie.

Anything aged fourteen to sixty-eight took the rake of his glance. Ankles to nape, he sized 'em up. Laid the gamey eye on. Nearly hop up on that, he thought. Nearly give that an auld lash of the baste, he thought. Nearly ate me dinner offa that, he thought. Oh, a rabid tush patrol he was on, with the peepers out on stalks, looking left, looking right, looking bang ahead, but . . . ah.

He didn't look behind him, did he?

No.

'Full whack on the fishmonger is the 'bino's word,' Fucker said.

'*Full* whack?'

'He been messin' with a missus, ain't he?'

'Long Fella don't like that.'

'He sure don't, Wolf.'

They ghosted through the Smoketown crowds and kept just a short ways back from their prey.

They knew to wait on the moment.

The fishmonger slithered into a shotbar.

He schlepped back a couple of mulekickers and tried to paw the plastik bazookas off the Ukrainer barkeep.

All the while he was watched from the street.

Wolfie had by this stage a punnet of fried chicken on the go and he offered Fucker a drumstick and Fucker took it and sucked it clean in one and tossed the bone and offered his greased fingers then to Angelina, who cleaned them good.

'I worry 'bout you an' that dog sometimes,' said Wolfie.

Fucker shrugged; Angelina drooled.

And Cantillon rode a string of dives but he bought nowhere, he was looking for the good price, and at length, as the boys and the dog trailed him, he hit towards the dune end.

Now the dune end of Smoketown is the cheaper line. There you will find a very low class of customer. The worst of the slagshops and the most insalubrious needle galleries are out there. Weird atmosphere on account of the system of dunes that rise just beyond and give the name to it. A spooky place that dune reef. Haunted by ferocious pikeys it is – their fires burn against the black night; sand-pikeys we call 'em – and the sea withers on, always and forever, insanely.

Fishmonger took a turn down an empty side street.

Bad move.

Suddenly, silently, Wolfie Stanners was at his side.

So sweetly:

'A word, Mr Cantillon?'

And yes there was Fucker Burke the other side of him.

All jaunty:

'Howya, Dec?'

And there was Angelina with a spill of happy drool falling.

Steered him down a tight alleyway, the boys, and a sea of rats parted underfoot.

Electric bristling of them.

Parting of the grey sea.

Angie yapped at the rats and was shushed by Fucker. Gently the boys arranged the man against a gable end.

'This about, lads?'

Fair play he even managed to keep the quake of fear from his voice. For all the good it did him. Wolfie took a wee lep off the dancers and was airborne, just briefly, but long enough to plant a perfect butt on the bridge of Cantillon's nose.

Soft explosion: muscle, sinew, blood.

The butt was a kindness; Deccie whited out – Goodnight, Smoketown! – and he slumped agin the wall and slid the length of it and was no sooner on the ground than Fucker Burke arranged the heel of a size thirteen high-top boot on his windpipe and mashed it down hard, and Angie on the leash was lapping already at the blood spilt.

Wolfie meantime worked his stormtroopers repeatedly about the man's face in neat precise stomps – happy in his work, the boy – so it would be a while anyways before this meat had a name put to it.

They lepped at the ribs also – they snapped easily as fish bones.

Angelina danced.

Boys walked out the dune end again. Glanced quickly left and quickly right and hit directly for the busier Smoketown of the riverside streets.

'I've a horn on me,' said Fucker.

'I'd ate,' said Wolfie.

Angelina lurched at the leash, she wanted to go back to the alleyway, she wanted more, but she was dragged along and scolded:

'Leave it, Ange!'

Smoketown juddered. The girls called out and the barkers hollered. Dreams were sold, songs were gargled, noodles were bothered. Wolfie Stanners and Fucker Burke and the Alsatian bitch Angelina melted back into the night, and as they passed me by, I saw the true-dark taint in their eyes.

It is at this hour that I like to walk the S'town wharfs myself. I like to look out over the river to the rooftops of the Back Trace and the Northside Rises beyond.

I like to see the river fill up with the lamps of the city.

11

The Gant's Letter to Macu

Dear Macu,

I saw you on Dev Street the other day. I wondered if I'd know you it's been so long girl but the shock to me was how little you'd changed. I ain't sure I can say the same about myself I'd say the years have gone on me sure enough it was always the way with my crowd the way we'd wear our lives on our faces. I want to cause you no unhappiness Macu. It was plain to me when I saw you on Thursday you been caused enough of that. I don't mean to pass remark on the life that you made for yourself I'd be the last one who could draw rosy pictures of a life for anyone. It doesn't mean that I have not dreamt of what kind of life it might have been if things hadn't happened the way they did. I saw you Macu and I wanted to go to you but it would not have been fair to you. Not yet I told myself not this time. Twenty-five year pass and leaves nothing at all hardly in your hand I don't know exactly when it was that I started to feel old but I feel it now true enough you can believe me I suppose there has been dark times for me as for anyone in a life but it is no good to nobody to dwell on the dark times. It only seems like weeks ago that I walked out of the place. A lot has happened to me in that time as you can well imagine since I took to the High Boreen that was a hard day believe me that day marked me. I am not in many ways the person that I was I have done things I am not proud of Macu. I have not married though I suppose there have been women. I have never settled anyplace. I am told you are without children and that is a sadness you should have been a mother it would have suited you.

I am living back on Nothin' now and it is my intention to settle here for as long as I have left may the SBJ grant that it is more than a season or two. I cannot say that I have known happiness since I came back here a few months ago I cannot say that I will ever know that again but there is quiet out here all the same that suits me and is a comfort to my old bones. You know that Nothin' has been a special place for me always. You know my feelings for this place and you will understand it was painful for me to be away from it so long. I come back here with no intention of causing you unhappiness.

I want to see you Macu. I want to look at you and not have to speak have to say stupid things I want to look at you and see what you've become. I want to hold you for a while. I am sorry to put these words before you I have no choice I must. I am a worm I know that to come back after all this time and what it must do to you it is hard and painful.

You said something to me once I wonder if you remember. You said that no matter what happened we would end up together. Do you remember that? It was probably just something a young girl would say and she was in love but I believed it for years it kept me together for years it kept me from the lip of the grave Macu.

I love you still. That has a horrible bare look to it I know when it is put down on the page maybe the truth is I do want it to cause pain for you. Maybe I believe there is some of that due to you. We make choices and we have to live with them. It might seem like madness that I would write those words after all these years but there you are you can deal with them I have had to deal with them so long.

When we walked the Back Trace and we were kids in Bohane I thought my heart was going to escape my mouth. Lay my hand on the small of your back and it was like stepping off a roof. Big soft grin on my face and I was suppose to be the hard boy in town. You were so slight. And the way that you talked to me low in a whisper almost and that it was so many weeks before you'd kiss me even.

We used to walk on those nights in the Trace and go down to the river. I can hear again the river on the summer nights and the way we'd sit on the stone steps and you would lean your head back onto my chest and rest it there. I thought that nothing that nobody could ever come between us Macu.

I tell myself that to come back here might be a way to break the hold on me you have still. The touch that I have felt on me these years in my dark times always it is your touch. I see you at seventeen, eighteen so perfectly clear every detail the tiny bones under the skin of your brow when you worried for me if there was trouble times in the Bohane Trace. I believe they were the wrong paths we took and what I have seen of your life here with Hartnett does not change that belief.

My days are quiet now. There are places that you would remember I'm sure from our own time when sometimes we'd walk out here. We would lie in the long grass do you remember Macu? As much as things change in Bohane things stay the same on Big Nothin'. The place I am living is no palace but comfort enough I sit like a true auld fella off the Nothin' bogs in front of my pot belly stove. I'd have laughed back then to see what I would turn into later. Though I will say again the same years I could hardly see on you on Dev Street the other day it took the breath from me you were so familiar. The way that you moved was just as I remembered. Do not think I was spying on you but when I saw you I could hardly be expected to look away.

I am back on Nothin' to stay and I wish to see you Macu. Even if it kills me I want to see you. What I ask is for a single meeting. The time and the place could be arranged as you see fit. If there are things I should say to you now after all this time then I could say them much better in person. Let me know through Mr Mannion if such a meeting can be arranged. All I can plead is that it would be heaven to see your lips form my name again.

That I may hear from you soon, girl,

The G

12

Who Gots the Runnings?

Dom Gleeson, the lardarse newsman, was on De Valera Street, fresh-shaven, his face still blotchy from the razor. He wore a baby-blue zoot suit and a pair of clicker'd heels that he danced in excitement against the pavement. He was nifty on the hoof for a fat lad and he gazed soulfully in the direction of Big Nothin'. He slowed his moves then and stilled himself. He looked down and regarded his small, sinister feet. He raised his fingertips to his lips. Nibbled them.

'The Gant's up top o' fifty, Mr Mannion,' he whispered. 'He's hardly gonna try and lay a snakey mickey into her at this stage, is he?'

Ol' Boy in a Crombie against the night chill, wearing a jaunty pork-pie hat, was sat up on the Dev Street railings, moocher-style, and he raised his eyebrows.

'Love can be so strange and enduring, Dom.'

'Then Hartnett is gonna have to be seen to act, Mr Mannion.'

'You ain't sellin' a spoof, Big D. He's got to throw down some class of a welcome for the Gant sure enough. The city's watchin'. The Authority's watchin'. And his missus is watchin' an' all, y'check me?'

The city's mood was a blend of fear and titillation. There was going to be an almighty collision, and a small world shudders when giants collide.

'He's been wantin' a bead on the Gant outside on Nothin',
Mr Mannion. An' I could hardly be seen not to oblige . . .'

'I wouldn't worry about the G out on Nothin', Dom.'

Ol' Boy smiled his reassurance, and there beneath the
Dev Street lights the Dom, amped on the city's intrigue,
tiptoed a dance step again. Shimmied his hips. Swivelled
them. Made gasping little fishmouths. Winked then, and
whispered:

'They say the missus' eyes straighten in her head when
she gets fleadhed, Mr Mannion?'

'They do so that, Dom.'

The Dom gurgled, and gazed to the stars, and he swirled
with them. Went kind of woozy and glad.

'Oh we got us a love mess on our paws!' he shrieked.

'We certainly have, Dom.'

The newsman swivelled his peepers over a shoulder as
though he might be watched from back there, and he leaned
closer then to Ol' Boy.

'An' o' course we got other problems, Gant aside.'

'Don't talk to me about the Cusacks, Dominick, please.'

Dom clutched himself tragically about the chest. Made
as though to drop and hit the stones.

'Oh my angina!' he wheezed.

Ol' Boy regarded him soberly.

'If the Calm breaks,' he said, 'we can all go an' whistle
for a Beauvista tram, Dom. And every last site for a manse
beside it, y'hear me?'

'Cathedral bells, Mr Mannion. Last thing Bohane needs
is a winter o' blood, like.'

Ol' Boy climbed down from the railings, and together the
men made aim for the S'town footbridge: it was the hour
in Bohane when gents would be inclined towards recreation.

'What we gotta be askin'?' said the newsman. 'Who's it truly gots the Bohane runnings right now?'

'Oh that's the question, Dom,' said Ol' Boy. 'I said that's the capital Q, y'check me?'

Big lunks of polis made a cordon at the entrance to a Smoketown alleyway.

Rubberneckers piled down the dune end and stalked out their eyes to see past.

'Back away to fuck'll ye!' yelped a polis. 'We need a stretcher backin' in here, like!'

Wisecracker in the crowd didn't miss a beat:

'More'n a stretcher that fella's needin'!'

A low round of chuckles ribboned out and even the polis good-naturedly joined in. Bohane was (and is) a perpetual source of amusement to itself.

Down the alleyway, a polis 'spector knelt by the bloody remains and peered closely at the bootmarks on blue flesh.

'Fancy,' he whispered.

He gestured to a raw polis, a mouth-breather not long off the Nothin' plain, and the young 'un crouched beside him.

'See this?' said the 'spector.

He showed in the pool of blood the particular shape of the clicker'd boot heels that had made their marks there.

'If this tells us it's an F-boy caper,' he asked the young polis, 'what else does it tell us?'

Mouth-breather was a quick learner, and he rose, and he faced the crowd at the alley's maw, and he addressed them loudly.

'S'lookin' like another suicide, lads.'

'Good boy,' the 'spector whispered.

Up from the river an assault of wind came knifing and it had a bone-deep chill in it for a sharpener.

That would be the winter in on top of us.

Girly Hartnett cued up a Mario Lanza flick from 1952 – Peg would have been eighteen; she dated the flicks always to her mother's age. *Because You're Mine* it was, the one where he sang 'Granada', a powerful set of lungs on the boy. She took a sip of John Jameson from her tumbler and she recapped the pill bottle. She relaxed her old bones to enjoy the rush of tranquilliser and the soaring of the young tenor's voice.

Girly was downtown.

Girly was seeing the lights.

Girly startled as a particular knock sounded on her door, the knock that always came late on, and she answered it with a single, sharp whistle.

Jenni Ching entered, and sat by the bedside, and poured herself a whiskey. She kicked her tiny lethal feet up onto the bed and Girly fondly laid a hand across them.

'Manners on 'em yet out there, Jenni-chil'?'

'Oh aye, Girly. Manners o' pigs an' dogs.'

Girly squinted then, and she made out the bite marks rearside of Jenni's neck.

'S'it the Wolfie kid been havin' an aul' jaw on ya, girl?'

Jenni took a stogie from the tit pocket of her white vinyl zip-up. Torched the motherfucker.

'For me to know,' she said. 'Now c'mere till ya hear the latest.'

She would tell the old bint as much as she needed and no more.

*

On Beauvista, Macu and Logan lay in the bed their long marriage had made and they held each other grimly against the coming of the winter. He sniffed hard at her as he sought a telltale smell – the taint of another – but he found no deceit.

'Don't you ever fucking leave me,' he said.

Fucker Burke and Wolfie Stanners walked the Big Nothin' plain in the great vault of dark. They came to the particular turn from the High Boreen and took it and it led to the ridge path that skirted the granite knoll and soon the Eight Mile Bridge loomed, and it was a moonless night surely as the tout said it would be, and they went by the water's edge and climbed down the bank and came underneath the arches of the bridge.

Tout waited for them sure enough.

He was tied by his ankles to a girder of the bridge, and his hands were tied also, and much of his skin had been taken off, and his throat was reefed plain open, and he was bled like a pig, with a pool of it congealing blackly beneath him, and the eyes were gouged from the sockets for badness' sake – draw a bead now! – and what was left of the skin hung in white rags and shreds from him.

On the stone of the bridge's arch where the tout was hung two words were daubed in blood:

WITH LOVE

Fucker looked at Wolfie.
Wolfie looked at Fucker.
They headed at pace for the High Boreen.

★

The night always on Nothin' brought dread with it and gusts of hardwind swayed the walls of the Gant's aluminium trailer. The bassoon call of a bittern sounded – that forlorn bird – and there were mystery rustlings and creakings outside, and the nerves were not a hundred per cent on the Gant just yet.

Pulse still up.

Head unsettled.

A roar of hot wind in his ears.

He shivered and tensed at every sound. He asked the night for forgiveness. His legs blazed with the cold aches of age and as he rose from his stool he moaned the same moan that had chorused his poor father to the grave. Even the moans get passed down. He heard the shrieks of the night critturs outside and droning voices among the reeds.

He wrapped himself in a buckskin and blew out the candles. He went to the darkness. He knew it was better to be among it and to be an agent of it than to sit and tremble with guilt in the trailer. He closed his eyes as he walked and he tried to attune himself to her proximity, her frequency.

He walked to a high vantage and across the bog plain the lights of Bohane city burned – was a Babylon on fire in the October dark.

II
DECEMBER

13

The View from Girly's Eyrie

Here was Girly, after the picture show, drugged on schmaltz, in equatorial heat beneath the piled eiderdowns, a little whiskey-glazed and pill-zapped, in her ninetieth – Sweet Baba help us – Bohane winter, and she found herself with the oddest inclination: Girly had a notion to get out of the bed. It was afternoon yet below on De Valera Street and she was determined to have a good old lamp at the place. Some fucker was playing a melodeon down there despite it all.

She shifted with a lung-quaking sigh the eiderdowns and the effort caused a dose of pins-and-needles across her shoulder blades that would put down a good-sized horse. The pins-and-needles, another of her daily trials, were symptomatic of thirty-odd years buzzing on off-script tablets, hard liquor and Hedy Lamarr pictures.

'Hell,' she said, but stoically.

She swung her legs out over the side of the honeymooners' special. She sat a moment, for breath, and regarded her legs carefully. It was Girly's opinion that she still had a fine pair of pins on her, all told, but it took a massive effort to plant the bastaring things on the floor and raise herself to an uncertain stand. This move in turn seemed to unseat a kidney. A dart of pain squirmed up through the small of her back on a zigzag course and it was as though the devil himself was jabbing at her with a pared stick. She sat back down again.

'Mother o' fuckin' Jay,' she said.

A frail arm she swung onto the bedside table and it upended a family-sized tub of tranquillisers. She fished a couple from the spill and aimed them at her gob. There was no great dignity here, of course. The pills that landed on her tongue – and she had a tongue like sandpaper today, whatever was after going skaw-ways in that department – she washed down with a swallow of John Jameson taken direct from the neck of the bottle.

So long, elegance.

Bravely she raised herself to a stand again and she endured a mighty assault of vertigo. She clamped her lips meanly against it. Then came a massive volt of lightness through her head. Girly had for many decades been suffering from attacks of what she called 'the lightness'. Also, there was shame. When you could not even get the whiskey into the tumbler, it was nearly time, in Girly Hartnett's opinion, to go and fuck yourself into the Bohane river altogether.

Of course the next thing was the walking.

Girly considered the vast Sahara of the beige-tone carpet that opened out between herself and the far window over-looking the Dev Street drag. She tested a step, tentatively, with her spider-veined feet. If the pins were holding well enough, the dancers were letting the side down rotten – Girly would not lie to herself. She moved a foot forward and tried her weight. If the one hip held out it would be a result, the two a Baba-sent mystery. She breathed as deeply as she could after ninety winters of damp penin-sular air. Her step was unsure and she tragically wavered. It was as if the Big Nothin' hardwind was inside in the room with her. She heard the whistling of the air as it went through her scoured cavities – Girly felt like a derelict house.

Strike that – a derelict mansion.

No panes in the windows and no fire in the grate and crows in the attic but there was grandeur yet, even so. A stately ruin was Girly. She settled again on the sad, squalling music of the melodeon below, a wintersong for foul December in the Bohane creation.

She was determined, and one quivering foot she put in front of the other, and she made for a view of the place. The great tragic armies of history had made it over storm-whipped mountain ranges quicker than Girly made it across that carpet but she persevered, and she reached, after an epic struggle, the drapes. She clutched, wheezing, at their long folds of blue velvet – dizzying, the flow of the fabric – and Girly whited out for a moment – the lightness! – and then regathered. She dragged the drapes apart the inch or two she had the strength for and aimed a hard squint down onto De Valera Street.

A December Tuesday. As miserable as hell's scullery beneath a soot-black sky. The nerves of the city were ripped. Bohane was looking at a total of eight young fellas reefed since the October bank holiday. Five of them belonged to the Cusack mob, three to the Hartnett Fancy, and the city simmered now with bitterness, rage, threat. Girly smiled. To keep Bohane at a rolling boil you just had to turn the heat up on the burner.

There were nightly rumbles in the Back Trace. There were skirmishes on the 98 Steps. There were random attacks in Smoketown hoorshops. Bottles and insults were being flung across the rooftops of the city. Fellas' sisters were being insulted. And mothers. It had drawn short, just yet, of an outright Feud, but the Hartnett Fancy and the families of the Northside Rises were close to it now.

Girly's reckon: a good Feud was just what the place needed.

In the high distance, she heard the Norries drone their ritual battle chants. She saw above the rooftops the flicker of their bonnas blazing. The Norries were letting it be known they were Feud-ready. Their chants were rhythmical, bass-toned, and punctuated by sombre handclaps. This was the music of taunt and resolve in Bohane.

Polis were everywhere on parade, with their riot sticks swinging, and the fear of the SBJ lighting their bog-crawler eyes. Poor goms of boys fresh off the bog and they were going to be duckin' shkelps and sweepin' innards to the far side of the year's turn.

The *Vindicator*'s evening edition was being hollered by the corner sellers – Big Dom Gleeson was scraping his violin and weeping hot prose for the maintenance of a Yuletide Calm.

Headline:

STOP THE MADNESS!

But the families of the Rises were united in a way they had not been for years and hard-prepped for a move against the Fancy.

Wistfully Girly looked on De Valera Street – ah, that she might have the strength for a good ruck yet herself – and the box windows of the El train zipped past then, the flick and yellow flashing of them, and the street blurred, and her mind went with it – the lightness – and Girly travelled to the Bohane lost-time.

The Gant Broderick she saw as a ten-year-old gypo child. A good-looking kid, blue-eyed and mournful. He was always scouring Dev Street for the main chance. A careful boy. Mind a mouse for you on a tramline. His father was a no-good Nothin' quaffer. His father was half his life nose-deep in a bowl of Wrassler stout and sentimental as a sackful of ballads. The family was in and out from the bog plain: half their time in Trace tenements and half in Big Nothin' trailer homes. The Gant kid was the oldest of them and soon enough he was running wild in the Trace. He took to knocking along with the sharps of the Fancy. Like a mascot he became. Went on errands for them. Was getting busy early on. Was getting into scraps with grown men on the wharfside stones. Oh, and watch the moves on it – you'd put your tuppence on the mannish boy in off the Nothin' rez. A gentle-spoken kid, but proud. Don't speak no pavee put-down if the Gant boy is around – he'd flatten your snout for you. Took to growing in spurts. Took to working a rep. Girly on a stoop one day in the Back Trace saw him come peltin' by on a badness errand and she stuck out a foot and tripped him up.

'Headed for, gypy-kid?'

Stood up slowly, the Gant child, and eyed her carefully as he backed away. He held the gaze on her all the same, he had the confidence for that, and not many could have said the same. Girly knew from one close look where this Gant boy was headed.

'Careful where you place your feet, son.'

Girly returned; she left old Bohane to itself, at least for the time being, but the past, she knew, was never still in this city, it continued to seethe and brew back there, and it gave taint to the present. How would the Gant's return play out? Now there was an intrigue.

She weakened, just for a moment, and she dug her claws into the velvet of the drapes. She took down a hard breath. She opened her eyes and strained for a view to the Aliados and she brought it into focus at just the moment she had waited for.

Wolfie Stanners and Fucker Burke marched out of the place. Girly kept an eye, always, on the young 'uns coming through. It was the young who shaped the city's moment. She watched the short, densely packed ginge – knew his mother – and smiled at the way he always walked with his wee fists bunched. You don't step in that boy's way, and the stringy galoot was beside, the boy of the Burkes, he'd put the heart sideways in you with that razor grin, and Girly thought:

There's little fear of the Fancy if we can keep this pair vertical.

Watched as the boys headed into the Trace and went northering. They were bound, she knew, for the 98 Steps. The Feud was to be officially declared.

In Bohane, at this time, if a Feud was to be engaged, it must be offered in writing, and accepted – acceptance, on behalf of the party challenged, was known always as 'the receipt'. There was an etiquette to the thing; we weren't savages. The Fancy's offering was in Girly's mannish hand.

She felt the strength come back into her. She straightened in her bearing. And as she looked down to the streets below she saw that Bohane had taken to the winter like an old dog to its blanket.

Bohane was *thrun down*, as we say, with winter.

Oh give us a grim Tuesday of December, with the hard-wind taking schleps at our heads, and the rain coming slantways off that hideous fucking ocean, and the grapes nearly frozen off us, and dirty ice caked up top of the puddles, and we are not happy, exactly, but satisfied in our despair.

It is as though we can say . . .

Now!

D'ye see, now, what it is we are dealing with?

14

The 98 Steps

Fucker Burke and Wolfie Stanners set their faces against the hardwind as they climbed the bluffs. Wolfie was zipped neck-deep into a velveteen puffa, and all to be seen was the vicious little head, with his eyes swivelling left and right to check out the sideways for lurking aggravators. Fucker was in a stripey dress shirt made out of a fine yellow cheesecloth – he was the sort of young fella who didn't feel the cold when a ruck was brewing; a strange fire burned inside. They clipped through the Trace and aimed for the 98 Steps. Eerie was the call of the hardwind in winter and the wynds of the Trace were deadhouse sombre.

Feel the chill moistness of the air – Bohane would be a hoor of a town for a lung infection now.

And of course feeling settles into the bones of a place – we know this – and the Trace had an odd, nervous shimmer to it this evening. It'll get this nauseous air when a Feud is on the short fuse.

Fucker and Wolfie made it to the 98 Steps. Ol' Boy Mannion had brokered an unmolested passage to the Rises for the pair but it was for this one evening only, and for this lone purpose.

The 98 is a steep, high-walled climb, and as they ascended, the Back Trace gave way by degrees to the Northside Rises.

From the broad and derelict avenues above the Norrie

voices scraped at the dank sky and the chanters droned an age-old warsong and the flames of the bonnas licked and spat.

Fucker and Wolfie neared the crest of the 98 and the voices faded a note and gave away now to a sequence of long, tuneful whistles.

Clear enough that the Watches of the Rises were marking the ascent.

Fucker Burke said a silent prayer to the Sweet Baba Jay that Mannion's word was good and that the passage was secure, and if it was not, and if he never saw or held his sweet Angelina again – never drowned again in the pools of her eyes – that she would find a happy berth, somewhere, and maybe after a time forget him.

Wolfie Stanners had recourse to no gods but to the even beating of his own fierce Back Trace heart and he stared hard and fearlessly about the Rises avenues as they cleared now the last of the 98.

The avenues of the Rises were broad, treeless, broken, and laid out to a vaguely Soviet pattern. The cement facades of the flatblocks were cracked from decades of freeze-and-thaw. Mean dogs patrolled the gutters, and still the slow whistles sounded, and a sharp voice cut out at them from the shadows of evening.

'Cunty fuckin' scum up outta da Trace!'

Wolfie smiled.

'That the best they got?'

High-rise blocks loomed either side of the broad avenue they walked along. There was a shimmering at the edges as they stared dead ahead – movement there – and yes, there were skangs all around then, evil little scuts of whistling Norrie young fellas, but they stayed back a way as the Fancy pair stepped along.

They hissed from behind and hoicked a few gobbers but they kept their distance true enough.

The melody of the whistles changed and took on an urgency and this told the boys they were coming in close on Cusack ground.

'Looks like we's gettin' a folly awrigh',' said Fucker, and there was a quake to his tone.

Wolfie, shrugging, remained entirely quakeless.

Behind them, the pack of skangs was growing in number by the minute and it was the way the melody of their whistles was so sweet was Fucker's worry.

From a roadside bonfire a rogue dog came at them, it hissed and lurched and bared its fangs, but Wolfie took a swift wee lep into the air and he landed a kick plumb on the cur's nose and it scurried away again.

'Norrie grapes on that crittur,' said Wolfie.

Taunts and threats sniped from the following pack but Wolfie turned daintily on his heel, a single swivel of a movement to grace any dancefloor, and he walked backwards, jauntily, and he smiled at the following pack, and they kept their distance despite the taunts.

Was said in Bohane this winter we're talking about there was no one quite so feared lately as Logan Hartnett's roaming lieutenant, Wolfie Stanners, the short-arse little dude with the ginger top and that evil motherfucker of a leer.

Wolfie and Fucker headed direct for Croppy Boy Heights.

This was the circle of flatblocks that was home ground to the Cusack mob. It was announced by an expanse of rough, untarred ground where barrel fires blazed and wild-eyed flatblock bairns were doing cats-tumbles off ancient pylons and there were severe gusts of Nothin' hardwind from the gaps between the blocks. A tang of menace sat heavily hereabouts.

From the basement of one of the blocks came the heavy throb of a Trojan dub bassline. They lamped it at once as the shebeen block and aimed for it: Fucker breathing shallow, Wolfie breathing deep.

On the Northside Rises, it was at this time the custom for each circle of flatblocks to have its own shebeen. This would be located in one of the flatblock basements, and there, the circle's young gents would drink beer, smoke herb, listen to dub plates, talk tush and practise knife tricks.

Wolfie and Fucker approached the Cusack shebeen.

A pair of goons were arranged in violent lethargy by its stairwell entrance. They carried tyre-chains, wore cross-slung dirks, and tugged idly at their pants. Fucker and Wolfie trained their eyes against the hard stares of the goons, there was a heavy beat of silence, and the goons parted, sure enough, but took their sweet time about it.

Now the basement shebeen opened out.

It was a low dive alright and wall-to-wall with Cusack filth. The family's allegiancers stood about with their bottles of Phoenix ale and their herb pipes on the sweet burn and a sinuous bassline thrummed on the air: feel it in the marrow of your spine.

Wolfie and Fucker did not need to be announced.

Quickly the dub plates were cut. The shebeen mob turned as one on this apparition in the doorway. Dark murmurs, hissed whistles, but the Hartnett Fancy was known always for its brazenness, its insouciance, and these boyos mounted it good:

Wolfie, hunched, beadily staring, with the little paws tightened into hard nuts of fists.

Fucker, hanging loose and limber, and wearing his trademark glaze of vast unpredictability.

97

The Cusack filth cawed like street birds – starlings were their symbol – but the mob did not step forward; it allowed itself to part.

The lights were turned up to a harsh, striplit glare.

A mighty bark sounded from the rear of the mob then and it was answered, ritually, by a mad volley of barks from all around the freaky shebeen.

In the cruel light the pocked skin of the Cusacks was all the worse for the badly inked starling tats it was covered with. (Complexions generally on the Northside Rises are nothing to write home about.)

Wolfie and Fucker looked around the enemy's lair:

Markings on the walls depicted the sacred symbols of the Rises: pit bulls in bout and the strange winged daemon-sluts of the flatblocks and there were memorials also to the dead knifemen of Northside lore.

Wolfie and Fucker looked massively unimpressed as they took a lamp on the Cusack mob:

Cusacks had settled this season on high-rolled denims and armless geansais and they had starling feathers – glossily iridescent, a greenish black – tucked into the bands of their pork-pie hats. Low brows were uniform and gave that vaguely puzzled look that is associated always with Northside knuckle-draggers.

The bark sounded again, was met by a volley of barks, and now it was Eyes Cusack himself, the king barker, who made his way through the mob.

Topless but for his gold chains, stoutly built, as near enough wide as he was long, with a mouthful of gold caps, he grinned malevolently as he approached the boys.

Stopped a couple feet from them.

Eyeballed Wolfie and took measure of the kid.

98

Nodded appreciatively.

'So the boy-chil' step up,' he said.

Rubbed his chin, thoughtfully. Came closer.

'So the boy-chil' workin' his own plan or he keepin' Fancy's affairs in nick?'

Sadly let his shoulders fall.

'Coz, boy-chil', it gotta be said, like? We got a rake o' Cusacks wearin' scars an' welts offa ye lot this las' while, y'check?'

Wolfie agreed.

'Been lively aroun' the place awrigh', Cuse,' he said. 'But there weren't no one got what weren't comin'.'

Hisses, caws, growls sounded – Eyes Cusack raised a hand to stop them.

'Boy-chil' . . . Reefins aside, like? There been floaters on the Bohane river down the years and them floaters got bruds and cuzzes in this place, y'heed?'

Wolfie bowed his head, briefly, and then turned his glance sombrely around the shebeen.

'I'm sorry for yere troubles,' he said.

The mob shook free of itself and came hissing forward but Eyes Cusack raised again his mottled hand, and he cried:

'Hup! Hup now!'

The mob eased up, despite itself, despite its awful compacted energy, and Eyes Cusack was admiring.

'The boy-chil' got grapes,' he said. 'Sure y'ain't got Norrie juice in ya someplace?'

Wolfie winced.

'Oney yella in me's what I piss in the mornins,' he said.

Eyes pursed his lips and raked a sconce on Fucker then.

'An' the galoot got a lash o' the pike in him, yep? Sketch the green eyes on it.'

Fucker spat, and flexed, and glared hard at Cusask.

'Business wan' doin',' he said. 'So don' min' the aul' bitchtalk, Cusey-gal.'

Eyes turned to his hissing mob and smiled and danced a wee skank.

'Oh the Long Fella don't rear no blouses for lieutenants,' he said. 'Sends me up a prize pair o' comanches. Don't do the walk hissel', though, do he? No, sir. Long Fella stayin' close to home, yep? Watchin' his yard. Am I right or wrong, ginge?'

'Mr Hartnett is indisposed,' said Wolfie.

'Oh aye?' said Cusack. 'What's he at? Straightenin' the eyes in his bint's head, s'he? Or he workin' a little plan with his mammy, like? He mammy's lil' boy yet, like? O' course the Hartnetts all for doin' business down the New Town these times, ain't they? Herb and hoors not good enough for the Fancy no more. No, sir. Now it's all trams and manses, ain't it?'

Wolfie raised a hand to signal the talk was at an end.

'We gots somethin' to put t'ye,' he said.

He reached inside his puffa and removed an envelope of silver vellum. It was embossed with the Hartnett Fancy's mark – a puck goat's head. Inside was the Feud's declaration.

Wolfie Stanners offered the envelope to Eyes Cusack.

Beat – a weird pause.

The pause suggested to Wolfie that confidence might not be all it should be among the ranks of the Cusack mob. But Eyes reached for the envelope then, and stuffed it in the waistband of his kecks, and from the arse pocket of same he took out a filthy scrap of paper that had been folded over twice, and he passed it to Wolfie.

Wolfie opened it out to find a drawing so crude as to be

100

done by a child's hand. It showed a skinny stick-man in cray-oned colours with a cock-and-balls attached to his forehead.

'The receipt,' said Eyes Cusack. 'See if yer man spot a likeness.'

Wolfie nodded most politely and with Fucker in tandem he turned to go.

'I'll let him know Feud's accepted,' he said.

'Do that, boy-chil',' said Eyes Cusack. 'An' we'll see ye down there, check?'

'Time o' your choosin', Cuse. All the same t'us, like.'

They walked again the pocked avenues of the Rises. There was a heat up in them now. There was a great thrumming on the air. There was going to be a Feud the size of which Bohane city hadn't seen in fucking yonks, y'sketchin'?

15

Black Crab Soup

The Ho Pee Ching Oh-Kay Koffee Shoppe, a whistle after midnight, and three steaming bowls of black crab soup were carried from the back kitchen by a wordless, scowling Ching uncle.

These were set with grave ceremony before:

– Mr Logan Hartnett, aka the Albino, aka the Long Fella, and he was sat there, breezing on the moment, and with a toothpick he worked lumps of cashew from the gaps between his yellow teeth. He was all got up in a wowser of a straight-cut grey vinyl suit – its sheen catching the Ho Pee's fairy-light glow – and there was a matching grey vinyl mackintosh laid over the back of his chair. *Dapper* motherfucker.

– Miss Jenni Ching, boss-lady of the Ho Pee ever since her black-mooded momma had tossed her small demented bones into the Bohane river (just a quick headlong dash from the caff), on account of dog-fight debts, some said, or because of a persistent strain of Ching family madness, according to others, and Jenni regarded the fatty, creamy soup her uncle offered with an as-if glare – on *my* hips? – and she pushed it aside. She was in a white leather jumpsuit up top of hoss-polis zippered boots, with her fine hair let down, and her hair was streaked and worn this season in a blunt-cut fringe that she blew aside with regular, rhythmic spouts of tabsmoke.

– Mrs Macu Hartnett, née Simhao, born to the Café Aliados, the queen of the Back Trace Fancy, with any amount of a cashmere jersey dress worn in a clingy fit beneath a thin crinolene duster coat (cream) that didn't cost her tuppence ha'penny in whatever high-faluting New Town boutique she scored it in, and she was eyeballing Jenni hard, and she was eyeballing Logan hard, and she was thinking: I'm forty-fuckin'-three and I'm sat around talkin' fuckin' *gang fights*?

'Many families Cuse gonna send down up top o' his own?' said Jenni.

'I'm guessing three tops,' said Logan. 'He'll have the McGroartys, sure enough. McGroartys are born latchiko. McGroartys would hop into a Feud on account of two flies fucking. He'll have the Lenanes also. That's a cert, coz the Lenanes can be bought, the Lenanes have always been bought. After that, well . . .'

Logan flapped a hand in the air, dismissively, to illustrate the thinness of the Rises' alliance.

'That's sure a lot o' chanters they got hollerin' for a three-family descent,' said Macu.

'If you wanted to be of a negative set of mind, love-o'-my-heart, you might think so,' said Logan.

In truth, he could not but hear them: the high bluffs of Bohane city were raucous with Norrie Feud-chants.

'A quare rake o' bonnas burnin' an' all, Logan? Saw 'em an' I comin' down from the house.'

Strings of fires all along the bluffs – Norrie families on a war footing was the message.

'They can light their little fires all they want. And remember this much for me, Macu, please – you never once in your fucking life had a good feeling the night before a Feud, check?'

'Maybe a time comes when there be one Feud too far, Logan, y'heed?'

He glared at his wife, but kept silent his anger, and he twisted it instead to aim coldly, smilingly at his girl-chil' lieutenant.

'Jenni-gal,' he said, 'I understand you're becoming quite a regular 'cross at the Bohane Arms?'

Jenni Ching didn't so much as flutter an eyelash.

'I'm findin' it's the kind o' spot you'd hear an interestin' yarn about the Bohane los'-time,' she said.

'Oh yeah?' said Macu. 'Concernin'?'

'All kin' o' caper,' said Jenni. ''bout how peoples come up and 'bout how they goes back down again.'

'My dear mother would have the sketch for you there sure enough.'

Jenni eyeballed Macu hard.

'An' 'bout where it was peoples come from. Originally, like.'

Laminate posters on the Ho Pee wall showed roosters, pigs, rats. The fairy lights were strung from wall to wall above the Formica tables and they burned a lurid note. Logan was smiling now as he spooned up his soup – he liked a catfight.

Macu, polite as the seeping of a poison, said:

'An' where's it the Chings is boxin' out of original, Jenni-chick?'

Jenni from her tit pocket yanked a stogie, clipped and lit it, sucked deep and blew a brownish smoke.

'Chings in Bohane goin' back an' again beyond the los'-time. S'town built offa Ching blood. We goes way back. We ain't in off the las' wave at all, missus.'

A motion she drew in the air then, slowly and looping,

with her cigar hand, to indicate the wave, and the smoke made signals indeciperable atop the Ho Pee's dreamy glow.

'Ye sure ain't,' said Macu. 'Chings been snakin' aroun' them wynds long as I got the recall. Gettin' the reck on everyone's business, like.'

'Ladies,' said Logan, 'please.'

He pushed back his soup. He knit long fingers across his slender belly. He always enjoyed the eve of a Feud. He knew that Eyes Cusack would not for long keep his mongrels leashed, and his mood was high and expectant. When you were running a Fancy, regular demonstrations of rage were needed to keep the town in check and, just as importantly, the Fancy boys in trim. Too much sweetness and light and they got fat, unpleasantly smiley and over-interested in the fashion mags.

Jenni Ching looked from Logan to Macu and back again.

Jenni Ching raised her brow and blew smoke to the tapped-brass ceiling of the Ho Pee.

Jenni Ching was thinking: This is what's runnin' the Back Trace motherfuckin' Fancy?

'Colours to be raised?' she asked.

'Absolutely,' said Logan. 'If we're going do it at all, we're going to do it properly.'

'Colours a pain in the fuckin' gee,' she said. 'Fuck we wanna be marchin' with flags for, H? This the Paddy's Day fuckin' Parade or what, like? Just get the fuck out there and reef the scutty fucks! Flags and fuckin' colours ain't gonna make no differ to the gack we welt outta the Rises filth no-how, y'check me?'

Logan sighed, was sweetly paternal.

'Jenni?' he said. 'We're not savages. If there's young fellas gonna be planted in the boneyard tomorrow, they ain't going

105

down without knowing who's responsible. Fancy's colours will be raised.'

'S'the kin' o' mawky shite that gets my melt off,' she said. 'Flags an' fuckin' banners . . .'

'I'm hearin' Girly talkin',' said Macu.

'True enough,' Logan smiled.

Girly Hartnett was long noted for nose-thumbing at tradition. Girly's reckon was that Bohane was far too sentimental a town. Of course, it didn't stop her spending a quare chunk of clock travelling to the lost-time.

'All I'm sayin', we've enough on us plates, like, without puttin' on the usual circus –'

'Jenni,' Logan was stern here, 'don't call it a circus.'

'All I'm sayin'–'

'Jenni? Just leave it, please?'

'But Girly says –'

'Don't mind fucking Girly! I'm running the fucking Fancy!'

'That so, H? Then why's it Girly gots to sign off on the Feud?'

His cold glare would strip a lesser child of its front but not Jenni.

'A nicety,' he said. 'Protocol. Keep her thinking she's involved still. It keeps her going, you know?'

A silence swelled.

Logan pussed.

Jenni smoked.

And Macu looked out into Smoketown's greenish night-time haze. It was the early a.m. parade of skinpoppers and inebriates and hoor-botherers. She wondered – against her will – if he was among the streets somewhere. And if she would recognise the gaatch of him. If he still carried in the same way. She had not replied to the letter. There had been

106

no further word. It was sixty days since the letter had been passed to her.

Jenni Ching slithered from her seat and made for the door. As she opened it a great surge of street noise rose.

'Time you givin' em till, H?'

'They won't need long, if I know Cusacks.'

'Fancy prepped?' said Macu.

'Stop your fretting, girl. Been weeks prepped if I'm right, Jen?'

'Fancy'd ate a child, H.'

He finished his soup and lay down his spoon and clasped his thin fingers across his middle.

'Go and make sure anyhow, Jenni-gal.'

'Feuds!' Macu cried. 'An' we a stretch pas' fuckin' forty!'

'It's the life, girl,' Logan said.

'For how long more, Logan?'

Jenni waved as she stepped outside.

'Tell Girly I was askin' for her,' Macu called.

Jenni mouthed a badness beneath her breath.

'Say what, girl?'

'Say nothin', Mrs Hartnett.'

'I'll be fuckin' dug out o' you yet, slant, y'hear me?' Macu said.

'Ladies, would ye leave it? Please?' Logan said.

'But d'ya hear her, Logan? About straightenin' eyes she's mutterin'!'

16

Wolfie: His Allegiances

Wolfie Stanners hung by the ruff of his jumper from a coat hook in the schoolhouse cloakroom. He squealed for help.

'C'mon to fuck will someone!'

But nobody came to free him.

He was ten years old, the tiniest runt in the creation, and the eyes rolled dangerously in his chickpea head as his feet flailed at the air.

'Please!' he screamed. 'Someone!'

Nobody came.

His breaths jabbed hard at the walls of his chest and tasted of sick.

'C'mon'll someone!'

Nobody came, and he swung from the coat hook, and he soaked in a panic sweat.

It was a lardy fatarse off the Rises that had hung him there.

'S'what ya get for sniffin' up sisters, filthy ginge!'

Wolfie in truth had tried to crawl up the gaberdine skirt of a wee Norrie sister – just for the sconce, like – but this was a harsh measure of justice.

'Please, someone!'

He hung there, and he jigged on the air, and he near enough throttled himself.

'C'mon, someone!'

But his screams came weaker now and hardly carried at all.

He stretched his arms behind his head but his reach was too short and fell shy of the hook. The jumper's ruff caught tightly at his throat and he tried to force his weight to rip it free but it would not give. And Wolfie turned blue.

'Fuck you doin' up there, Stanners?'

The Burke kid at ten years old was already a long-legged galoot and a gommie sort with it. He was a blurry apparition down there below Wolfie in the cloakroom, and the small boy squinted to bring him into focus, and he lamped him as that beanpole from the wynds – Fucker, he was known as.

'C'mon t'fuck an' get me down offa here'd ya!'

His spindly arms had no more than the girth of chopsticks, Fucker Burke, but might have been threaded with steel wool for the strength in them, and easily from his tiptoes he lifted Wolfie clear from the coat hook, and the runt staggered into a corner of the cloakroom and spluttered his guts on the floor.

'Min' yer shoes,' said Fucker Burke.

Wiping the drool away, Wolfie turned to Fucker, and he cleaned his gob with his sleeve, and he was awestruck in the presence of a saviour. He said:

'Y'help me get him?'

Fucker liked the gaatch of this gingery kid – even if he couldn't tell exactly what it was that made him smile (it was the dense, packed *menace*) – and he said:

'Know where we can get diesel an' all, y'check me, gingey-pal?'

Later:

The lardy-boy off the Rises wobbled along the wynds of

109

the Trace and headed for the 98 Steps on the dreck after-noon of a winter's day. Lunatic gulls dive-bombed his nosh bag but he batted 'em away with an impatient, pudgy arm. He had a duck's walk, the chubster – here's me head, me arse is comin' – and he chomped on a lump of macaroon so hard the jaw-motion made a thundery roar in his ears. He didn't hear Wolfie Stanners step up the one side of him, nor Fucker Burke the other.

Fucker gripped and twisted the boy's arms and locked them behind his back and he marched him down a dead-end wynd.

'Th'fuck, like?'

Typical Norrie squawk of fear in there, sketch?

'Big fella now, aintcha?' Wolfie said.

Fucker held him steady, and Wolfie kicked the boy's shins until they gave from under him, and the lardarse was on his knees then, whelping, and Fucker knelt in behind, and he held the boy's arms locked with one hand and with his free hand scrunched the boy's hair to get his head back.

The boy screamed hard and showed his fat pink tonsils to the Bohane sky.

Wolfie poured diesel from a can into the opened gullet. Lardarse choked on it and spat and Wolfie slapped him; Fucker chortled.

Drizzled the diesel on the boy's clothes and hair, too, most carefully – he'd a dainty touch for badness, Wolfie – and he produced the matchbook with a flourish, and he signalled for Fucker to back off, sharpish, and as he did so, Wolfie ripped a match, sparked it, and flicked.

So it was a lardarse kid on fire sprinted tubbily the wynds of the Trace and he ran onto the dock and leapt head first into the roaring blackwaters of the river. Flapped and splashed and gurgled, and the sight caused a wailing commotion on the wharfside stones – auld dears out of the Trace market threw their sprouts and cabbages in the air and roared a great commotion, coz it wasn't every day you saw a fat child in flames, not even on the Bohane front – but then a hero of a dock polis came pounding along, with his porter-gut swinging, and by 'n' by the lardarse got fished out again with a winch hook.

Lay on the quay, then, quenched but sizzling.

Ain't been a pretty sight since, the same lardarse, face on him like an S'town burrito, and plenty more in the city suffered at the same hands as the years turned, and as many as were left sucking the air and could tell the tale, the same amount again were fattening maggots down the eerie boneyard. Was the way of things Trace-deep since Wolfie and Fucker took to working in tag.

They realised that day that no matter how fast their hearts might beat at the brink of an atrocity they would not pull back from it, not ever, and Wolfie saw where this gift could send them in Bohane.

But now it was the eve of a Feud, and in the small, ominous hours of the night Wolfie walked the Back Trace, alone, and he felt a creep of grim knowledge:

No Bohane Fancy ever had two names to it.

He tried to put manners on his thoughts – the black surge of them was malevolent as the river's. Walked through the 98er Square and he felt the dip of the glance from the quare-hawks who were gathered beneath the winter-bared trees in their greatcoats, with their sacks of tawny wine, and he knew that his name was spreading, its power building, but he realised that it had Fucker's maniac strength behind it, too. He knew there were others in the ranks had ambition to match his own. He knew there was no viciousness to match his but for Fucker's, but for Jenni's.

Hardwind was up and Norrie chanters sounded in the distance and the Fancy was mobbed 'cross in Smoketown. He would go to the ranks soon enough. He felt an icy tinkling at his spine – thought he sussed a follow – and he looked sharply over his shoulder but he saw nobody, and he told himself it was just Feud juice that had him edgy.

He decided on a quiet drink in a groghole down a Trace wynd. Pushed in the door to a brood of silence. There were just a couple of old sorts at the low tables. Wolfie sat at the bar and asked for half a Wrassler stout and the ancient dear serving said it would put the iron in him sure enough, boy, medicinal for ya, and the smile Wolfie showed as the stout settled to its blackness put a certain end to all conversation. Sat with his half and his thoughts and it was as quiet a night as you'd get down the Trace – with the Feud so near, as many as could had cleared out already. Wolfie sat there all soulful and bothered in the half-light of the dank old bar.

Wolfie wore:

A neatly cut Crombie of confederate grey above green tweed peg pants, straight-legged, a starched white shirt, collar open to show a harlequin-patterned cravat, and a pair of tan-coloured arsekickers on the hooves that'd been imported from far Zagreb (them boys knew how to make a boot, was the Fancy's reckon; if the Long Fella wasn't walkin' Portuguese, he was walkin' Croat).

Wolfie sipped at his Wrassler's smoky bitterness. There was a sulk to his mouth. It was never far away, not since his ninth year, and the night that his mother, Candy, got herself kicked to death in the Trace. She was a quick-fingered thief and a scuttery drunk and she wasn't shy with a blade in her paw. She worked the snakebend line of De Valera Street. He used to stand up on a street bench to keep decks for polis. He smiled over the stout as he thought of Candy inside in Horgan's Department Store, whipping eyeliner pencils and tubs of mascara to flog to the Smoketown tushies at low bars in the afternoons. Drinking money. And nightly, then, their roaming of the Trace. The way she'd drag him close to her when she was boozed up and croon old songs, the tunes of the lost-time. He felt yet the hard beating of her heart and the way she nuzzled his neck. Later in the night she'd disappear for a while. The night came that she didn't come back. She was found by the 98 Steps. Wolfie was brought there by Trace women and he did not cry at all but he lay with her for a few minutes, where she'd been stomped, and already he felt the way the cold of the ground rose up into her. Then he got dragged away and Candy got shovelled up.

He blamed Norries, and he finished the Wrassler, and he called another. Drank sombre; brewed foul thoughts.

Another old sort arrived in off the wynd and blew on his hands and brushed past Wolfie – want to watch himself – and he took a seat barside. Called for a hot Jameson. A big-boned old sort, voice like an actor, like something out of the Crescent Hall, and Wolfie noted the hands on him; the hands were massive, scarred, gnarled.

Wolfie kept an eye on the old sort in the mirror over the bar.

Half mad by the looks of things. Mouthing off to himself. Square-cut chin, as handsome as an old actor an' all, but gone to daftness. And then the old sort took a half-swivel on the high stool.

'Wolfie-boy makin' a move?' he whispered.

An actor's whisper – hushed yet loud. Wolfie didn't so much as grace it with a look. Kept face.

'An openin' for the boy-child?' said the old sort.

Wolfie turned an eye to him now and glared. The old sort smiled and nodded.

'Ne'er a sign o' that bead, no?'

A chill came into Wolfie then.

'Madam? Lay up another Wrassler for this kid. He's after comin' over class o' pale-faced.'

Wolfie stared straight ahead and felt for the four-inch dirk in his waistband – it was gone.

'Pale as his master,' the Gant said, and he took the dirk from his inside pocket and slid it along the bar.

'Be more careful with that,' he said.

Wasn't often Wolfie Stanners had the gob dry up on him but it was dried up now sure enough.

'You'll have got the message, Wolf?'

The others in the bar supped up and ghosted from the place, lively, and the ancient barkeep arranged herself as far down the end of the counter as was possible.

Wolfie didn't answer the Gant Broderick – he just stared at him.

'Underneath the bridge, Wolfie?'

The Gant shook his head sadly.

'Mercy on that poor man's soul,' he said. 'Shockin' end he came to.'

Wolfie's gut told him to flee the place but the Gant's dark stare mesmerised.

'You working a plan, Wolfie?'

Wolfie turned from him and looked straight ahead.

'You'd want to be at this stage, child. The way the Fancy's gonna break up?'

Wolfie didn't answer.

'Come back along with me here,' said the Gant, 'and maybe we can talk a little.'

The Gant went to a low table in the rear dim of the grog-hole, and Wolfie found himself slipping from the high stool, and going quietly to join him there.

17

The Shortest Day

Solstice broke and sent its pale light across the Big Nothin'
bogs. A half-woken stoat peeped scaredly from its lair in a
drystone wall and a skinny old doe stood alert and watchful
on a limestone outcrop. Sourly lit, a cruel winter scene – a
raven clan soared and watched for scavenge, and there was
a slushy melt to the hillside as the distant sun burned, and
a puck goat chewed morosely on a high mound there.
Bohane river ran as ever it did and fed off the bog ice that
quaked into it as the shortest day's sun came still higher.
Surge of the water was all to be heard as Ol' Boy Mannion
stood in the first of the year-turn light on a high bank of
the river and pensively urinated into it.

He finished, and trousered himself, and he stood a while
longer to listen.

It was among Ol' Boy's more esoteric opinions that the
bog plain had over the course of the years become weirdly
. . . *untamped*. These times, the city of Bohane was powered
largely on its turf, and the bog had been cut away and reefed
everywhere. Who knew what passages to its underworld
had been disturbed? The bog's occult nature had been inter-
fered with, its body left scarred, its wounds open, and might
this also be a source of the Bohane taint? It would not surprise
Ol' Boy Mannion one bit.

He tied the string of his pants and he let the hardwind

come in rearside of him and he aimed his boots in the direction of Eight Mile Bridge.

There was a tingle of excitement in Ol' Boy this morning and he knew it was caused by the prospect of bloodshed and he was shamed by that.

Oh, the Bohane taint darkened each and all of us – even a long-tooth as honourable as Ol' Boy.

He had sent a runner-child to the city to watch on developments overnight. A Feud was like an ember lying low in a tinder of straw – no telling when the spark would ignite, but that it surely would, and Ol' Boy sure as the Sweet Baba bled on a cross wasn't going to be around when it did. Ol' Boy had long since slapped a preservation order on hissel' – a long-tooth out the tip-end o' this western peninsula was never by accident, always by design. A long life was a decision to be made.

The child was about due back to the inn at Eight Mile and Ol' Boy marched for it and he kept an eye on the angle of the sun to know the hour.

Ol' Boy wore:

High-top boots expensively clicker'd with gold taps, a pair of hip-hugging jodhpur-style pants in a faded mauve tone, an amount of gold chains, a heavy mink coat to keep out the worst of the hardwind's assaults and a goatskin beanie hat set pavee-style at the crown of his head.

Truth of it – this was as suave an old dude as you'd come across in the whole of the Bohane creation.

He went to Eight Mile via the hills. It was his tactic always to keep to the higher paths. Ghost around the place as best as you can – that was the way to stay alive out on Nothin'. His shadow as he climbed the hillsides was long and needling in the white winter sun. He was not at all immune to the dark magic he walked through.

Nothin's colours in low December:

The soft gold of the withered reeds – pale as an old wedding band's gold.

The bluish mica glint of the stone knolls – the same precise glint as a gull's eye's.

The purples, discriminating, of the sleeping gorse.

Ol' Boy walked on and the winter light came across Big Nothin' slantwise and grudgingly – the bog plain was a whole heap of distance from the sun, and it had all the odour of that distance. It was a grave's wet musk.

Mannion chewed on his thoughts. His hope was that the Feud sparked up fast and was over as quickly and that it would have the rejuvenating effect of a gorse fire. Then he could go back and pad a downtown prowl. See how things settled.

He walked the high reaches and skirted the boundary of the pikey rez and wondered what messages those sombre folk had been reading lately in the arrangement of cloud-fall and the scattering of the stars.

The pavee kind knew sure enough when there was Trouble a-brew.

He began a descent towards Eight Mile and walked for a time on the river's high bank and was mesmerised by its remorselessness. He came at length to Eight Mile Bridge and he crossed the great stones of it and the Bohane thundered for the city. He waved to the scatter of inebriates beneath the bridge's arches: the red-eyed habituals of the scene, suckin' tawny, and these were intimates of Ol' Boy, too, but then who wasn't?

He descended the three stone steps to the inn and pushed through the door.

Turfsmoke, hidden nooks, ale fumes.

He went barside and nodded to the innkeeper. She was a stout-thighed widow with a game eye on her and she gave him the flash of it sure enough.

Ol' Boy caught a kiss as though she had blown one and gently caressed it onto his cheek and winked.

'Pour me an amber, sweetness,' he said, 'an' pour it slow so's I can have a good aul' lamp at ya.'

She laughed for him, huskily.

'Ya never lost it, Boy Mannion.'

Ol' Boy had made his parade of life without ever knowingly failing to flirt with a serving lady. Even if they were plain, he viewed it as a necessary courtesy. If we do not have manners in this life, we do not have much. He took the glass as it was served to him and slapped down a shilling piece. She moved her hand for the coin – a shiver of lust in the auld dear yet, though she must have been pushin' forty – but he slapped his hand over the coin at the last moment and hers fell onto his. Let the moment sit, did Ol' Boy, and he winked for her once more.

'Ne'er a sign o' that runner-child, missus?'

The innkeeper took on a look of fright and crossed her arms across her bosom and allowed one hand to rise and clutch hungrily her throat – this was a peninsula woman's semaphore to indicate troubled times.

'Sure ain't we all waitin' on the same young fella, Mr Mannion?'

Ol' Boy took his glass of beer, and winked again, and he skulked about the premises. The usual Big Nothin' quaffers lurked in the smoky corners. There was a good crowd in for this hour of the morning – all knew that word was expected on the Bohane situation. Ol' Boy took a seat by the fireplace nook and sipped at the bitter Phoenix ale and he waited.

119

Sipped.

And he waited.

Listened.

He sipped.

And just before noon the door fell in and a welt of hard-wind in a flash filled the room and raised smoke from the fires and as the door was kicked closed and the turfsmoke settled again everyone turned to see if it was the runner-child who had arrived but indeed it was not – it was Big Dom Gleeson.

The fat newsman stood in the middle of the floor in an emerald frock-coat and knee-high patent boots and closed his eyes and shook his great jowls in distress and sounded a bull-elephant's moan.

'Oh!' he cried.

Staggered – *staggered!* – over to where Ol' Boy sat and collapsed – *collapsed!* – onto a chair beside him and he let his frail, pudgy fingers reach for Ol' Boy's arm and he trembled.

'Oh . . .' said Big Dom.

'I know, Dom,' said Ol' Boy, 'your angina.'

The innkeeper brought a bowl of brandy for Dom and he wept – *wept!* – thanks to her and clutched her hand and lay it against his brow.

'Yes I know, Mr Gleeson, I know,' she said.

As she departed, raising her eyes, Ol' Boy raked a knowing look over Big D, and he smiled.

'So you been inside watching the ructions?'

'Indeed I have not,' said Big Dom. 'They ain't seen my arse for dust in that horrid, horrid town!'

'You got out awright then?'

'I did, Mr Mannion,' he said, and he patted with a wink

his stout legs. 'Early yesterday, I took to me getaway sticks. I thank you kindly for sending the word, sir.'

Ol' Boy sipped.

'So if you ain't been inside watchin' the Feud, what explains your distressed condition? Don't tell me, Dom, that you've been hiding out in some Ten Light knockin' shop?'

Ten Light was the village of the Nothin' hill country where the rural hoor-parlours clustered.

Dom shut his eyes in mortification, and grimly nodded.

'Let me guess, Dom . . . Suckin' on a dream-pipe . . . skullin' French brandy . . . an' buried to the maker's name in buxom jailbait?'

'Oh I'm a weak, WEAK man!' cried Big Dom.

The door fell in again, and the hardwind again set the smoke from the turf-fires billowing, and it settled as the door was kicked shut and this time, true enough, a biteen of a young fella was revealed: it was the runner-child.

Child at once dropped flat onto his back in the middle of the flagstone floor.

Child stared hard and with great derangement at the ceiling and had terror in his eyes.

Child went into a trembling fit.

Ol' Boy went to him and he knelt and cradled the child's head in his hands and he cried out to the innkeeper.

'Slug o' the Beast there, missus, an' lively!'

She brought from beneath the counter a bottle of illicit green spirit – the Beast – as was brewed in the high reaches of the Nothin' massif by a pair of retard brothers who had the gift. Everyone in the inn gathered around the child. Innkeeper passed to Ol' Boy the bottle and he uncapped it and he filled the cap with the noxious fluid and he held it to the child's trembling lips. Drizzled it down carefully. The child gasped and spat and retched and then swallowed a wee sip and brightened just a shade. He opened his mouth for another drop or two. Ol' Boy allowed him some. The runner-child it was clear had been witness to Dark Events.

Big Dom most professionally – grant him that – slid from the inside pocket of his frock-coat a spiral-bound notebook and licked the nib of his pencil.

'Easy now,' said Ol' Boy. 'And try and tell it for us, yes?'

As the Beast went to work, it brought slowly some colour and strength to the child. He tried to shape a word and everybody leaned in closer.

'Bo . . .' he said.

Silence was deathly in the room as the child struggled with the word. A little more of the Beast was drizzled into him. Fire of the spirit lit the word.

'Bo . . .' he said, '. . . hane!'

'Very good,' said Ol' Boy, drily. 'But what of it, child?'

'Bohane,' said the child, 'is gone . . . to . . . to . . . to the Sweet Baba!'

Ol' Boy took the child's hand and stroked it gently.

'Tell as much as you can, son.'

Child was stronger now by quick degrees. He was feeding well off slugs of the Beast and off the attention also.

'Polis blockin' all roads out,' he said.

Low whistles caroused the turf-smoked inn.

'High Boreen?' Ol' Boy prompted.

'Cordon up, sir,' said the child.

'How'd ya get out, son?'

'Came crossbog.'

Shivers in the room at the thought of the runner-child coming crossbog in low winter. That would be a trial for a fit and grown man. Wonder a swamphole hadn't devoured the wee cove. Big Dom happily flushed as he sketched notes for a *Vindicator* colour-piece.

'Way's she blowin' in there now, child-o'-mine?' the newsman whispered.

Runner shut his eyes and slowly he let the story come.

'All the night through bonnas is leppin' off the Rises like dogs for the lick of a bone, sir.'

'Ah sure we know that,' said Ol' Boy. 'Sure the bonnas were seen from as far back as the plantation road.'

'Come first crack?' said the child. 'First the Norrie whistlers marched out, then the fife drums . . .'

'Uh-oh.' Big D was loving it.

'Then the Norrie chanters came down, sir. An' as many as never's been heard!'

'Go on, runner. More.'

'Nex' thing I seen? An' with me own peepers, like? Seen . . . an . . . an . . . an . . .'

'Say it, child!'

'I seen an . . . an *eight*-family descent, sir.'

The inn collapsed into delirium, wailing, tears. And the Big Nothin' drinkers, as at all times of Trouble, turned immediately to religion:

'Oh mother o' the Sweet Baba!'

'Oh Sweet Baba won't ya come down an' protect us!'

'SBJ be good!'

'SBJ be faithful!'

'Oh Baba don't forsake us said don't forsake us now!'

'Baba-love be with us!'

'Baba-love always be with us!'

'Ah shush it, will ye, for fucksake!' cried Ol' Boy. 'Herd o' bleatin' fuckin' lambs!'

He leaned down close to the runner-child.

'Speak to me now, son, please. Twas an eight-family mob, you're sure of that? You counted *eight*, like?'

'Eyes Cusack, sir? He got the McGroartys, the Lenanes, the Dillons –'

'That's not news at all. He's always got them fuckers.'

'But he got the Halpins, sir, he got the Fitzhenrys, he got the Lenihans too –'

'Sweet Baba-love don't desert us now!'

'Baba come down among us! Said Baba come down!'

'Please!' cried Ol' Boy. 'Will ye lay off the bollockin' Baba-love! Baba won't help ye now!'

Runner-child's eyes focused on Ol' Boy's, and locked, and Ol' Boy knew it was truth the child spoke.

'An', sir? He got the McGraths an' all, y'check me?'

'That's the eight.' Big Dom whistled low and made the note – eight (8) – and confirmed it with a tick mark.

Ol' Boy Mannion didn't like the sound of this one bit. All around him in the inn there was disbelief, awe, terror. Tell ye this for thruppence: many a yella moon had shone on the glorified pig's mickey that is the Bohane peninsula since we had seen the likes of an eight-family mobbed descent off the Northside Rises.

'Eight families . . .' said Ol' Boy, calculating. 'That could mean anything up to . . . I dunno . . . what are we talkin', Dom . . . a hunnerd an' fifty latchiko headjobs?'

'Easy,' said Big D.

'At least that, sir,' said the runner-child, 'if'n yer to go by what these peepers ha' seen.'

'That'll be plenty to take the Trace,' said the innkeeper.

'I'd nearly want to be thinkin' about a thirty-two-page special,' Big Dom sighed.

'Shush, will ye?' said Ol' Boy. 'Let the child tell it.'

'Happens they gots the Trace awready, sir.'

Consternation in the inn at this, and more wailing, but Ol' Boy raised a firm hand to stop it.

'What're you sayin', son?'

'Hartnett deserted the Trace, sir . . . He left it to 'em!'

Shock at this, and hisses of anger, but Ol' Boy smiled.

'Fancy's where?'

'Ain't seen it meself, sir. But it's said the Fancy's mobbed yet 'cross the S'town footbridge.'

'And he has the Trace all locked down, am I right?'

'Every las' tenement in the Trace shut and bolted agin the Norrie assault since before first crack, sir. Fancy didn't send a sinner out to meet 'em, sir.'

'I see,' said Ol' Boy. 'Looks like the Long Fella wants the Norrie mob to blow itself out.'

'You've lamped it in one, Mr Mannion,' said Big D. 'He's lullin' 'em!'

'At least that's what we hope, Dom. You get a look on the families close up, child? It have the look of a mob that means business?'

'Blackthorns. Hatchets. Hammers,' said the child. 'Dirks flashin' and bricks being lobbed. They's layin' into anythin' that moves Trace-side but not much does move, sir. Bar a few dogs an' drunks, like.'

'Ain't it shockin',' said the innkeeper, 'for this manner a caper to be goin' on in Bohane an' we oney three days to the birthday o' the Sweet Baba Jay? What do be wrong with us at all?'

'There are those, ma'am, who'll say it carries in off that river . . .' Big Dom mused.

'Stow it!' barked Ol' Boy. 'Go on, child.'

'Cusack's mob is makin' shit o' the Trace, sir. Smashin' it up bad now. Startin' fires in the squares.'

'And they're on the rant already, I suppose?'

'An' hard on it, sir. Suckin' at carry-sacks o' moscato and batterin' the herb-pipes goodo. Gots some o' their wenches down awready and havin' a lash off the jiggy in plain view o' the wynds.'

'Oh they've got no class!' cried Dom Gleeson.

'Norries can't even rent it,' Ol' Boy concurred.

'Bohane sliced in twain,' sighed the innkeeper, and she too was loving every minute of it.

'An' is Hartnett prepped, y'reckon?'

Child paused for a slug of the Beast. Wee fecker had a tongue got for it so he had.

'Is said it's the man-chil' Stanners is callin' the Fancy to order.'

'Ah,' said Ol' Boy.

'No sign o' Long Fella hissel' just yet. Is said the ginge gots the Fancy about eighty strong and mobbed beneath the colours. Waitin' on a whistle is all.'

'They're beneath the colours, they are?'

'The purple and the black, sir.'

'Indeed,' said Ol' Boy, and as he felt the full horror of the day, he felt also the great pride of it.

'Polis tactic?' Big Dom enquired.

'Cordon gone up every which way, sir. Everythin' Traceside o' Dev's a no-go zone.'

'They're trying to contain,' said Big Dom. 'Good luck to 'em with that.'

'Could it spread to Nothin'?' The innkeeper was fearful now.

Ol' Boy considered.

'That's a tricky call to make, ma'am. We know what Big Nothin's like. Sympathies out here might switch with a lick

126

of the hardwind. A lot of us got peoples in the Trace but a lot of us got peoples on the Rises too. My gut's read? It won't spread bogside till one or other of the mobs is suffering an' suffering bad.'

The runner-child had by now greatly recovered. He was placed on a stool by the fire and was coddled there. He was fed hot milk and further slugs of the Beast. Big Dom leaned in close and coaxed from the child some further background detail. There was great pride in the child at having witnessed the outbreak of a Bohane Feud. And the inn this winter's day had suddenly about it a most festive and excited air.

Ol' Boy left the crowd to its gossiping and its chirruping and he took a quiet high stool in a snug. Was it wise, he wondered, for the Long Fella to allow the boy Stanners such a prominent role upfront of a massed Fancy?

Big Dom, reading over his notes, came to join him.

'Looks like y'picked a wise day for a spot check on yer Nothin' bureau, D?'

'I thank you again for the word, Mr Mannion.'

They sat amid the flickers and turfsmoke and they let the situation hover before them a moment – picked at it silently. Then:

'Way you readin' the Hartnett tactic, Dom?'

Fat newsman's eyelashes fluttered.

'Leavin' the Wolfie-boy step out? Seems to me like he's droppin' a hint he's set to move along, Mr Mannion.'

'Droppin' it for who?'

'His lady wife?'

'Could be you're right, Dom.'

'Maybe she wants him spendin' more time above in the yard, y'check? Helpin' with the rose garden.'

'Or goin' at a more respectable line o' business. Of course,

127

it must be hard to balance family life with the Fancy's runnins. You'd have sympathy there.'

'He don't wan' to be leavin' any gaps on the home front . . .'

'Indeed. But ain't it weird, hah? That the Gant comin' back might spell a lucky season for the Wolfie-boy.'

'It is strange, Mr Mannion, what can bring change to a Fancy.'

'A change to the city with it.'

Thoughtful, the pair, as they considered love's quiet but decisive manoeuvres, and how an entire city might be shaped by them, a fiefdom, a world. Ol' Boy called another amber; Dom, a French brandy.

Was the Wolfie-boy coming through, then?

It is at times of the Bohane Feudin', after all, when Bohane reps get made.

18

The Light That Never Goes Out

Looky-here:

The Gant Broderick, without a lick of sleep to his name in three weeks solid, walked the deserted streets of the New Town, in foulest December weather, and he aimed his hopeful toots for the Beauvista bluffs.

From the Trace, distantly as he climbed, he heard the hollers and taunts of the Norrie fiends.

Fancy, meantime, held to an S'town stand-off as it waited on the sure mo' and the 'bino's call.

The Gant had spotted a gap sure enough.

He was after an assault of the midwinter blues. Each sleepless night in the trailer's cot had been an infinity. Each morning he had felt as if he had fought a war. The Bohane taint had lost no drag on him in all the years he'd been gone. Violent thoughts reared up in his ham-faced noggin. It had been as much as he could do the night before not to throttle the little ginger cuss on the spot – spare him the wait for a sure fate ahead. But he had work to do, the Gant. There was a job agreed to, a price to be paid for his passage of return.

He could not settle. The level of drooling lust was unspeakable. Nostalgia was off the fucking charts. He was calling out his daft thoughts to the four winds. He was in fierce debate, at all angles of the clock, with the very many versions of himself. He was flatulent, he was baggy-eyed, he was hoarse with emotion. And here he was, despite it all, presenting himself for love.

Rum, Gant.

Scaled the Beauvista ascent by 'n' by and came to the more genteel Bohane – the austerity of the trees here along the grand terraces, their tangled limbs bared in winter and hazed in rainfall, this was unspeakably beautiful, and a tear trailed softly the Gant's cheek. All the great turrets and chimneys leapt at the foul winter sky, and he knew where to head for, sure enough, because it wasn't his first climb of the bluff this season.

He had watched her in shade and silhouette; he had watched her the winter through, but from a distance.

With a dart of his tongue he wet a thumb the width of a tab-box and he smoothed back the cow lick that fell onto his forehead always, but then he thought that maybe it might work to spark her memory of him, and that he should let it fall unchecked, boyishly. Then he chortled. He almost choked on the harsh comedy, at the teenage turns his mind was taking; he felt so young again. The Gant was the length of fifty and here he was in a moony love-flap.

All the winter through he had prepared the first words he would speak to her. Rolled them out and weighted them. Offered them to the Big Nothin' moon and the roaming puck goats. Tried to foresee the read she'd take on the words – tried to see them *go in*. Nights unending he had tried to gauge the meaning of her silence, her refusal to answer the letter. It signalled there was a fear in her, surely, a fear of what his return might mean, and that fear for the Gant spelt hope. Tricky the paths that a long love might follow, like the spiral-down twists of a raindrop on a windowpane.

He came to their terrace. His belly swollen with fright, he was ill with nerves – it could all end right here and now – but as with death, you look away from the approach of a darkness, and he was at their door, and he knocked, and all the words he had prepared were in that instant lost, forgotten, gone, and he was reduced to a single word – almost at once she answered – and he said the word:

'Macu.'

19

Logan and Fucker Meet the Sand-Pikeys

Shortest day worsened as it went on and by threat of evening it was about as dreck as you'd get it in the creation. There in the black pit of December the rain came side-on and whipped its cold assaults. The hardwind was bossing about the place belligerent as a hoor's broken-faced mother. There was an icy mist ghosting from the ocean that'd just about freeze the tongue solid in your gob. Logan Hartnett and Fucker Burke walked through the squalls and wallops of weather and they were largely oblivious to it being Bohane aborigines both.

They went out the back end of Smoketown and made it onto the track that led to the dune system. Track was an ancient one. There was a time – it wasn't today nor yesterday – when young folk walked down it to take the sea air, fly kites and get fluffy with their sweethearts. But long gone in Bohane the days of the kites, and Fucker turned to Logan, and he said:

'The fuck we doin' callin' on them fuckin' sand-pikes, H?'

'The fuck we're doing, Fucker,' said Logan, 'is we're thinking on our fucking feet, check?'

'Ah but the sand-pikeys, Mr H? In all fairness? There's low an' there's fuckin' low again, like.'

Logan allowed the boy a dismal shrug. His calculations of the day a misread, he was in no mood to debate sand-pikey morals with the galoot Burke.

'I know that you have high standards, Fucker,' he said, 'so I'll explain the tactic again. What we're dealing with is an eight-family descent from the Northside Rises. I said eight! We ain't seen that many wall-bangers hop down the 98 Steps since back in the lost-time. But as many as they've got, they have the old flaw in them still. Just listen to 'em back there . . .'

He jerked a thumb over his shoulder, and despite the howls of the weather, the Norrie aggravators could be heard to roister still in the Back Trace.

'These young gentlemen, they've no sense of . . . *restraint*, Fucker. They think that we've fled and left it to them. They're taking knee-tremblers in the wynds. They're bothering booze and pipe like booze and pipe just been invented. Another hour or two of that and they'll be more than a little sapped. As long as we've the numbers to match them, it'll be a simple cleaning-out operation.'

'Still, H . . . Sand-pikeys for back-up? Sand-pikeys allegianced to the Back Trace Fancy?'

Logan stopped up short then; Fucker made the reck a note later.

On a high dune above, in the gloom of dusk, a line of sand-pikeys had noiselessly appeared.

Ye sketchin'?

Sand-pikeys – so silent there in the thickening light.

Now out on the Bohane peninsula, there were those who'd say your sand-pikey was just about the cutest devil of the lot. Say your sand-pikey had it made out there on the dunes, so hidden it was. Your sand-pikey was of the pavee kind but specific to the tip-end of the peninsula, a thin sliver of land out beyond Smoketown where a sequence of towering dunes is knit together with marram grass – great ropey chains of

133

marram as thick again as the cables the sea rides on – and the dunes have a bad-luck air to them, by legend, but it was the sand-pikeys always that talked up the legend. Maybe they just wanted to keep the place to themselves.

They stood a dozen strong on the high dune and with their braids and feathers and markings they had the look of strange birds indeed.

'I'll do the talking, Fucker,' said Logan.

And so at duskfall on the shortest day Logan Hartnett and Fucker Burke climbed the duneside and the line of pikeys stood and silently watched their approach and an orphan clutch of pine trees sang in the dark haze as hardwind careened off the crested dunes.

Sand-pikeys wore armless jerkins year-round, their hair was braided thickly and dressed with magpie feathers, and their torsos were covered with ash markings – unreadable to all but their own kind. They were martyrs to the sweet herb and as noiseless and wary as the dune hares they had for neighbours and sometimes, in the hard times, for prey.

'How're we now?' cried Logan Hartnett, cheerfully.

Our sand-pikey brethren settled the dunes way back. They had a forge out there in which they made weaponry for their protection and for trade. They built also six-bar gates they sold to the farming fraternity: the Big Nothin' fermoiri. They drank elderflower gin and married at fourteen years of age and enjoyed the maudlin scrape of a fiddle. They didn't get mixed up in Feuds too often, but when they did?

Was said there was no sight on the peninsula quite so fearsome as that of a sand-pikey at the business end of a scrap.

Logan and Fucker were close enough to make out the faces now. Creased, typically, a sand-pikey's features – this was from squinting out for generations into the dusty expanse of the dunes, and the decades of fine sand blown hard at them gave an odd, silvery sheen to the complexion, as though your sand-pikey was born of some distant planet altogether, a place made of different minerals and gases.

No answer was made to Logan's call but he could see the pikeys looked serene enough.

It was known that the sand-pikeys in the evenings listened intently to the wind's tune and divined what messages from Big Nothin' it might contain. If you had e'er a drop of the pikey blood in you at all, it was Big Nothin' was the spirit-home, was the bog-maternal, check? The sand-pikeys also read messages in the sky at night – Word was delivered to them in the arrangement of the stars. Logan knew that if he was to secure their aid this evening, much would depend on what they were hearing in the wind and reading in the sky. This was the level of it when you were dealing with the sand-pikey kind.

Logan and Fucker stalled a few yards from the pikey line.

'Smile, Fucker!'

Fucker pasted what he could of a grin across his chops and the hardwind dipped and there was momentarily an awful silence and a grey hare passed along a dune crest down the way and rose on its hind legs and was frozen still as it watched the men and the mystique of the dunes was stored, somehow, in the stillness of its stringy frame.

Your sand-pikey, it so happens, was given also to super-stitious thinking about the significance of the grey hare – but that is a bag of sticks we are as well keeping for another, less trying day.

'That's not a bad evening at all!' called Logan Hartnett.

135

Was there a leader among the sand-pikeys? There was – it was the fattish lad that styled himself Prince Tubby.

He stepped out now from the pikey line and he was a big cuss of a young fella for sure. He was the same width across the shoulders as a dray-horse would be. Was known he kept eight wives, aged fourteen to forty-six, and they were all lookers, one as black-eyed and sharp-boned as the next, and three of 'em sisters, and a head count of twenty-two bairns had thus far been bred off them. Twas as if Prince Tubby was out to explode the sand-pikey population with just the lash of his own member.

He eyeballed Logan and Fucker.

He silently chuckled.

He went blank-faced, vague, mystic.

'I-and-I's de Far-Eye,' he said.

Prince Tubby wore his braids waist-length and as thick as the marram and his filthy red velvet lowriders were tucked into leather boots and up top he had his jerkin open across a broad, bare chest on which was tattooed with Indian ink an evil eye.

'Fuck's he sayin', H?' said Fucker.

'It's just their old cant,' said Logan. 'Hush, child.'

Prince Tubby came down to Logan and Fucker, side-footing the duneside neatly in the sand-pikey style, and close up he had the look of a full-blown howler.

'Tis the 'bino I's talkin' at, tis?'

'Logan Hartnett, Prince. And this is my boy Fucker Burke.'

The sand-pikey pulled a slow hand through his braids and the hand he bunched into a fist then and bumped it sardonically with Logan's.

'Awrigh'?' said Fucker.

The Prince smiled at him benignly and Fucker dipped his

eyes. Could a pikey tell at a glance, he wondered, if there
was pikey blood in you yourself, like? The Prince signalled
to his ragged crew behind that they could remain at ease
and he gently regarded Logan and he raised his eyes in polite
questioning.

'Maybe a quiet word we'd have?' said Logan.

'T'ain't needed, 'bino.'

'Oh?'

'I-and-I's de Far-Eye.'

'You were saying.'

'Far-Eye cop a reck at de Bohane mash-up.'

'And what are you making of it, Prince?'

Prince Tubby shook his head in sadness.

'I-and-I gots the feelin' de 'bino facin' a manky shake o'
uptown aggravators.'

'You're speaking the truth, Prince.'

'I-and-I don't need tellin it's truth he speak,' Tubby softly
corrected. 'All that come from de I-and-I is truth and Baba-
sent. I-and-I's de Far-Eye.'

Logan placated:

'My visit to you is no surprise then?'

'T'aint, 'bino. An' dere's a price I can name an' all, y'check
me?'

They trailed down to the pikey camp. Women 'n' childer
scurried forth from the darkness, wide-eyed, to watch: there
were strangers on the dunes. Of course, sand-pikey children
were an odd breed – they didn't walk till they were seven
years of age but were quick as lizards on the four-hoof crawl,
and they came about the Fancy pair, and made hissing noises.
Fucker, frankly, was a little shook, and all the more so when
he heard a strange rattling, a kind of keening nearby.

'What's it, H?'

'Lurcher cages.'

'Do they really exis—'

'Stow it, Fucker!'

They came to the bonfire in the central pit of the sand-pikey camp, and sharp-pointed posts 'bout yea high, maybe ten foot tall, were arranged to a ritual design around the fire, and atop each post a scalp was nailed.

Sand-pikey old-timers looked up from their haunches by the bonna, and passed wee bottles of the Beast around, and there was a heady aroma of bushweed, and some old cove hollered a ballad of the pikey lost-time, and the surging throb of the forge was palpable nearby.

Logan maintained as best he could; Fucker kept his eyes down.

'Said you've a price in mind, Prince T?'

The sand-pikey menfolk all took to crouching by the fire, all went to the haunches, and Logan and Fucker joined them, and Prince Tubby for a while whispered.

Sand-pikeys didn't come out of camp all that often. Sure, they might head off for a time, after a few palominos, perhaps, or for a rendezvous with some mustachioed diesel seller in Clare or Galway, but they would be back again to the dunes, soon enough, with fresh scars, a good bake on them, and more bleak tales for the telling. And more often than not with new scalps for the posts. They were not to be crossed in business, and the Long Fella knew it, and so he nodded in agreement as Prince Tubby named his price.

It was spat on and shook.

And so it was that less than a half-hour later, the runnings of life on the Bohane streets were set to a different and yet stranger course. For their willingness to help clear the Back Trace of Norrie aggravators, Logan had sworn to the sand-pikeys a third of a share in the Smoketown trade and a role in its daily management.

Fucker Burke could not take his jaws from the ground.

'Pikeys, H! With a third the business o' Smoketown?'

'Just shut your fucking pipehole, Fucker, please!'

A demon vision was to be seen come nightfall. From atop the high dunes, led by Prince Tubby, came a line four-dozen strong of sand-pikeys, and they were armed for Feudin'.

Carried hatchets and iron bars and lengths of ancient fender and blackthorn sticks soaked in brine for the hardness and bricks and shkelps and rocks and hammers and screwdrivers and they carried these items with a lovely . . . insouciance.

Fucker Burke and Logan Hartnett kept to the rear of the line.

Fucker carried a forlorn and puzzled air.

Logan carried a length of rope.

20

Beauvista Interior

The entire structure of the old manse had been scooped out to leave a vast and sombre space. From the limestone flags to the wooded vault of the ceiling was maybe a forty-foot climb along the rendered walls. The leaded windows were thin and pointed, stern as church, and of a dark, opaque glass. A mezzanine platform circled the room entirely, two-thirds of the way up, and it was reached by a pair of spiral stairways, set opposed to each other across the room, and the entire platform was lined with clothes rails, hundreds of them in dizzying rows around the circumference of the room, his 'n' hers, and the rails were hung with all the colours – some seasons gaudy, some muted – of capricious fashion. Peninsula symbols marked the hangings that were tied to the oak beams of the ceiling. A great length of chimney breast ascended from a central hearth to the high vault of the room. A blaze of Nothin' turf lengths burned in the hearth space and the flickers danced on Macu, who sat by the hearth, on a low settle, with her legs crossed, her slenderness unchanged, and her age showing.

Macu wore:

A pair of suede capri pants dyed to a shade approaching the dull radiance of turmeric, a ribbed black top of sheer silk that hugged her lithe frame, a wrap of golden fur cut from an Iberian lynx, an expression of wry bemusement about the eyes, and about the mouth an expression unreadable.

The room was lit, at Gothical intervals, by candelabras mounted agin the buff render of the walls on cast-iron brackets.

Gant's eye was drawn morbidly to the bed space. It was tucked away in a nook down back, and was heaped with furs and rugs, and there was a headboard cut from driftwood.

Nausea sent a spike to his throat.

A single, enormous photograph was framed above the hearth – it was as outsized as its subject: a great Irish wolfhound of doleful mien.

The Gant said:

'Who's the dog?'

Macu regarded him evenly.

'Why're you back, G?'

He took to a settle opposing her by the hearth – he took to it before his legs gave out. He could hold her glance for just a moment at a time. Every gesture, every piece of weather that passed across her face was pain to him. He saw clearly now the age that had crept on. He saw the faint crowlines and the puckering that would tighten and dry out as the dreck seasons passed.

'I can't answer you,' he said.

She had opened the door as to one expected. She stood aside and let him enter the great vault of room. He felt conscious of his every movement. He felt nineteen again, and he tried not to carry himself like a Big Nothin' gombeen.

'Dog's Alfie,' she said. 'Was Alfie. Got a slap of an El train.'

'Logan's?'

'Ours.'

'Handsome.'

'An' stupid.'

'Often the way those'd go together, Macu.'

The flicker of his humour he could see was a reassurance to her. But careful, Gant, he told himself, don't go tossing out the wiseacre lines now; you don't need to impress.

'Look at you,' she said.

'I know,' he said.

'Where've you been, Gant?'

There was no quick answer to that. Except to say he had been to the darkest caverns, where ogres loomed.

'Been away over,' he said.

'I know that,' she said. 'We'd have . . .'

The regal 'we'.

'. . . got word the odd time.'

He rubbed his hands together to distract them from trembling. Every word that spilled from her spun him back to the lost-time. It was better if he didn't look at her – better to let the dream persist.

'I moved around a lot,' he said.

'No settling in those bones.' She was sly here. 'A rez boy born true.'

He was sly right back.

'Whiff o' the campsmoke to a lotta blood 'round this place, Mac.'

The pale boy Logan had not long been in the Fancy's ranks. He was tall, he was skinny, he was stylish. Vicious as a mink and cute in the noggin also. What you did, in the Fancy, with one you were afraid of? You kept him close, and so it was that Logan became a lieutenant for the Broderick

Fancy. The Gant was wary of him and he set him the trickier errands. Maybe hoped he didn't come back from them, maybe he had designed it just . . . Ah but talk to her, Gant, don't let her see you travelling back. Don't let her see the weakness of that.

'See you got scary boys about the Trace?'

'Norrie trash,' she said.

All of the feuds in Bohane go way back, the Gant thought, as he sat there on the settle and dried out in the warm fug. Such a childish town.

He recalled the lad who was tarred and feathered on the dockside one night by Norries – it was the Gant found him, writhing in the black goo, a nightmare bird he had the look of. The lad belonged to the Gant and there was vengeance required. It was callow Logan was sent to take it. After the vengeance he took, there was even Fancy boys could not look him in the eye.

'You know I wrote you.'

'You know that I got it.'

'Not just that letter, Macu. Hundreds of 'em. Decades of 'em, girl. I never did send 'em though.'

Logan was quiet-spoken.

Logan didn't parade no Fancy-boy machismo.

Logan was . . . cooler.

'I've seen him about the place,' he told her.

'Guessed you'd been hauntin' the shadows, G,' she said. 'You were always handy at stayin' hid . . . for a big unit.'

'It's a knack,' he said. 'He doesn't look happy.'

'Who is? In fuckin' Bohane . . . You think I am?'

The dark girl he had known resurfaced, for an instant, in her glance but he knew now – he saw it with migraine intensity – that their time was gone.

Logan had dressed a little differently to the rest. It would be the flourish of a neck scarf maybe. Or a different cut to the boot. If everyone else was wearing a square toecap, nothing would do Logan Hartnett only to arrive into the Aliados in a winklepicker, and the sly puss on. The other Fancy boys would look at him, study him, see what was coming next. The Gant had the finest threads himself, of course, but he couldn't help feeling he wore 'em like a turf-cutter.

'I'm sorry I didn't send you word,' she said. 'But what was I suppose' to say?'

He remembered the way she had snagged on Logan. He could see it happening – right there in the Café Aliados. Logan down back of the bar, by the jukebox, summoning up a slow-mover of a calypso tune. He'd kick at the corner with his 'picker, a deft little toe-dink to take the life out of a maggot. Soon as they were all wearing winklepickers, Logan Harnett would be dusting off the square toecaps.

Nights, the Gant would talk to Macu about Logan. He sensed the double-feeling in her when he talked. The Gant could hide nothing from his own face. He knew that Logan would be meaner to her.

'Macu, I don't need to . . .'

He could not find the words. The Gant flailed in the strange and sombre room. She looked at him and held the look and smiled. She was beautiful but forty-three.

'No taking it back, is there?' he said.

All the years he had been gone, he had remembered their talks word for word:

'You get so long in this place and no more. Maybe it's time we took to the High Boreen, girl?'

He could not stay in the city without falling to its taint.

144

Logan would never leave, and Macu, too, was Bohane to the bone. Macu was a stayer.

'I asked you, remember?' He came back to the Beauvista hearth. 'I asked you to come with me.'

'Ah, Gant, please . . .'

'I knew that you wouldn't.'

She edged forward on her settle. She clasped her hands and held them a moment to her mouth. She spoke to him now very gently.

'Gant,' she said, 'we went out together for three weeks.'

Spike of nausea.

'I know,' he said. 'I know that's all it was.'

'Oh why're you here, G?'

The firelight traced out the lines of her aged skin. She was no longer what he needed or wanted. Reality infected him with its sourness and truth. A new course swiftly presented; it had its own sweet and vengeful logic.

'I'll tell you exactly why I'm here,' he said.

21

Feud

The Hartnett Fancy was mobbed beneath its colours
out the Smoketown dune end. It was first-dark of the longest
night. The Fancy was edgy. The hot charge of adrenalin
rushed, mitts were flexed, knuckles cracked, jaws clenched,
and the ranked banners in the wind's assault made an
ominous rattling. The purple and black of the banners had
an ecclesiastical look, neo-Romish, and upon the banners
were daubed the symbols and the slogan of the Back Trace
Fancy:

Symbols –

A puck goat's head.
A scimitar dirk.
A dog-star moon.

Slogan –

Truth Or Vengeance

S'town was agog, and freaky-eyed hoors amped on Feud-
juice shrieked their XXX-rated tributes to the Fancy boys
from the high windows.

Fancy boys waved back to the hoors and attempted a
semblance, at least, of blithe spirit.

Among the Fancy – as was remarked, with awe and suspicion, in the S'town grogpits and herb-parlours – the fearsome sand-pikeys now were mingled.

Sand-pikeys had about them the calmest of airs. They shook out their limbs, and performed calisthenic stretches, and tossed their hatchets for show in the air, and caught 'em again behind their backs, and filled repeatedly their neck-pipes with bead-sized nodges of blackest hashish, and sucked deep on the fill – these were the Dreadlock Assassins of the dune system.

Fancy regulars and sand-pikey buy-ins were of a number, combined, that'd be a match, but just about, for the eight families of Norrie aggravators roisterin' cross-river in the Bohane Trace.

Logan Hartnett suavely walked the ranks and he offered his smiles and his whispers of encouragement. There was confidence to be read in the sly pursing of his lips, and atop a most elegant cut of an Eyetie suit he wore, ceremonially, an oyster-grey top hat.

Mothers and sisters and lovers of the Fancy boys meantime passed through the mob, shedding tears and Sweet Baba Jay medals as they went. The medals were for protection.

Fucker Burke was bouncing about as though on springs, and he hissed his encouragement to the Fancy, and he kept on an extendable battle leash his Alsatian love, Angie, who pranced, and drooled, and whose eye-gleam gave back the glow of December moon. Fucker was bare-armed beneath a denim waistcoat and wore his finest brass-toed bovvers and he felt the racing currents of pride, emotion, fear. Angie had been kept without a feed for three days.

Jenni Ching pinballed about the assembled mob and

screamed crazy Mandarin curses. Jenni Ching carried a spike ball on a chain and swung it above her head. She wore an all-in-one black nylon jumpsuit, so tightly fitted it might have been applied with a spray-can, and she smoked a black cheroot to match it, and her mouth was a hard slash of crimson lippy.

Wolfie Stanners, however, was widely acknowledged to have taken the prize. Wolfie was dressed to kill in an electric-blue ska suit and white vinyl brothel-creepers with steel toecaps inlaid. Four shkelps were readied on a custom-made cross-belt. He danced along the ranks of the Fancy, and he eyeballed each of the Fancy boys in turn, and he gestured to the Back Trace beyond, where the Norrie aggravators could be heard to howl their taunts and curses.

'Ye takin' that?' Wolfie hissed. 'I said ye gonna fuckin' well take that, like?'

Logan approached the boy then, and he embraced him, and he whispered to him; Wolfie aye-ayed.

Yes and it was Wolfie that blew a short, three-noted whistle then, and a great wealth of feeling settled that moment on the Fancy.

The whistle was a plain melody that rose once and then fell, that was melancholy, that was sourced from the lost-time in Bohane, that had a special power to it – a power that I cannot even begin to explain to those of you un-fortunate enough not to come from this place – and it was answered after a silence had for a moment held, it was answered in sweet, sad sequence by the Fancy, and by this plain music they swore allegiance to the Back Trace, and as one they moved to reclaim it.

Man – even the sand-pikeys were zoned on the mo'.

And as the mob marched out across the S'town streets,

the whistled melody was taken up as a general tune, and it carried across the footbridge, and in the wynds and alleyways of the Back Trace the uptown aggravators knew their assault was not to go unanswered.

That drained the blood from the bastards' faces sure enough.

Trace families barricaded in their tenement homes for the length of the assault heard also the Fancy's whistles, and they rushed to their rooftops, and their breaths caught with pride as yonder across the Bohane river they saw the hoisted banners come steadily closer – the purple and the black – and the night had cleared, as though on cue, and all of cruel heaven's cold stars were flung gaily about.

Logan Hartnett, kingly outlaw, arranged himself towards the rear of the marching Fancy. The Eyetie suit was sharp enough to slice an eyeball open, the top hat rakishly set, and he was unencumbered by weapons save for that same coil of rope wrapped loosely about his shoulder. Hard not to be floored by the nerveless elegance of that slender old dog.

Fancy made its way onto the footbridge and it crossed onto the Bohane front and the ranks of hoss polis clustered along the dockside kept their mounts and their backs discreetly turned. Looked in the opposite direction, the polis. As though it was the pretty streets of the New Town where the Feud was to be played.

Fucker and Jenni and Wolfie pelted up and down between the advancing lines of the Fancy and motivated the fighters. Wolfie winked for Jenni as they passed, and he blew her a kiss, and he hit a high-hand salute with Fucker.

But it was Wolfie that took the general lead of the Fancy as it made its way across the wharfside cobbles to the Trace, for he was bone-Trace, that kid, he had Trace wynds for bloodlines.

And Wolfie sounded a ripper of a Back Trace howl and everyone behind him heard it in their deeps and they were fortified by it.

Shkelpers were unsheathed and chains were swung and blackthorns raised.

Sky itself was about ripped by the Fancy's cries.

Wolfie turned on his heel and trotted backwards so as to face the moving lines and he performed most jauntily a natty-boy skank – the signature move of the Hartnett Fancy – and the cheers that rose had a raw, terrifying jaggedness to them, a want to them, and it was a want for blood, y'check?

Wolfie turned again and entered the Trace.

A flashbulb's blue shriek lit the sky and caught his battle scream.

22

The Note That Macu Left For Logan

This is the end Logan. You are too sick now. The jealousy is poison. How could you do such a thing to that poor man? He came here tonight and if you could see him it would break even your sick fucking heart. I can't be with you any more. I can't hear your voice any more. I don't know where I'm going to go but I'm going and I would say do not try to find me but I know you'll try to find me. You'll have your boys come looking for me just like they did the last time just like they follow me always. But this is the end Logan. Do not try to find me. You cannot change my mind no more. You must leave me alone now Logan. Please will you just leave me, Logan?

23

The Darkroom

The longest night simmered, and the Feud raged, and the hunchback Grimes pelted about the wynds of the Trace and laboured under the weight of a medieval Leica.

The hunchback, Balthazar Grimes, watched the great surge of the Fancy as it ran into the waiting lines of the uptown aggravators, and fearlessly he shot the clash.

The hunchback, Balthazar Mary Grimes, lensman supreme of the *Bohane Vindicator*, had worked a share of Feuds in his day but few to match this one for belligerence.

When it was all but done he took from the Trace on his short, quick, twisted legs and he darted through the polis cordons on De Valera Street.

Took the smirk of a fat polis:

'Tasty one, Balt?'

Shook his head woefully, the hunchback, and he kept running – there was a thirty-two-page special on the cards for sure, and it wanted filling.

The offices of the *Vindicator* were located on a New Town street, a block of stout Edwardiana in prim greystone, and Balt Grimes descended to its basement along the rusted iron stair.

Shut the door of his darkroom behind him and leaned back against it and felt the lightness of relief and the pride of an assignment completed.

He set about unspooling the reels and soaking them.

From the pools of developer – brought in from the Lisbon route now, most often – a succession of images rose from the blue fluid. The images were lifted from the pool and pegged along the line. The hunchback Grimes walked the line, thoughtfully, as the photographs dried, and he made notes for the captions.

He saw:

– The Fancy's mobbed ranks enter the Trace . . . their gobs violently agape as they hollered (per tradition) random names of the Back Trace dead . . . interesting . . . the way they had the look of young crows out for a feed.

– The boy Wolfie Stanners as he led a squall of followers into the 98er Square, his hackles heaped like a rabid dog.

– A Norrie line, barechested, as they hissed and cawed . . . oh and a lovely detail: the way their tongues were held as bits between their teeth to make the sound . . . and upon their scrawny chests crude renditions in charcoal of starlings, their symbol.

– Close-up: what looked like a Cusack–McGroarty cross-breed – the hunchback Grimes squinted – giving the come-on to the Stanners kid directly, with his eyes rancid and herbshot, a scrunchy look to him, a classic Norrie scobe.

– Close-up: same boy on his knees, a moment later, with his face busted open by the sling of a chain, and Wolfie whispering to him as he prepared with a scimitar dirk to slit his throat. (Just a boy he was – sixteenish?)

– A scraggle of shit-faced McGroartys in a wynd's shadow looking none too sure of themselves.

– Wolfie appearing to hover in the filthy air – prime shot, page lead – as he made for the McGroartys in a lung-busting dash.

– A broken face.

– A gaunt Norrie lad with a dislocated shoulder: lovely, the way his features were caught in a rictus of animal pain.

– Distant shot of Trace women and bairns on the rooftops as they roared encouragement – no good, too fuzzy.

– A gouging.

– A kicking.

– A shkelping . . . this one too much . . . the spilt innards visible . . . bin it.

– Wolfie, again, so low-sized, and neck-deep now in Norrie gore.

– A sand-pikey, his dreadlocks flailing as he went hand to hand with a Lenane bro' – there was only going to be one outcome.

– The boy Burke – Fucker, known as – with an Alsatian on a battle leash, in the 98er Square, fending off a pair of Norries with his boots as the Ala feasted on a gore spill.

– The Ching gal – prime shot, page lead – as she lands a flying kick to split open the noggin of Eyes Cusack hissel' with a steel toecap.

– Close-up – page lead – Eyes Cusack, bleeding, as reality dawns.

– Close-up – Logan Hartnett . . . the Long Fella . . . the 'bino – a page lead – leaning back against the wall of a wynd, arms folded, a rope coiled and waiting on his shoulder, and not a single fucking hair out of place. Smoking a tab.

– Wide-shot: cackling sand-pikeys chase down a gang of fleeing Norries.

– Close-up: Fucker, a hank of hair in his paw, looking . . . sexual. Bin it.

– Close-up: Angelina drooling.

154

– Ching gal – prime shot – with Eyes Cusack in a headlock.

– Wolfie bricks a scuttling Norrie weasel on the back of the noggin – a comic turn, page . . . 6?

– Triumphant Fancy lads doing a natty-boy skank in the 98er Square – lovely, a double-page spread.

– Close-up: Fucker's forehead raw and scabbed from headbutting.

– Close-up: the Long Fella, stony-faced beneath his top hat.

– Jenni Ching arriving into the 98er Square – prime shot – with Eyes Cusack before her, a shkelp to his throat and his hands tied behind his back.

– Peach: the high arc of the Smoketown footbridge, its shape beautifully embossed on the dark of night, just as Fucker and Jenni hoist Eyes Cusack over the railings, while Logan makes the knot, and Wolfie waits.

– Peach: Wolfie slips on the noose, delicately, and this one's an interesting study, his expression is almost . . . saintly – one for the portfolio, certainly, coz Eyes maintains a dignity too. Fair dues to him.

– Wide-shot: along the dockside, the ranks of hoss polis as they keep their mounts discreetly turned. Lovely.

The hunchback Balt Grimes came to the end of the line and wryly he smiled. Norrie bluster, it seemed, was of a moment's lasting, and Back Trace class was permanent.

– Front-page shot: Eyes Cusack is hung by the neck from the Smoketown footbridge.

24

22 December, 12.01 a.m., Bohane Authority

Each of them ashen-faced, each with bloodshot eyes and trembling hands, the twelve members of the Bohane Authority sucked on high-tar tabs and drank a dose of filthy coffee from paper cups. Talk ran madly the length of the conference table as the Feud's aftermath was reckoned.

'What're we talkin', boys?'

'It's lookin' like a dozen dead.'

'An' twice that lamed, blinded, or generally crippled.'

'SBJ wept! As if our fuckin' name wasn't bad enough!'

'Oh those bastards outside in the Nation Beyond will be laughin' up their sleeves tonight!'

'It's the end of a Beauvista tram!'

'Think the NB tit was gone witchy on us b'fore? It'll be witchy on us now mos' certain!'

'Ne'er a sign o' Mr Mannion, nah?'

'They're at it again! That's what they'll all be sayin'! One half o' Bohane tryin' to ate the other half!'

The Authority men were desperate and ill-paid souls who lived as peaceably as they could in the modest terraces that ascended towards (but did not reach) the Beauvista heights. They kept always to the New Town side of De Valera Street. They went nervously about their business in an animal town. Their business was to keep the place in some manner civilised. It was a job of work.

'What do we know of the kid Stanners?'

'Came up rough. Orphaned early. Runs with the boy of the Burkes.'

'Fucker, known as. A regular savage.'

'But not much of a brain, really, just a viciousness. It's said the Wolfie runt is as smart as he's vicious.'

'We know he's attached to the girl of the Chings.'

'Sweet Baba Jay float down and preserve us!'

There was plenty to be bothered about in Bohane at the best of times. The El train must be kept running, and the sodium lights must rise for whatever few hours of the night could be afforded, and occasionally – if only that – the gutters must be swept clear of dead dogs, jack-up works, and mickey-wrappers. The Authority men truly cared that the once great and cosmopolitan city of Bohane should retain at least the semblance of its old civility.

'Polis need to be kept tight on the Norrie families. We don't want some halfwit of a young fella coming down the 98 to make a martyr of himself on account o' Eyes Cusack.'

'Agreed.'

'Is Mr Mannion on the El train?'

'That's the word we have – he's just in offa Nothin'.'

The men of the Authority wished that the docks be kept open and working. They wished for beer to be brewed and sausages packed. They wished that relations between the factions be kept just a shade short of murderous. They wished that the gentlemen of Endeavour Avenue be allowed to go about the administration of their business. They wished that the lost-time in Bohane might with the years that passed fade into less painful memory.

'What way is the Mercy holding?'

'What doctors we have are called in. The Mercy's handled worse than this.'

'Did Girly give nod to the pikeys?'

'Must ha'! Logan's the babby-boy yet. He couldn't call in the pikeys without Girly's say-so.'

The door of the conference room fell open then and it was Ol' Boy Mannion that stylishly appeared. The Authority men rose as one and came about him in a great kerfuffle.

'Ah shush, will ye!' Ol' Boy cried. 'Barnyard fuckin' fowl ye're like.'

He quietened them, and quickly, for he was practised in the art, and soon all were seated and smoking again around the long table. Ol' Boy stood at its head and raised his palms once more for hush.

'Now let's not get this out of proportion, boys,' he said. 'There were minor disturbances among juveniles in the Back Trace area of the city. We can get past this. We get the bodies down to the riverside smokehouse under cover of dark. We get the corpses burned off before first light. How're we fixed for diesel?'

It was confirmed that sufficient supplies could be rounded up for the purpose.

'Good. Now we need to let Eyes dance on the air for an hour or so yet. The Fancy will want to linger on the sight – leave them to it. We don't want to rile the boys when they're in a celebratory mood. They'll have the calypso records out and the herb-pipes burnin'. Tomorrow, we'll let the *Vindicator* special go ahead, coz the town has an appetite for it, but I'll have Dominick cut any mention of a body count. A nice few gorey pictures and Bohane will be happy enough – you know the way of it, gents. Of course, the polis will have to keep the 98 Steps especially tight for the holiday period. We'll want every unit out: hoss polis, dog polis and the knuckle-draggers general.'

The Authority clucked a henhouse concensus.

'Do we know,' Ol' Boy continued, 'what level of brute animal violence has been committed to the properties of the Trace?'

He was informed of what damage was known.

'At least the market canopies seem to be intact. That's something. If an old dear can pass through the market of a morning and snag herself a stalk of sprouts, it seems as if all is right with the world. Next thing is Girly.'

Shudders around the table, which he acknowledged with a sad closing of his eyes.

'There is no way around it. We need to send a delegation to the old rip. We need it made clear that if the sand-pikey element is to be allowed a share of the Smoketown trade, then they have to be kept in some way decent. We can't let the place go to hell altogether. We might suppose, of course, that the Fancy's promise to the sandies is half-hearted at best and they'll attempt to fob 'em off with the run of a couple of hoorshops and a few vouchers for a tickle-foot parlour . . .'

Pale smiles surfaced – the first of the night. Ol' Boy's grasp and control was so reassuring.

'But that would be a dangerous game for the Hartnetts to play. There is nothing so terrifying to behold, as those of us ever so slightly longer in the tooth know, as a sand-pikey feeling hissel' to be double-dealed. Now I mean no disrespect to their ethnic heritage . . .'

He raised his eyebrows.

'. . . but we don't want them lightin' bastards getting any sort of a foothold. Bohane's name is bad enough. And I am not suggesting for a moment that it is altogether unjustified. This is a bad-ass kind of town.'

The Authority men shrugged in sad agreement.

'All I'm saying,' Ol' Boy went on, 'is the last thing we want to be known as is Pikey Central. Things are bad enough, lads. We need to get Girly onside agin the pikey influx. Now. With regards to the Gant Broderick . . .'

The Authority members edged forwards in their seats.

'. . . situation, I've spoken to him more than once but I confess his motives are still a mystery to me. I don't know for sure why the Gant is back. What I do know is that he's causin' sleepless nights for a certain pale-face. And the way I'm figurin'?'

Ol' Boy shrewdly grinned.

'We got the Gant, and the Long Fella, and lovely Macu. So think on, boys-a-mine. It's a rum ol' love mess for certain and it could make fine distraction for the Bohane people this weather. Could make 'em forget an aul' Feud quick enough . . .'

Slowly the Authority men nodded as they grasped the sense of it.

'Hear this!' Ol' Boy cried. 'Bohane city don't always gots to be a gang-fight story. We can give 'em a good aul' tangle o' romance an' all, y'check me?'

III
APRIL

25

Babylon Montage

A hot scream cut the April night in S'town.

Logan Hartnett, the sad-eyed Fancy boss, looked drowsily to the high window of the dream salon's booth. The window was open to the great swelter of spring and the air was pierced by the white syllables of the scream. Heartbroken in the cruel season, Logan as he lay on the settle bed felt the scream along the tracklines of his blood as though carried by an army of racing ants. His true love had left him, and he closed his eyes against the scream, and the pink backs of his lids pulsated woozily. He felt the slow, negotiating trickle of a single bead of sweat as it rolled from his forehead along the line and tip of his nose, dropped to the indent above his thin lips, trickled slowly across his lips to leave a residue of salt burn, and rolled onto his chin to be removed with the single neat swipe of a toe by Jenni Ching.

He opened his eyes to the girl.

She winked as she drew back her foot again. She sat on her haunches, at the far end of the settle, facing him. She took up the pestle and mortar and grinded still more of the poppy bulb's paste. She spread it on the burner of the dream-pipe, and she came to him along the length of the settle – see the slow and sinuous movement of her as she brought balm for his soul's ache – and she placed the pipe to his lips, and she sparked the flame.

'More,' she said.

The scream ripped the air again but it broke up as it caught at its source, and it became a hacking cough, and a boy of fifteen doubled over in a dune-end alleyway. His thin hands clutched at his sides and his fingertips kneaded his ribs and on each knuckle a numeral was marked in the pale blue of Indian ink:

2 0 1 1
2 0 5 3

These were the dates of his father's span. It was in the same alleyway his father was stomped to death by Fancy boots. The boy Cantillon knew that vengeance might cost his young life to exact but his screams told the need for it. He felt inside the waistband of his lowriders for the shkelp – the reassurance of its bone handle – and he wondered how long it would take for the moment to present itself. The wooziness of the spring night was all about him and a silence held briefly to worry the moment.

Then a round of roars and chants surged on the measured beat of handclaps from a pikey-run grindbar nearby.

Sand-pikey floor show was in full swing:

A slave-gal lurcher, painted with lizard motifs about the face, was chained at the waist. The chain's end was held by her handler, a hooded dwarf. She writhed and twisted in a diamond-shaped pit marked out with burning reed-torches. A fat gent got up as a dog-demon, in full pelt, then entered the pit on his fours – whoops and hollers rose – and the pair cavorted, frankly, and at great, unsavoury length, and they kept a good rhythm with the handclaps as they went.

All the while, the lurcher ranted for the tiered punters a devil's babble – it was learned to her in the dune cages – and her eyes were livid in the dim of the pikey joint.

The dwarf handler fed out lengths of chain at certain moments, and withdrew chain at others – this so as to assist and steer the design of the cavort. The punters clapped out a steady, three-beat rhythm, and whistled and hissed, and they sucked on herb-pipes – squinting through the greenish fug of their smoke – and they lapped up a three-for-two offer on bottles of Phoenix ale.

Lurcher had the telltale welts of captivity on her back. Type that would have been taken as a girl-chil' from the high reaches of the Nothin' massif, and dune-raised. Such were the sad old stories you'd get out that end of the creation. Gal the likes of the lurcher might have been bought for a few bottles of the Beast and a box of colouredy bangles.

Get 'em young – that was the sand-pikey reckon when it was lurchers they was talking.

Yes and the sand-pikeys held all the hottest tickets out the S'town dune end this season. The lurcher and her dog-man were tonight but a curtain-raiser. It got lowdown and brutish altogether as the night stretched out its hairy arms, and the trick-ponies emerged, and the big lasses in harness, and the biters, and the maulers, and the double-jointed chap with the moustache what styled hissel' 'The Magician'. You would blush to even repeat the details of that man's act – suffice to say there wasn't a cat safe for miles.

And all the while Prince Tubby, the Far-Eye, kept sconce from the doorway, and he tallied a head count in the tiered seats around the pit. There was a couple of stag parties in, which was always a help. He reckoned the toll he'd taken in door tax and he nodded serenely.

Prince Tubby was offering cheap entry, credit lines for repeat custom and rotating deals on Phoenix ale, Wrassler stout and Big Nothin' bushweed. Ambition lit the Tubster like a star this weather. He had taken to city living. He placed a hand in the pocket of his velvet loon pants, and he felt the weight of coins there, and he set them merrily a-janglin'. He scratched his balls and he wanted more – more! – and he brooded on the weakness he perceived in the Trace Fancy. The 'bino was down to lonesomeness and the dream-pipe, and the Fancy boys were whispering.

Tubby went outside for a taste of the night. He took a sniff at the S'town air. His guards were stationed all along the dune-end alleyways – the Fancy was not to be trusted – and he felt the reassurance of them. He ate a lungful of mineral wind. Raised his eyes and read the stars. Briefly, in Bohane, there was that feeling again of stillness.

And then a nightbird's strange call from the treetops.

Bird's call had the neat, rapid, whirring sound of an old motor, and it carried a distance along the tops of the scarred trees, and it was picked up by others of its kind, and answered. The call – this sequence of whirrs and tiny, deep-throated clicks – ascended thus the gable-end of a fetish parlour, and crept through the window of a top-floor suite, and Big Dom Gleeson, the stout newsman, heard it as he lay on a bed with his belly-side down. He suckled on a sour French brandy from the nipple of a baby's bottle, and he sweated profusely as a seventeen-year-old tushie whipped him a hundred strokes on the raw of his arse with a pearl-encrusted hairbrush.

'Oh I am a weak, *weak* man,' the Dom sighed.

166

The pouty tush weltered him and muttered the count:

'Seven'y-sic' . . . seven'y-se'en . . . se'eny-ate . . .'

And Big Dom between soft moans and sucks on the bobba's tit pondered the weird, precise whirring of the night-bird, and he made it as a blow-in from an ocean storm – it was the season for them. He groaned, in happiness and in shame, and he enjoyed as always the slow turning of the season, the opening out of the Bohane year.

'Se'eny-noine . . . atey . . . atey-wan . . .'

Oh, this one had a wrist on her! And as he succumbed – once more! – to his weakness, and as he – oh snivelling, oh putrid Dom! – relished the . . .

'Atey-foe . . . atey-fi . . .''

. . . measure of pain the tushie extracted from his sinful bones, he started to think about supper, too – would I ate a lump o' halibut? – and the way the whirring of the strange bird had the sound of the hunchback Grimes's old Leica – didn't it? – and also his proposed editorial comment . . .

'Noin'ey . . . noin'ey-wan . . .'

. . . for the following evening's *Vindicator*. A succession ruck was brewing in the Fancy – no question. This marked a difficult moment in the city.

The boy Stanners.

The galoot Burke.

The slanty-eye Ching.

They were all making shapes. They were all manoeuvring. Even in victory, Logan Hartnett had shown a weakness – he'd gone beyond the Fancy's colours for back-up. Such a plain display of weakness was in Bohane oftentimes fatal. But Dom's editorial, he decided, would plead for patience, for the Long Fella to be left in place for a time yet, for the status quo . . .

'Noin'ey-sic . . . noin'ey-se'en . . .'

. . . to be maintained. After all, you could say what you liked about the Long Fella, but at least he had class.

'Noin'ey-noine . . .'

And there was the fact that he made a very fine picture. A tall man, thin, a clothes horse. Strange, but he'd be missed. Dom braced himself for the last stroke of the brush, for which she always retained a special venom, and indeed she raised the arm high for it, and a whack of pleasure with great fury was landed.

'A hundert even, Mr Gleeson!'

Moaned loudly, the Dom – shamed, yet again! – and his fat-man moan carried through the window, and floated downwards, softly, until a lick of the hardwind caught it and threw it above the rooftops of Smoketown, sent it across the blackwaters of the Bohane, and it faded as it carried, and it reduced, and it was succeeded on the Trace front by the sound of the meat wagons as they crossed the cobbles, the iron rut and clanking of them.

As they sketched the wagons roll out from the arcade market and head for the slaughterhouse – the night shift already was in swing – Ol' Boy Mannion and the Gant Broderick leaned back against the stained brickwork of an old warehouse, and they spoke crankily against the din.

'You been soundin' kinda bitter this weather, G. If you don't mind me sayin', like?'

'It's bred into me, Benni.'

'Ah, stop, will you? The fuckin' martyrdom!'

Gant sourly shrugged.

'It's this place, you know?'

Ol' Boy's read: the way the Gant trained his stare on the

black surge of the river was a worry. Mesmerised, he seemed. And not in a good way. Ol' Boy trickled some beads of soft talk from his velvet bag.

'A *place* ain't gonna be the cause of all your woes ever, Gant. Y'hearin' me sense now? And a place ain't gonna solve your woes neither. You been puttin' too much faith in –'

'A dream is what you're sayin'.'

'We all dream of being young again, Gant! Dancin' in the pale moonlight and claspin' a pawful of fresh fuckin' arse! Fact it ain't gonna happen makes it all the sweeter! But don't let yourself drown in that old stuff, boy. Get over it! I mean to say, Gant, you were with the bint three fuckin' weeks! But you've come sluggin' down the Boreen with a fixed notion on you and the mad little eyes all lit up inside your head –'

'She jus' didn't want to know, Ol' Boy.'

'Ah, Gant, what did you expect?'

'But that ain't the cruellest of it.'

'Oh?'

'The cruellest of it? I didn't even want her.'

'Coz it's been twenty-five fuckin' years! Ya plum fuckin' ape! A lot happens, Gant. A life happens. A girl don't stay girl in Bohane for long. An' then, you know, we gotta make . . . arrangements with ourselves? Else how can we put up with the things we done, choices we made? Likes a fuckin' Bohane . . . ah look . . . this is a hard town . . . it's a place . . . an' okay, okay, I know. Here I am sayin' just the fuckin' same . . .'

The Gant slyly winked for Ol' Boy then.

'You think I came back o' me own volition?'

Silence played a long beat as Ol' Boy weighed this.

'Sayin' what to me, G?'

'You think I'd ha' been given the pass?'

A chill of recognition for Ol' Boy.

'What you're sayin' . . .'

The Gant shoved off from the warehouse and aimed his toots for the Trace-deep night.

'Sayin' I got work to do, Benni.'

Looked back with an evil smile.

'But don't worry, Mr Mannion, sir – things to occupy me . . . I'm workin' a plan, y'sketch?'

Ol' Boy smiled at the very notion of a plan – as if the Mad-Town of Bohane was amenable to design.

'You wanna make me laugh, G?' he said. 'Then just go ahead an' tell me those plans o' yours.'

Watched him go:

A big unit, with the splay-footed gaatch of an old slugger, and he turning down a Trace wynd . . . the carry, the burliness, the country shoulders rolling. But even a creature as canny and brave as the Gant could not make Bohane concede to his wishes, and Ol' Boy felt a darkness imminent.

Sadness was the breeze that came off the river and warmed his face.

And then, despite himself, he fingerclicked a snare beat, for the clanking of the meat wagons worked nicely as percussion to the shimmer of a calypso rhythm that travelled from De Valera Street.

A pack of wannabe Fancy boys – fourteenish, hormonal, all bumfluff 'taches and suicide eyes, with the wantaway croak of bravado in their breaking voices – traced the hip-sway of the rhythm outside the calypso joint, drew circles in the air with the winkled tips of their patent booties, passed along a coochie – eight of 'em drawin' on it – and they kept watch – so shyly – on the Café Aliados down the way.

170

You might see Wolfie Stanners pass through those doors, or Fucker Burke with his prize Alsatian bitch, Angelina, or – swoon of swoons – the killer-gal Ching from the Ho Pee.

These were the legend names on the lips of the young ones in Bohane as the spring of '54 came through.

And the spirit of the humid night at a particular moment caught the boys, and the badness (the taint) was passed down, and they broke into an old tune that worked off a doo-wop chorus – it fit nicely up top of the calypso beat – and they sang so hoarsely, so sweetly, and their young faces were menacingly tranquil.

Yes and the song carried to the old dears hanging out washing on the rooftops of the Trace, and they paused a mo', and smiled sadly, and sang croakily the words also: '*It's a bomp it's a stomp it's a doo-wop dit-eee . . . it's comin' from the boys down in Bohane cit-eee . . .*'

And a whisper of change travelled on the April air with the song, it went deeper and on and into the Trace, and the ancient wynds came alive with the season.

Dogs inched their snouts out of tenement hallways and onto the warming stoops.

Upon the stoical civic trees in the Trace squares a strange and smoke-streaked blossom appeared, its flowers a journey from sea grey to soot black, and the blossom was held to work as a charm against our many evils.

Beyond the city, the sea eased after the viciousness of springtide and softly, now, it drew on its cables – its rhythms a soft throb beneath the skin of the Bohane people.

Night in the Back Trace shimmered with dark glamour.

The Gant passed through the Trace, and he turned down a particular wynd, and he entered there a grog pit. He met in its shadows, by prior arrangement, the galoot Burke, who was hunched traitorously over a bottle of Wrassler stout.

Sidled in beside.

Eyed the kid.

'Been havin' a little think about what I said to you, boy?'

Fucker nodded.

'We can go a long way together,' the Gant said, 'if you got things to tell me?'

It came at a great surge then the Judas testimony of Fucker Burke:

'Long Fella, he come 'roun' the dockside evenins, late on, I mean you be talkin' pas' the twelve bells at least when he come creepin' the wharf, an' that's when you'd catch him cuttin' Trace-deep, an' he walk alone, sketch? An' it's like maybe he head for Tommie's – you know 'bout the supper room, sir? I can make a map for ya – or if mood take him maybe he haul his bones 'cross the footbridge, stop in at the Ho Pee, that's the Ching place, he might suck on a dream-pipe, coz Long Fella a martyr to the dream since the wall-eye missus took a scoot on him, and the Chings is known for the top dream, like, but o' course you mus' know 'bout the Ching gal, Jenni, the slant bint that been workin' her own game, if you askin' me? An' she got my boy Wolfie in a love muddle 'n' all, and that ain't like Wolfie, no sir it jus' fuckin' ain't, like, and the way I been seein' it, Gant, what's goin' down with the Back Trace Fancy, or I mean say what's on the soon-come with the Fancy, if it all plays out the way I'm expectin' . . .'

Mercy, the Gant thought, there's no shutting the kid up.

26

The Burden

Logan Hartnett on an April morning walked the stony rut of his one-track mind:

Where does she sleep now?

The shadow of his disease was beneath every inch of his skin. Since she left him, in the winter, he had realised the true extent of it. She had left him when he tested her, and maybe he had designed it just so. Maybe he wanted his sourest fictions to come to life.

Where does she sleep?

He crossed the S'town footbridge. He walked the Bohane front. He was dream-sick in the morning, and his nausea fed on the squalling of the gulls, the slaughterhouse roar, the clanking of the meat wagons. He turned onto De Valera Street. Blur of the street life, the faces indistinct and greenish. He aimed for the Bohane Arms Hotel. The street people still dropped their eyes as he passed but a questioning note combined now with the fear.

His jealousy had weakened him.

A night of fever-dreams and half-sleep was behind him at his berth above the Ho Pee Ching Oh-Kay Koffee Shoppe. He didn't climb the Beauvista bluff any more – he couldn't face those lonesome walls. He just sent Jenni now and then to fetch some fresh clothes.

Logan wore:

A pale green suit, slim-cut, of thin spring cotton, a pair of burnt-orange arsekickers with a pronounced, bulbous toe, a ruffle-fronted silver shirt open at the neck, a purple neckscarf, a pallor of magnificently wasted elegance, and his hair this season swept back from the forehead and worn just slightly longer, so that it trailed past the ruff of his jacket. Also, a three-day stubble.

Was the Long Fella's opinion that, if anything, his suffering made him even more gauntly beautiful. He had all the handsome poignancy of heartbreak.

He hoicked a mouthful of green phlegm at the gutter – the pipe was affecting his lungs. XXX-rated images came at him randomly as he walked – they showed Macu in hot-mouthed abandon with a phantom sequence of young lovers – and he relished these pictures as does the tip of the tongue the gumboil. A burning sensation in his throat, a hollowness.

Where does she sleep?

Through the warm caffeine waft and dust-moted quiet of the shaded hotel foyer he passed, and he was watched by an Authority tout from an old suede lobby couch. They were waiting on his fall. Tout's excited eyes jerked up from behind a conspicuously raised *Vindicator*, and Logan blew a thin-lipped kiss for the gombeen fool.

He ascended – hear now the dreary clank and groaning of the age-old elevator as it works its frayed ropes; Logan heard the workings slowed down, drawn out, dreamily – and he came along the corridor and knocked his particular knock on the suite's numberless door.

'Get in t'me, ya long fuckin' ape!'

Girly was propped on a dozen pillows in the honey-mooners' bed. She was apparently well fuelled: she had the weird crimson colour about the cheeks. When she was sixty, he had worried that the colour spelt her imminent death. She had lately turned ninety. Logan took the bedside seat, and she watched him, and she held the glance, and she puffed her cheeks then in exasperation.

'Night I'm after puttin' down?' she said. 'You wouldn't put a fuckin' dog through it.'

'A bad one, Girl?'

She let her eyes roll tragically in her head.

'I'm between sleep an' wakin' all the night – y'know that kind o' way? The dreams is gone halfways fuckin' alive on me. Four o'clock this mornin', I was convinced Yul Brynner was on top o' the bedspread tryin' to claw in at me and have his way. In the days of the hair.'

Logan, impatient – he had heard it all so many times – rose again, and he went to the velvet drapes, and he shifted their weight a fraction, and he moved a little on the balls of his feet, shifted from one to the other, and he looked out to the rooftops of the Trace wynds.

Was she Trace-deep somewhere? The city was big enough, but only just, to get lost in.

'Things ain't looking so tasty away yonder,' he said.

'An' the nex' thing your father appears. In all his glory. Fuckin' Patcho! Las' toss-bucket I wanna set me peepers on. An' he's above on that wall there on top o' the light switch playin' his little trumpet? About the size of a stood-up rat. Dreams! An' me eyes wide fuckin' open, like?'

'I'm being squeezed,' Logan said. 'I got the sand-pikes getting ambitious in Smoketown. Same time, I got the Norries working up a sour fucking brood for vengeance.'

'Mind you, he could make that trumpet talk, yer aul' fella.'

'Never met him,' Logan said. 'And of course every

swivel-eyed runt in the Fancy with a shkelp to his name and a nobber the size of a peanut is weighing his chances.'

'Well, you're hittin' fifty, aintcha?' she said. 'Then I had the sensation, this was about half five, I'd say? Sensation that I was bein' sucked into a bog-hole. Me! Ousside on fuckin' Nothin'! Being swallied by a mound o' wet turf! Me what ain't left Bohane city since back in the lost-time. Sweet Baba! How many yella moons gone since I saw the Nothin' plain, Log? Not since one o' the times you went missin' out there, I'd say.'

A lonesome kid, he would walk out the Boreen – he ghosted about the rez, the massif villages, the backlanes, the haunted cottages, their roofs all caved in. See him in a field of reeds – at ten years old – his pale face above the burning gold of the reeds caught in drenching sun, and the reeds ride slowly the sway of the wind.

'I haven't been able to find Macu,' he said. 'There's no word from her even.'

'She ain't slidin' a pole in S'town, no?'

Out on Nothin', as a kid, he would listen to the old dudes at the rez fires, and in the shebeens, and he would watch the way they held themselves, and the way they carried themselves. That stuff didn't get taught in the schoolhouse.

'If I don't find her, I don't know that I can go on.'

Girly made a fist and bit down weakly on its bunched knuckles. For patience.

'Comin' along about seven bells?' she said. 'Gettin' light out, the gulls havin' a yap, the early El clankin' a beat? And I came up outta mesel' again.'

Logan winced at the bleach of morning sky over the Trace.

'I don't know what to do, Girly.'

'Lay off the fuckin' pipe for a start,' she said. 'Anyways I came outta mesel', and I floated out that same window you're stood at with a gommie fuckin' puss on ya. Saw the rooftops. Saw the mornin' get itsel' all worked up. Saw the rush in S'town, saw the suits on Endeavour at their little cups o' joe, their pinkies stuck out, and I saw the Rises women build their fires in the tower circles. An' I saw a way to work it all yet, y'check me?'

He turned to her, and smiled. Girly in her floating visions so often spied a new course. He came back to the bedside chair, and folded his bones into it, and he crossed his legs neatly. He wasn't the world's most masculine man. He leaned forward. Weighed his chin in a cupped palm.

'Tell me, you old witch,' he said.

She reached across and slapped his knee, and the move had a playful note, and playfully he slapped her hand away. But the slap and parry – they both knew – had a deeper meaning in freight: it was for the consolation of touch.

27

The Ancient & Historical Bohane
Film Society

It is not often that I get a good-looking woman in here. It is more usually men who are my patrons. The women can keep their feelings tamped a little more. But the men get to a certain age and it becomes too much for them. They must reach again for the whimsical days of their youth, and for the city as it was back then.

Mine is a small premises of the Back Trace. You will discover it down a dead-end wynd, with an unprosperous old draper to one side, his hands shaky now on the measuring tape, and a rotisserie the other, the charred smell of chicken skin wafting from ten in the morning. It is a glass-fronted shop, but the glass is a smoked grey, opaque, and on the door there is just a small title on a piece of white card, with the lettering of the Ancient & Historical picked out in gold ink. I do not need to advertise.

This particular April morning, the bell announced a customer, and I came forth, sighing, from behind the curtain, expecting the usual sad-eyed gent, the usual droop-of-mouth, the usual plea.

It was natural, then, that my breath should catch a little at the fine lady who appeared on the bell's tingle. She was tall, Iberian, green-eyed, one of the eyes turned slightly in – but the quirk an emphasis, somehow, to her attractiveness

– and her lips parted just a fraction, and I inclined my head patiently for her words, but she hesitated.

She wore:

A light, silken, springtime wrap of pistachio green turned just so across her shoulder, a scoop-neck top, French-striped, a pair of three-quarter-length buckskin hiphuggers that accentuated her tallness, and wooden clogs with a wedge-rise that lengthened the ankle beautifully.

Upon the right ankle, I noted at a glance – I don't miss much – there was a small tattoo, in Indian ink, of a Bohane dirk.

'How does it work?' she said.

I merely nodded, and smiled, and I raised the hatch on the counter, and with a gesture (priestly, I fancy) bid her enter.

She came through, and I parted the curtains, and I led her into the back room. It is a silvery, mica tone of dark-ness that persists there, and the room contains just the drawn-down screen, and an easy chair, and to one side a hatch that leads to my projection room.

'When?' I asked. 'Roughly.'

She sat in the easy chair, and removed the wrap, and the bareskin of her shoulders had a glisten in the silver of the gloom, and she crossed her legs, and she named the era that she longed for.

Anxiously, then:

'Can you do this?'

I nodded.

'The footage goes into the Thirties,' I said.

Discreetly, I withdrew to the projection room. I flicked through the cans of reels. I had transferred onto these reels what had been rescued from the street cameras. I called to her, softly, through the hatch:

'De Valera Street? The Trace?'

'Dev,' she said. 'Maybe there by the Aliados?'

'Where it gives onto the Trace,' I whispered, soulfully.

I picked a favourite compendium; a really lovely reel. It shows the snakebend roll of Dev Street, deep in the bustle and glare of the lost-time, at night, with the darting of the traffic as it rolled then – ah, the white-tyred slouch-backs, the fat Chaparelles, the S'town cruisers – and the crowds milling outside the bars, the stags and the hens, and it was a different world, so glaringly lit.

Of course, it is a silent footage always in the back room's replay, and so I cued up an old 78 on the turntable I keep by the projector, and I played it as accompaniment. It was a slow-moving calypso burner that gave a lovely sadness, I felt, to the scenes it worked with.

Discreetly, through the hatch, I watched the lady as she watched the screen. She was mesmerised.

And though I have watched this reel thousands of times myself, I was as always drawn into it, I was put under a spell by the roll and carry of the Dev Street habituees. If all had changed in Bohane, the people had not, and would never:

That certain hip-swing.

That especially haughty turn-of-snout.

That belligerence.

28

The View from Fifty

An old Bohane proverb:

The beginning of wisdom is first you get you a roof.

Of course, the Gant knew that a rez-born long-tooth can escape his wandering nature about as easily as outrun the length of his shadow, but he was willing to try. Big Nothin' had over the winter months become too much, too lonesome. He had felt like he was losing the sense of himself again – the old darknesses were seeping once more through the cracks of his life. And so, quietly, he had taken a room in the Back Trace. It was a place to breathe in the city and see what feeling he could take from it. The room was the attic of a tenement; it was maybe fifteen feet along by ten feet wide, with a sloped ceiling. It contained a single bed and a sink and damp-warped old floorboards that creaked and sang as he paced them. The bed was an insomniac's heroically rumpled nest, the sink for pissing in. A small window set in the roof gave a view over the Trace: the up-and-down of it, the rise-and-fall, the skewed calligraphy of the Bohane skyline, the dead pylons and dead cables, the half-dead birds with their spooked eyes, the strange dark blossom that trailed over the rickety zees of the fire escapes and the deep green voids of the wynds. The sense of being high above things gave to the Gant a feeling of breathlessness and abyss.

He had put the hard word on Jenni – Jenni had not turned.

He had put the hard word on Wolfie – Wolfie had not turned.

He had put the hard word on Fucker – Fucker said, what's in it for me, like?

The Gant shook his head at the kid's foolishness. He hoped that he would leave the place now. Take to the Boreen and head due east and never look back over the shoulder, not even once.

That's the mistake, boy: the looking back.

The day persisted, outside; the world persisted. The gulls belligerently called – *mmwwaaoork!* – and morning sounds rose up from the Trace. The bustle and pep of the arcade market. The old dears as they milled and chirruped. The veg prices hollered, the stony-voiced haggling. The old dudes out on their stoops with wind-up transistors tuned to Bohane Free Radio – where it was always yesteryear. The old love songs, the slow calypso rhythms that triggered the sense memory of dance steps that were still wired into his bones, and that he tried out, now and then, laughing, on the warped floorboards.

The snatches of song opened him up. The streets below were for the Gant a memory hoard. Every kiss, every reefing – it all came back to him. The detail was close up, halluci-natory, blood-warm.

It was just three weeks they had been together. The night she left him he remembered in a visceral way. He could summon it at will. The colours of the lonely street that night; the nausea of defeat. He knew where she was and who she was with. He experienced again every moment of it. He saw it so clearly. The facts were plain:

She was eighteen, and Logan was cooler.

There in the attic room the Gant came back to the moment and he seethed again with youth's intensity. The shallow fucking bitch. In the glare of spring, he was seeing things plain. He feared now he had come back to extract a revenge from Macu as much as from Logan. He had wanted to make her fall for him again, to make her sway, to make her world come loose. But on the longest night of the winter, on Beauvista, he saw that time had already from Macu taken its revenge.

He glared out over the rooftops.

Shallow fuckin' town.

He watched now the young ones in the April morning as they roamed down there. You could pick out the blow-ins so easily: the arrivistes, the hard-eyed adventurers. They would by long tradition head for the city of Bohane in springtime – they brought their shkelps, their herb-pipes, their dreams. See the way they tried out a walk – getting the roll of the hips just right, and the loose carry of the shoulders, and the glide of the feet; you didn't want to arrive Trace-deep on the stride of a cow-hand. He smiled but knew in his own way he was still trying out a walk. Still trying to fit into his own skin. At fifty! Oh hapless G, oh neurotic Broderick, oh the comical shame of this never growing old.

And still the lost-time music rose to him, remorselessly.

The Fancy boys had packed away their Crombies and wore sleeveless tanktops in bright pastel colours. The tattoo shops worked overtime – he could hear the zit-zing-zinging of their needles. And see the girls down there – the young stuff – in their wedge heels, their vinyl zip-ups, their spray-on catsuits; all trying to work it like Jenni Ching. Yes a shallow fucking town.

Now, critically, something shifted, a new pool of clarity opened, and the Gant as he watched the girls go by saw his revenge tack to a richer course.

He saw a slow way to hurt Logan.

29

The Intrigue in Smoketown

Jenni Ching whipped from the tit pocket a fresh cigarillo, clipped it and lit it, and she winced against the glare as a dose of filthy sunlight filled the Smoketown wharf. She looked yonder to the Trace across the Bohane's charismatic waters. She leaned back against the old cinnamon ware-house – it was lately got up as a grindbar – and she closed her eyes in long-suffering. Bit her pretty lip. Then she opened her eyes again, and blinked hard, and she turned to the sand-pikey bossman who was slouched beside her. This was an arranged meet, and his dreadlock brethren from the near distance warily kept guard. They fingered nervously their dirk sheaths. They kept careful sconce on the slanty bint. She scraped at the scummy cobblestones with a six-inch spike heel. She sucked from the lung-blackener what patience its tars might give. She said:

'Tubby, I wan' ya to hear this now. I don' care what fuckin' savagery ye practise out on them fuckin' dunes, y'check me? Ye can chant yere fuckin' pikey curses and ye can skin yere fuckin' hares for the stewpot and ye can build yere little six-bar fuckin' gates for the Big Nothin' fermoiri an' ye can hang yere fuckin' scalps and paint yere bollix blue an' have a read o' the fuckin' stars. Ye can train yere lurchers and hose out their minty fuckin' cages. Fine! Coz I don' have to fuckin' well look at ye while ye're at it. But lissen up, fatboy, and lissen good, coz yer in the fuckin' city now, right? I said look around you, Tubs! Them's buildings, them's streets, them's human fuckin' peoples! I'm tryin' to keep things a bit fuckin' civilise aroun' this joint, ya hear what I'm sayin' t'ya? So let's keep it all fit for biz, lardy-boy! Heed?'

The killer-gal glare she trained on him would put the scrotum hairs standing on a lesser gent but Prince Tubby just smiled serenely. He reached for the herb-bag that hung from his neck – fashioned, in the pikey way, from the skin of a goat's testicle sac – and he took out a bud, and he crumbled it expertly into the bowl of his pipe, and he pulled the draw-string on the herb-bag to secure his supply, and he lit the bud with his Zippo – the lighter of choice, always, for the Bohane smoker, no other providing sufficient protection against the hardwind's abrupt gusts – and he drew on the pipe. He glazed beautifully. He eyed Jenni Ching. He said:

'I-and-I's de Far-Eye, Jennie-sweet, y'check-back? I needs oney state dis one and true belief – de woman must not serve de man when she seein' de moon.'

Way it was in S'town, this weather, Prince Tubby had his sand-pikey goons doing the rounds of every grogpit and shothouse and dream salon, and they were questioning the women who worked in these places about their menstrual cycles. Sand-pikeys held the belief that women were unclean when in flow.

'It's us way, Jen-chick, y'get me?'

Jenni Ching, defender of womankind, spat her cigarillo.

'Y'ain't nothin' but a pikey fuckin' throwback!' she cried. 'People's got their fuckin' privacy, check?'

Tubby displayed his palms.

'Said it's de sand-pike way, Jen,' he said. 'An' what's our way is de Smoketown way dese times, heed?'

186

She let a scowl devour him.

'Oh we'll see about that,' she said. 'Now g'on down the dune end an' watch yer fuckin' back, y'check me?'

She pushed off from the grindbar's wall. Prince Tubby watched her go, and he glazed again on his draw, and he nodded slowly, appreciatively, at the clip of her spike heels, and the way she carried that high 'n' tight slanty-chick can.

Jenni felt his glare and turned to it over her shoulder.

'An' don' even fuckin' dream it,' she said.

Jenni wore:

Black nylon ski pants, a sheer black nylon top, a silver dirk belt, and a pork-pie crownsitter perched jauntily up top.

She aimed for the Ho Pee Ching Oh-Kay Koffee Shoppe. April sweltered, and there was a glisten of sweat on her forehead. The burn of his eyes on her rear end had planted a notion. In springtime, the city was opened to the elements like a wound and the sky bled its rude light on her as she walked. Manic birds hovered and cawed. The Ching gal plotted.

This seeing-the-moon caper was the least of it. That the sand-pikeys were opening credit lines for repeat customers was an even greater taunt. Not to mention their specials on brew and bushweed and particular methods of fornication. They were also, in Jenni Ching's opinion, spreading all manner of superstition among the hoors, the dream sellers and the trick-pony boys. Then there was their general demeanour. They were fire-eating in the sideways and blowing perpetually on their horrible didgeridoos. Jenni reached the Ho Pee. She stormed through the swing doors of the place. She found Wolfie Stanners settled in a booth over a plate of gingered cuttlefish. He raised a moony look to her.

187

'Stow the love-eyes,' she said. 'I gots enough on me fuckin' noodle, check?'

'S'up with ya, girl-a-mine?'

He laid down his chopsticks and pushed back his plate. Attentive, husbandly, lost to first love – it gets even the Wolfies among us – he reached for a cup and poured her a fill of jasmine tea from the bamboo-handled pot.

'Sand-pikeys!' she cried. 'They ain't got no fuckin' class, Wolf!'

He sighed. He thought for a moment, and then he winked slyly. He placed on the table a small, scarred hand, the palm down, its fingers splayed, and with his other hand he drew a four-inch dirk from the inside pocket of his Crombie. He jabbed the dirk first slowly into the wooden tabletop between his splayed fingers, and then more quickly, and then at a furious pace until the knife became a blur. Knife tricks rarely failed to distract his girl from her troubles, but today she could raise only a wan smile. She laid a hand on his to still the blur. She spoke in a low voice.

'Pikeys sendin' Smoketown straight to fuckin' hell, Wolf. An' I'm suppose to stand around and look at the fuckheads while they's at it?'

Jenni lit another cigarillo. She bopped smoke rings from her pouted lips. Wolfie became aroused beneath his gaberdine peg pants. He replaced with trembling hand the dirk in his inside pocket.

'I think I know what you're goin' to say to me next,' he said.

'Where's the change we wan' to see comin'?' she said.

'That's what I knew you'd say to me,' he said.

She had been laying it on since the year-turn. Every day and every night. Jenni would lean in a little closer to him, and she would bring her lips to his ear, and she'd lick the lobe briefly, just once, with a single dart of her tongue, and then whisper to him:

'The change, Wolf? Where's the change we been wantin'?'

Now in the Ho Pee afternoon she saw there was too much loyalty in the boy. He was not ready to move. And Jenni made a decision. The sand-pikes without a leader would be headless and fatally degenerate. The Fancy without her boy-clutch, Wolfie, would be still riper for the taking. One or the other, Tubby or Wolfie, would not survive a collision. If her luck was in, both might fall.

'What I wanted to talk t'ya about, Wolf . . .'

She turned her glance from him, and assumed a tragic aspect, as though too wounded for speech.

'What's it, girl?'

'This Tubby, y'know? He ain't got no fuckin' respec', like.'

'How'd ya mean, Jen?'

She jerked a thumb over her shoulder to indicate the S'town beyond.

'Not five minute since?' she said. 'He oney goes and drops the hand on me, don't he?'

Homicidal rage at once travelled the short length of Wolfie Stanners. It forced him to a stand. His freckle-puss crimsoned. He gripped the booth's tables with his tiny, scarred fingers.

'He did . . . fuckin' . . . *what?*'

30

The Beak of the Law

See a busted-nose smirk from a Bohane polis. See his great slabs of ham-bone arms crossed on the station's high counter and inked with tats showing the symbols of the polis fraternities:

A truncheon with a snake's head.
A length of coiled chain.
A Judas coin.

Was a bottle of Phoenix ale on the counter and he raised it and sucked deep on it and burped a cloud of kebab breath (mutton flavour) and he placed the bottle down again, wiped his mouth and smacked his greasy lips and a wee lizardy tongue emerged and tickled the air; see the searching tip of it.

Logan Hartnett was stood up on the other side of the counter and he winced, delicately – his gut was already unsure from the dream-pipe – as the cloud of polis breath meatily lingered.

'You've got the fucking rot in you, friend,' he said. 'Not long for the beat would be my call.'

Polis smirked even more slyly – the arrogant chops of the fucker creased to a fold there beneath the bleached glare of the stationhouse strip lights.

The station walls were painted an institutional green and old bloodstains were dark inkblobs against the green. Polis reached beneath the desk and brought up a bottle of state whiskey; he showed it. Logan shook his head – he wouldn't shame his throat with that tangerine-coloured pisswater. The polis fathead nodded politely – no offence taken – blew another damp, liverish breath, and lightly, he said:

'Mr Hartnett, why's it you're here again, sir?'

Was the thinnest of smiles Logan allowed the fat polis.

'I think you might have someone I need to see.'

Long Fella was working the latest plan from Girly's play-book. Goal: the immediate pacification of the Norrie kind. The Norries in humid springtime were restless, wounded and brooding, and a play was urgently needed.

'We picked her up,' the polis confirmed, 'but that's a dangerous game on the Rises, y'understand? When tis a Cusack kid we's talkin'?'

Logan slid distastefully a fold of notes to the polis. The fathead smirked, and took the fold, and raised it to his porcine snout and sniffed it, and then stood from his desk.

''Course it was Mr Reid the master butcher did the job itself,' he said. 'Said to say t'ya tis a favour answered.'

'Whatever that might mean,' Logan said.

Polis picked a ring of keys from the wall with his tab-stained fingers. Swung the ring as he trailed down a dank, urine-smelling corridor. Strip lights overhead buzzed, failed, briefly came to life again, and failed again. Corridor sang with old spirits. Logan as he followed the fat polis closed his eyes – he was tapering yet from a Ho Pee dream – and heard the screeches of age-dead Fenians seep from the walls. No shortage of ghosts in this place. There were occult fre-quencies in the Back Trace heard only by dogs and the 'bino.

He came with the polis on the cell rooms down back of the station.

Polis slid a key from the ring into a cell's lock and the lock clacked, unclicked, and the polis flicked a switch outside and as they entered a dim bulb found a young girl on a straw pallet. Polis winked for Logan and went and crouched down by the girl. Polis took her wrists and turned her palms to show Logan the fresh marks that had been skilfully cut in:

A pair of clover-shaped stigmata.

Logan nodded, painfully – his mother was such a sick old fuck; the skewed logic of her derangement was beyond even him – and the polis rose and left the cell, sniggering.

The girl looked up at him. She was hard-eyed as any Norrie bint but she could not keep the scare from her voice. She said:

'I'll do what you wan' me to, 'bino . . .'

Logan got down on his haunches to meet the girl with a level and reassuring gaze.

'I know that, sweet,' he said. 'And you'll do fine work for me.'

She cried despite herself.

'Hush, lovie,' he said. 'Now I hope that fat polis fuck ain't been taking no undue liberties . . . Was it painful for you, child? With the butcher?'

She looked at her palms – shrugged. No more than twelve, and a pure Norrie hard-face, but awed, all the same, by his proximity. In Bohane, you make your name and let your name do the work.

'We need to get this trick working, Little Cuse,' he said. 'You've been missing for three days and three nights, check?'

'S'right.'

'You were drawn to Big Nothin',' he said. 'You felt a strange

192

drag from the bog plain. Something brought you to the High Boreen – it was a particular star in the sky, a bright, bright star. And then, upon a high knoll . . . do you know what a knoll is, Little Cuse?'

'Nah.'

'Class of a wee hill,' Logan sighed. 'And out there, in the night, on this *knoll* you came across a puck goat – you know what a puck goat is . . .'

He turned his own palm and showed on the inside of his wrist the finely inked tat of a puck's horns – symbol of the Trace Fancy.

'I know that awrigh', 'bino.'

'And the goat spoke to you, Little Cuse. But as he spoke to you, it was the words of the Sweet Baba you heard, y'check me?'

The eyes of Little Cuse widened.

'Baba took the form of a puck, 'bino?'

Logan inclined his head respectfully.

'He most certainly did, girl-child. And now His Perpetual Sweetness has left the mark on you. Do you understand?'

Mouth open, eyes popping, she displayed the faked stigmata – Logan liked this kid.

'And listen good now,' he said, 'because the Sweet Baba has passed to you a special message for your people.'

'What's it, 'bino?'

He leaned in, and he whispered to her a moment, and the message was understood. He let it be known, too, what would happen should she fail to comply precisely with his instructions. He stood then and he led the girl from the cell. The fat polis leaned back against a corridor wall and smiled like the fondest of uncles. Gestured to a back door down the far end of the corridor. Logan brought the girl there and he kissed his bunched fingertips and he placed the kiss lightly, so very lightly, on her cheek. He trailed then his fingertips along the filigree down of her arm's fine hair, and this touch was electric, his eyes closed; he felt youth, he felt vitality, he felt the sense-memory of Macu, when young. His eyes watered, his gut lurched. His throat screamed for the dream-pipe. He turned the girl loose to the dusky streets. He had made a decent connection, he felt. He came back down the corridor. Fat polis grinned, and he said:

'Baba due an appearance, Mr H?'

'Sweet Jay on the comeback trail,' Logan said.

He went again to the evening and he walked the Back Trace shadows. Girly's shrewd reckon: gullibility on the Northside Rises was to be fostered and worked with. Long Fella admired her canniness as he walked the darkening Trace.

The Back Trace was the brain of the city, and he felt the wynds' pulsing: an arterial throb.

Pitbull behind a chain fence lurched for him.

He hissed at the dog.

It barked a yard of stars.

31

All Our Yesterdays

Big Dom Gleeson, the corpulent news hound, and Balthazar
Mary Grimes, his hunchback lensman, were on official
Vindicator business in the Bohane Trace. It was dusk of the
same hot April evening – with a mango wash to the sky
above the rooftops – and Dom was breathing hard and fret-
fully as he followed his snapper down a dizzying tangle of
wynds and turns.

'Go handy on me, Balt, please! I am not a young
gentleman!'

'You're thirty-eight, Mr Gleeson.'

Through the dank squares they went, and they were deep
in the foul and ancient maze, and they came at length to a
certain tenement building in the shadows of the arcade
market. Dom took from the fob pocket of his mustard-
yellow waistcoat a piece of paper on which the address was
scrawled, and he showed it to Balthazar, and the hunchback
turned from address to tenement, and back again, and yet
again for the triple-check, and he nodded.

'S'the place awrigh', Mr Gleeson.'

Dom gathered himself with a couple of deep breaths and
he pushed in the heavy door of the tenement.

'Sufferin' Baba above on the cross,' he said. 'The heart
would be skaw-ways in you, Balt?'

Balthazar shrugged, and grimly lugged his medieval Leica

through the door, passed by his boss, and set first to the stairs.

'He knows we're comin',' he said. 'Let's move.'

They climbed a flight of the old stone stairs, and then climbed again, winding at each turn, and climbing again, and the building was deadly silent, with an eerieness palpable, and Big Dom was frankly unmanned, his bottom lip quivered babyishly, but he was set all the same to his task. There was prize copy for the taking.

'All Our Yesterdays' was by far the most popular and prestigious column of the *Bohane Vindicator*. It was penned by Dominick himself, in a limpid and melancholy prose, and its stock was reminiscence and anecdotes of the Bohane lost-time. It appeared – twenty-seven inches of nine-point type over three column drops – in the Thursday evening edition, and the queue for it formed early outside the paper's office and snaked far down the streets of the New Town. This week's column, Dom was certain, would attract a record readership.

'What I'm wonderin', Mr Gleeson,' Balt panted against the climb, 'is why's he agreein' to the interview jus' now?'

Dom rested a moment on the turn of a stair. Smiled; sweated.

'Ol' Boy's worked his powers of persuasion,' he said. 'What we're tryin' to do, Balt, is distract the town from atein' itself alive.'

'But what's in it for the man hissel'?'

Dom shrugged as he began to climb again.

'It lets a certain party know he's back in town, don't it? An' that he ain't afraid to show his jaws.'

The Gant Broderick appeared then on the landing at the top of the last flight of stairs. He had to bend a little against the angle of the low ceiling. He looked down without expression to the climbing pair, and he gestured lazily to indicate the door to the garret space behind, and he turned and went through.

'Mercy,' Dom whispered as he climbed the last haul of steps, 'but he's still a powerful cut of a man, Balt?'

Balthazar nodded grimly.

'Big unit,' he agreed.

They entered the spartan garret. Gant sat on the bed and he eyed them calmly and he massaged with one massive hand the other. Dom removed his pork-pie hat in greeting.

'Mr Gant . . .'

'Gant is fine,' said the Gant. 'Jus' Gant, okay?'

'Yes, sir. Gant . . . sir.'

The Gant eyed the hunchback as he went about propping his Leica and mounting its flash. The Gant looked to the window set in the garret's slanting roof, and said:

'We got a nice aul' tawny light comin' through yet. Probably don' need that flash, y'heed?'

Balthazar looked to the evening light, and he nodded.

'Might be nice alrigh', Gant . . .'

'It'll be lovely,' the Gant said. 'And don't be shy. You can come up good and close.'

The Gant turned expertly then his square jaw to the tawniness of the light as it poured through, with dust motes rising atmospherically about him, and the hunchback crouched in close, and he framed the old scoundrel so that he loomed, poetically, and the G allowed to form on his features a poignant, dark, unknowable glaze.

Click-and-whirr of the old Leica's motor:

Prime shot . . . peach . . . one for the portfolio . . . manly gravitas in haunted black-and-white.

197

Dom Gleeson meantime sat on the garret's one hardback chair and nervously he licked the tip of his pencil and turned to a fresh page of his spiral-bound notebook. With a nervous croak to his tone, he began:

'Mr Gant . . . Gant . . . It's been a . . . been a stretch o' lonesome moons since ya last hauled yer bones aroun' the city o' Bohane, sir. So what I'm wonderin' is –'

'Twenty-five years such a long time?' the Gant said.

'Well, we ain't talkin' yesterday nor today, sir.'

'No,' the Gant handsomely smiled. 'That we ain't.'

They spoke then at length of the Bohane lost-time. They talked of the great feeling for it that had drawn the Gant to the creation once more. They talked of those who had passed, and of how their spirits persisted yet and carried always on the air of the city (or lingered, maybe, away yonder on the bog plain). Dom Gleeson felt that the Gant spoke lyrically, yes, but guardedly, and at length he sucked up the courage to launch an especially toothsome question.

'I s'pose what a lot o' people would be wonderin', Gant, is . . . ah . . . Well, sir, about these pas' twenty-five year, like . . . Where the hell you been, G?'

The Gant as the last of the evening light began to fail smiled wryly at the fat newsman, and at his hunchback accomplice who sat cross-legged now on the floor, and he said:

'Over.'

Jerked a rueful thumb easterly.

'Crossed the water.'

The Gant confided that he had roamed for many a desperate year England's cheerless marshes. He worked the dark cities of the north for any who had the price of a shkelping. Got older. Got sadder. Got fatter. He came out of that rough trade with the sure scars of it. Worked the riverboats for a while . . .

'Like many a Bohane émigré before ya, sir,' Gleeson said.

. . . worked the Tyne, the Mersey, and the Clyde. He spent a cruel infinity staring into the smoke-coloured wind that blows always across those dead rivers. He saw the Wigan riots of '36, he saw the ascendance of Borthwick in Macclesfield, and he saw the bloody last days of D'Alton's Humberside Fancy.

Balt Grimes whistled low.

'Now that was some fuckin' massacre!'

He spent long nights, he said, walking the backstreets of strange cities. Skunk hours in the demon mist. The Gant walked every street of every city and they were never his streets and when the streets are not your own they are not for dreaming. He admitted that he had seen too much. He allowed that he had found solace, for a time, in the arms of the Sweet B.

'Happen a lot of lads when they go over,' said Big Dom, kindly.

'I renounced the blade,' said the Gant, and he smiled against the dark that seeped then into the attic room.

He told that he had spoken the Word in the West Midlands for a time. Found a congregation of swayers, swooners, shriekers. Spoke out against the violence of life. Spoke out against the lust. Spoke out against the lies. Oh yes, there he was, stood up on a beer crate, in tragic Wolverhampton, with tears in his eyes, and he hollering the Baba-love.

'A man with a good brogue,' said Big Dom, 'would get a start easy enough at the preachin' over.'

'Didn't last at that trade neither,' the Gant chuckled.

'Oh?'

'Bothered a pawful o' young tush an' got ran out o' Brum.'

The roofops of the Trace beyond were ghostly as they settled into night's shade; bitter, the memories that settled in the Gant. A taste of Macu, in her youth, had left him with an insatiable taste for girls of that age. This was not the least of her crimes against him.

'I was on life's great turning wheel,' the Gant said, and Big Dom scribbled furiously.

'The longer the past receded, the clearer it became in me mind's eye,' the Gant said.

Philosopher we got on our hands, the hunchback Grimes reckoned.

'I was drawn back to the lost-time,' the Gant said.

'And did you find it a dangerous place to linger?' Big Dom showed his skill.

'Yeah,' said the Gant. 'It's too sweet back there.'

Big D thinking: headline –

LOST-TIME TOO SWEET FOR THE LINGERING

Beneath them, the wynds simmered with life in the oily night, and the savour of a sadness came up; the men quietened, and listened.

'Been changes around here sure enough,' Dom sighed.

'It's all change.' Balt, too, fell woebegone.

'Not all change is for the worse,' the Gant smiled.

'Oh?'

'Mean to say,' the Gant said, 'I see these young girls workin' it now in the Trace an' I got to tell ya?'

'Yes?' Dom was interested.

'Them girls the future in Bohane.'

A strange glint in the Gant's eye.

'You reckon, Mr Broderick?'

'An' on the soon-come too, y'check me? Change be good for Bohane sometimes.'

Dom and his lensman quietly regarded each other. Dom said:

'But I'm wonderin', Gant . . .'

'Yeah?'

'Why's it you've come back . . . *now*?'

But the Gant just smiled, and he began to speak again, softly, of the lost-time, of the old butchers and bakers who had premises once on De Valera Street, of all the shebeens and herb-shacks, of the life of the street as was. Emotional Dom Gleeson lapped it up. Big Dom remembered the dogs and cats of Dev Street. Dom would be happy to talk about the old Bohane until the clock came down the stairs, and there on the hardback chair he rocked to and fro, rhythmically, as he made notes from the Gant's powerful recall, and the hunchback Grimes, too, was set adrift on memory bliss – ah youth; he'd been a puckish spirit in his youth, Balt Grimes; the hump hadn't kept him from his share of tushies (your Bohane tush anyways tending to incline towards a bit of strange) – and the three men cut across each other, and prompted each other, and riffed; when a reminiscence got going in the Back Trace, nights, it worked like a freestyle morphine jazz.

32

Wolfie Got a Brood On

Wolfie Stanners prowled an S'town beat.

Wolfie Stanners worked a vengeance plot.

Wolfie Stanners was amped to wade in the Far-Eye's blood.

Drop the hand on a fiend's clutch – in this town – and you'd best be ready to meet your manufacturer. But there was a kink in the plot – the sand-pikes kept their premises, and their leader, well guarded, and Wolfie would need help to get a clear shot at the dreadlock bossman in his dune-end fastness.

He aimed his bovver boots for Ed 'The Gypo' Lenihan's hoorshop.

Afternoon, yes, in an April swelter, and this was as quiet a time as you'd get in Smoketown, but there was a scatter of degenerates around all the same – skin-poppers, tush-maulers, dream-chasers. Wolfie-boy as he made his parade of the cobbled streets breathed deep to take in their savour: Smoketown smelt of chemical burn, untreated sewerage and sweet chilli noodles. There were faint back-notes, also: pig, brew, oxen, coriander. The atmosphere generally was riverine and as Wolfie walked the wharf there was no small amount of poetry mingled with violent intention. Was the prospect of violence that stirred the poetics in Wolfie.

He approached a two-storey, narrow-shouldered, old town house, an S'town leaner, and he knocked on its door

– it was quickly answered by the aged hoor-ma'am of the place.

'Mr Stanners,' she said.

The 'mister'! To be addressed as 'mister' made him as aroused almost as Jenni Ching's cigar-flavoured kiss.

'Gypo about?' he asked.

He did not make eye contact with the hoor-ma'am. Truth be told, Wolfie had a secret fancy for these handsome older ladies, and he was shy of them.

'Mr Lenihan's above with the girls,' she said.

Edmund 'The Gypo' Lenihan had blown a gasket since the sand-pikeys arrived into Smoketown. Pikey himself, and proud of it, he was dismayed at the intrusion of the dune breed. Ed Lenihan was the oldest hoormaster in the creation. He had been trading in tush since the lost-time. Nobody knew S'town like the Gypo Lenihan. The Gypo knew the backways of the red-light streets, and the nuance of the double-jointed lingo, and the whereabouts of the secret passageways. He waited, smiling, as Wolfie made it to the top of the hoorshop stairs. The upper floor was given over entirely to screened slots with rush matting for beds. The girls present at this hour were using the afternoon lull to wax themselves. They squealed mightily as they waxed. The Gypo called to them:

'Arra jus' fuckin' do it, would ye!'

He sighed.

'I'd have a pack o' gorillas to me name if I didn't keep on top a things, Wolf.'

'Runnin' brassers ain't no easy life, Gyp.'

They fist-bumped. They set to a smoke by the sash window overlooking the S'town run. The Gypo's filmy eyes widened as the boy explained – in tooth 'n' claw detail – his intentions with regard to Prince T the Far-Eye.

Ed Lenihan whistled low:

'It's a radical plan of action, Wolf. I'd say that for it. And while I'd be very much in favour, technically speaking, it ain't gonna be a cinch to pull off, y'heed? He's well guarded down there.'

'You know the dune end, Mr L.'

'I surely do but –'

'You can get me close in, Gypy-pal. If we wait on the mo', like?'

'Could be a longish wait, kid.'

They talked it through.

'Certainly they're lowerin' the tone, Wolf. Which is some fuckin' trick in S'town. And decent Baba-fearin' premises the likes a me own can't compete. All I'm offerin' is clean, fresh-shaven girl. Which ain't good enough for Bohane no more. No, sir! Now we all wants to be ate alive by slave-girl lurchers! But still an' all, Wolfie, you don't want to go off on no loolah mission just on account of a sand-pikey –'

'He dropped the hand on me clutch, Mr Lenihan.'

'As you've been sayin', boy.'

'Jenni's me all-time doll, y'sketch? I wanna start a fam'ly with the bint an' all, like.'

Silently, the Gypo Lenihan tried to imagine the likely spawn of a Ching–Stanners union, and he shuddered.

'That's very lovely, Wolf,' he said.

A strange moment, then: the boy-villain seemed to come over a little bashful. Stared at his bovver boots a pensive moment.

'Actually, Mr Lenihan, that's somethin' else I wanted to ask your advice on, sir.'

'Oh, Wolf?'

'Mr L . . . You've run a share o' Chinkee chicks in yer day, check?'

'Certainly,' said Ed Lenihan. 'Our oriental is a powerful cut of a hoor.'

'And what I wanted to ask ya, Gyp . . .'

A blush! Lenihan could hardly believe it – there was a blush on the demon's cheek!

'What's it, Wolf?'

'Your Chinkees,' said Wolfie, 'they'd a gone down from time to time with the, ah . . . with the carryin' o' childer, like?'

'Of course. Any young lady can get herself caught. The precautions aren't what they were, Wolf.'

'Okay,' said Wolfie, and he breathed deep, 'so what I wanted to ask ya was . . .'

He pointed to his fine-cropped red hair.

'D'ya ever come across a Chinkee gettin' bred off one a these?'

Ah, thought Ed Lenihan, the boy has a brood on. He was young for that. But they know, sometimes, in Bohane, that they may not be long for the road.

'D'ya mean, Wolf . . .'

'Off a ginger, Gyp. D'ya ever come across a Chinkee bint gettin' bred off a ginge?'

Lenihan smiled.

'What is it exactly you're asking me, Wolf?'

Shyness glowed all over Wolfie Stanners. Fear, also.

'Could the chil' not come out skaw-ways, Mr L?'

Sympathy for the little demon, Ed Lenihan found he had, and he placed a fatherly arm around Wolf's shoulders. Felt a tremor in the boy at this touch, a recoil.

'When yer lookin' to start a family, Wolf, you just got to pack away your fears and throw it all to the fates, boy.'

'But what y'reckon, Gyp? Would it come out ginger or would it come out Chinkee, like?'

As he led Wolfie back towards the stairs, with his hoors yelping as they waxed themselves smooth, he leaned in, and said:

'Wolf Stanners? When any child o' yours appears 'pon the face of the earth, I don't think there's gonna be e'er a doubt about it.'

'Thanks very much, Mr Lenihan.'

By the doorway then, the Gypo consented to be the boy's guide to the dune-end backways, and to get him close in on Prince T. Wolfie's blackbird stare told him he had no choice.

And so it was that a lightness in the step was evident as Wolfie walked out again through the Smoketown streets. He didn't notice the sand-pikey watches who eyed him from the doorways and the rooftops there, and who knew already of his intention.

33

Jenni Ching, Superstar

This was the year all the girls in the Back Trace started to dress like Jenni Ching. They wore white vinyl zip-ups tighter than sin, or black nylon catsuits as though fitted with a spray-can, or gym shorts worn a handful of sizes too small over sheer silver stockings, and always there would be a set of custom steelcaps fitted to the high-steppers: groin-kicker boots for bad girls. They all started chewing on stogies, too. And in the Dev Street salons de coiffure, if you wanted a blunt-cut fringe while keeping some length and body in back, you asked for a Jenni.

Next thing?

The girls started to run in a wilding pack in the Trace. There were all-girl roisters in the midnite yards. You were a girl in Bohane, in the springtime of '54, you had a shkelp in your inside pocket, and a stogie on the chomp, and you walked the wynds with that Ching-patented S'town glide. And you did not kowtow to no fuckwad boy-chil'.

Witness:

The girls skanked in the wee hours to dub-plate cuts blasted from the Trace rooftops.

The girls walked the snakebend roll of De Valera Street and they kept their mangle-dogs on chain leads.

The girls took from the malevolent surge of the river its defining taint, and fed on it.

207

Their talk travelled and lit on the usual nodes of adolescence
– rage, lust, shame – but always this season, in the city of
Bohane, it circled back to the one subject, again and again
and again:

'I seen her crossin' the S'town footbridge an' she got like
a pair o' wedge heels workin' off a pair o' pedal pushers in
like a lemony, like a tangy shade, an' she got like . . .'

'Heard ya can get in the Ho Pee awrigh' but not pas' the
caff bit, like. Y'gots to get the connects right afore they lets
ya to the upstairs rooms, like, to the dream salons an' Jenni'd
be up there mos' . . .'

'Is said she gots the Long Fella stashed up there an' all,
y'sketch?'

'Gots him hangin' on a string, like.'

'Gots the Gant on another.'

'An' Wolfie besides . . .'

'Is said she gots a dozen, maybe thirteen, scalp to the
shkelp belt, check, an' that's oney wots known o', like.'

'She's a size six tops, like . . .'

'She gots the bes' cheekbones in the whole o' Bohane,
like . . .'

'An' tell you this, heed?'

'S'that, gurl?'

'She's a fuckin' *mega* dancer.'

34

The Succession

Ol' Boy Mannion braved the top-floor suite at the Bohane Arms Hotel. He found himself at the foot of the honeymooners' bed. He stood up straight. He held his hat in his hands. He had brass enough – but just about – to keep his eyes locked on Girly's. She raised a tumbler of neat John Jameson to her lips.

'S'pose you know he's gone fuckin' loolah?' she said.

'Ma'am?'

'As a bucket o' cats,' she said.

Ol' Boy shaped his mouth sadly, and shrugged – it was not for him to pass remark on the Long Fella's mental status.

'I blame the thunderin' rip he married,' she said. 'Gave him delusions of grandeur, didn't she? Trace not good enough, oh no. He's got to be up on Beauvista like some fuckin' Protestant, ain't he? Swingin' off the rafters o' that fuckin' manse. And I wouldn't mind . . .'

She paused, sipped.

'Wouldn't mind but Immacu-fuckin'-lata is the spawn o' fuckin' dock trash off a fuckin' tuna boat, ain't she? And the hoor of a mother she had was from the wrong end o' the Trace an' all, wasn't she? With the smell of a thousand fuckin' campfires off her.'

Ol' Boy sighed.

'Marriage is a hard old game at the best o' times,' he said.

She eyed him in silence a moment. Saw that he held yet her gaze. Tickled her upper lip with the tip of her tongue.

'Course now she's gone off in a hump and he's lying about on a Chinkee settle horsin' the dream-smoke into hissel' like there ain't no t'moro and the Back Trace Fancy is runnin' around like a fuckin' rat with its hole on fire.'

Ol' Boy soothed:

'The Hartnett family still has the runnins o' Bohane, missus.'

'Ah yeah,' she said. 'For now anyways.'

She laughed then, miserably, and wheezed, and paled. She said:

'I see you got the Gant all over the paper?'

'I'm trying to distract the town, Girly.'

'From what, Mannion?'

'From badness.'

'Best of luck with that,' she said. 'How's our tram comin' along?'

'To be honest, it looks like the NB is long fingerin'.'

'Well, that ain't no surprise, is it? When we been actin' like a pack o' savages! An' you know what's comin' next, don't ya? A royal scrap out back o' the Aliados as all the little Fancy fuckheads try and put their call on the handle. Oh I seen it more than once in my time, Ol' Boy. They'll be pullin' hair and gougin' eyes all the way to the far side o' fuckin' Crimbo. An' while they's at it? Some wee bollicks off the Rises or some sand-pikey dickwipe outta the Smoketown dune end is going to march through the town and take care o' business. Or how's about some gang o' wildin' gals from me own fuckin' Bohane Trace?'

'I have been meanin' to ask about Jenni . . .'

'Y'know the latest, Ol' Boy? She's encouragin' them girls!'

'This is all we need.'

'You're tellin' me! It's as much as I can do to keep a halter on that friggin' Chinkee bint.'

'I understand ye're close.'

Girly smiled, so fondly, despite her hard words; Ol' Boy could read the love. He worried where it might send the town.

'Way I am with Jenni,' she said, 'dunno whether to put in the adoption papers or take her slant eyes out with a six-inch dirk.'

'She's impressive,' Ol' Boy admitted.

Girly hacked out a chuckle.

'S'the way she hold me gaze an' all, y'know? Ne'er let it flit at all, like. Stone cold!'

'I hold your gaze, Girly.'

'Yeah, but you're all act.'

It was the lines that came with a smile that stung, and Ol' Boy duly winced. That he recovered as quickly was the mark of his skill. Gauche, he knew, to ask, but he could not resist.

'So who'd you reckon on, Girly? If Logan's done his time . . .'

Girly creased again with laughter – as though she'd answer! The laughter was torture but slowly she recovered, and she poured another whiskey, and she lit another tab, and she said:

'Tell ya this, Ol' Boy. S'been keepin' me awake nights. But I'll keep ya posted on me call, y'check?'

35

On Riverside Boulevard

Take a left out of the Yella Hall station – as so few of us
ever do – and you will come quickly to a long, curving
run of pathway known as Riverside Boulevard. It follows
the Bohane river along the last of the city's bluffs until
the river opens out to a vague, estuarine nowhere. Haggard
seabirds hover above the empty walkway, and the air is
ghostly. It is a place few of us go to because of its strange-
ness. You will encounter there an overwhelming sense of
déjà vu. Invariably, that odd swoop in the spirit occurs,
and you are flung back to an inner lost-time that you can
never quite place. It is a frightening sensation – one senses
an odd lurch within, a movement that can feel almost
nauseous. Thoughts come loose. Souls hang on the air.
Warps occur. And Logan Hartnett, dream-sick in April,
sold to the pipe and heartache, had begun almost daily to
haunt the place.

He walked it; he fed on the weird. He chased with clouded
eyes the flight of the demon skuas. Hummed softly. And he
made – with pale lips moving – his dark reckonings.

Now a particular afternoon of April presented, and the
'bino was again on Riverside, but today he was not alone.
He sat on a bollard, as the hot river wind blew, and he gazed
up, most pleasantly, at a very nervous Fucker Burke.

Fucker hung his limbs from the chainlink fence that edged

the Bohane river hereabouts and he slapped at imagined bugs on his neck.

Logan regarded him with a loving smile.

'You'll notice a certain feeling, Fucker?'

'This place, Mr H, it's like . . .'

'Is it sendin' you, Fuck?'

Fucker had in his voice a child's quiver:

'Ain't feelin' so hot now, Mr H, if I'm bein' honest with ya.'

Fucker threw a hopeful glance towards the Bohane downtown – its rooftops loomed royally in the near distance – but the Long Fella shook his head sadly; there was no going back.

'You'd pass along this way much yourself, Fucker?'

Spoke to the boy in the sweetest hush, as though whispering a lullaby, and Fucker felt a chill dampness at the base of his spine.

'No, Mr Hartnett.'

Logan nodded, firmly, as if that was the best tactic the boy could choose.

'So tell me about Wolfie and Jenni,' he said.

The jaw lolloped on the galoot boy Burke.

'What would I know, H?'

'Are they rock-steady, Fuck?'

'W-wolfie is.'

'Got the hook in his gut, he has? I thought as much. And Jenni?'

Fucker made an attempt at indifference.

'Dunno, Mr H. I mean she givin' him the whiff of it, like, but . . .'

Fucker's words trailed off. His eyes rolled some. Logan let a silence hover, for just a moment, and he watched carefully to see where it would send the boy. Fucker Burke had a routinely Gothical West of Ireland childhood under his belt, and it was there again, his own desperate lost-time, beneath the glaze of his green eyes. He was sent to it. The horrors he had seen, and those by his own hand begotten. There was no way to escape the tingling of his past; it was ever-present, like tiny fires that burned beneath the skin.

'Come back to me now, Fucker.'

'You think the Baba'll wan' me for a finish, H?'

'Shush, boy, and come back to me – the Baba loves you.'

Fucker Burke swung down from the chainlink and shuffled his feet uselessly. Shifted his weight from the left to the right and back again. Logan raised a hand to still him.

'What do you think of the situation with Wolfie, Fuck?'

'Situation how, Mr Hartnett?'

Logan smiled delightedly, as if a notion had just occurred.

'Would you say we should do away with him?'

There were dried flecks of spit at the corners of the 'bino's mouth – they cracked as he spoke.

'But H, Wolf is like the Fancy's bes' –'

'Are ye close still?'

There was a wrinkle to the 'bino's collar, and his kecks were unpressed.

'Close ain't got nothin' to do with it. Jus' ain't seein' what Wolfie's done.'

'Loyalty is a tremendous asset, Fucker Burke.'

'I don't like it out here, Mr H.'

There was a greenish wash to the 'bino's deadhouse pallor – the colour of a mould.

'Oh I know that Riverside feeling, boy. Things rise up in you, don't they?'

214

Swallowed hard, Fucker, a crab-apple of terror descending and then rising again the length of his throat.

'We strollin' back, H?'

'And what about Jenni – should we do away with Jenni Ching, Fucker?'

'I wasn't brought up to mess with no Chinkees, Mr Hartnett.'

'You'd be as wise not to, child, under normal circumstances. But what I'm hearing about Jenni Ching?'

He shook his head slowly.

'She's got plans, ain't she, Fuck?'

'Don't know about that, H.'

'Do you not? I see.'

Logan stood from the bollard and approached the boy and he placed his hand on the back of the boy's head and pulled him close. He leaned in, brow to brow. He said:

'Let me tell you a few things, Fucker. All this?'

A wee swoop with the palm was shaped – a gesture to take in the world as was.

'All this is going to pass away from you so quickly now, hear me? You've been in your glory, Fucker Burke. A set of grapes on you and a few bob put away and I dare say certain females who've been deranged enough to put themselves at your disposal. You've had your lovely dog, Angelina. And I understand what you did, Fucker. I do. It felt as if your life would never start but in fact it's been racing past you all the while. But this ain't for play no more. What are you, eighteen?'

The certainty of what was to come apparent, Fucker's tone was flat now with resignation.

'I'm seventeen, Mr H.'

'Oh that's a beautiful age to be, Fuck. You think you're going to live forever . . . Well, I'm here to tell you that you ain't.'

Logan made an O with his lips, and he blew a slow, steady whooshing, like the wind through the hollows of a wood, and it was aimed directly at the boy's face.

The breath lingered as a foul breeze – Fucker smelt the pipe-burn and the Ho Pee on it, and the rot of an old outlaw that he would never be.

Logan said:

'Look at me, Fucker. Look at me, sweetness. I can't say that I ain't had the luck. I've been twenty-five years with the Fancy to my name. I've been reefed six times and I'm still sucking at the poison air. An accident, do you think?'

He smiled, and the pale blue of his eyes showed the colours of sky and water, refracted.

'Did you think I was fit to move on from things, Fucker? That I'd go and play a few hands of rummy and dribble my moscato and get fat?'

The boy's lips greyed in expectation. He felt again the breath of the Long Fella on his face, the cold hand on his throat.

'Why did you do it, Fucker?'

A mark of the city that it was not fear that flushed the boy's face now but shame.

'Mr H, I never meant nothin' by –'

'Gave the Gant everything you had, Fucker.'

'H, please.'

'I know what you told him, Fucker.'

'Don't have to do this, H, please . . .'

A strange glow came to Fucker: what little of love and intimacy he had known in his life surfaced for a last time and gave succour for the journey ahead.

'I know because the Gant told me, Fucker.'

The air on Riverside was washed by the Atlantic gusts

216

that came over the estuary and it carried all the dread of its ghosts. The Bohane all the while ferried a drag of gravel and stones and the drag swirled drunkenly deep down – it had the sound of chains being swung.

Logan slid the dirk slowly and let it sit heavily in the boy's gut. Then he worked it from side to side, a neat and easy movement, and he held the boy, gently, as his head slumped forward, and he whispered to him.

He stepped back, and with a deft wrench removed the dirk, and the vitals flowed as he kept the boy propped still.

He felt an oddness then, Logan, it was a kind of . . . lightness, and he near enough succumbed to it.

He took a breath down, hard, and held it.

Let his brow lean in to the dying boy's again and rested it there a moment and asked forgiveness.

He stepped back and the last of Fucker Burke was left to slump where it would – like a useless hand puppet – and he stepped nimbly aside. With a stick from the ground and the blood that had spilt he daubed on the path by the body the word 'Judas' – it was written in his big, nervous, childish hand.

He scaled the chainlink fence then and descended a set of thick stone steps cut into the river wall.

Daintily with forefinger and thumb he raised the ankle cuff of his trouser leg and dipped a Croat boot into the water to wash it clean.

Saw a red vibrancy mingle with the tarry brown of bog water and so quickly disappear in the great mass of the river.

36

Macu's Dilemma

Then it was night-time in the Trace.

She walked the wynds, and she came at length to a small, deserted square, and she sat for a while on the wrought-iron bench. Dead lovers' names were scratched into the wooden seat back. The growth all about was so fervent, so cloying, so diseased. Fescue grass gone to the black rot, and the cat's tail that climbed mangily the tenement walls, and the sickly perfume of the clematis that persisted, even yet, and trailed from the rooftops; petals on a grave. Late spring was a rude throbbing as the Bohane creation ascended to the peak of its year, and ever closer to its precipice.

The pulsing of April brought a soreness to her glands.

Sometimes, in the good times, they didn't even have to speak to know what the other was feeling. A child would have put fear in the town, sure enough, and would have given to the marriage a motive force. But a child never came, and the space was filled by his jealousy.

He would come back to the Beauvista manse in the small, dim hours, and he would say:

Were you out at all?

Did you see anyone?

What have you been doing?

What did you do today?

Where did you go today?

Who did you see today, Macu?

Who did you see today?

Were you out at all?

Where did you go?

Who did you see today, Macu?

It had made a child of him. He began to lock her in. She said that she would leave him if he turned those locks on her again, and he stopped for a while, and it drove him all the madder to stop, and he could no longer sleep at night.

He sat in the dark and watched over her.

Were you below in the town, Macu?

Who did you see today, girl?

He had the Fancy boys follow her. She would walk the New Town, at the hour of the evening paseo, and catch a sconce of Fucker Burke and Angelina acting blithe in a sideway – and Fucker wasn't born to *blithe* – or Wolfie Stanners at a discreet distance behind, with his thyroidal eyes bulging.

She said:

This is not a life for me, Logan.

He dreamed up new ways of testing her. There was nothing he could do any more that would surprise her. Only the persistence of her love for him was a surprise to her.

Was she strong enough now to stay lost to him?

37

Speak a Dream

Midnight.

The Ho Pee Ching Oh-Kay Koffee Shoppe.

An upstairs salon.

And Logan Hartnett lay on the settle, and he placed softly the tips of his fingers on the back of Jenni Ching's hand. The girl put the flame to the pipe for him. He drew deeply. She placed a dampened cloth on his brow.

Jenni said:

'So you'd been doin' her yet, y'had? Till she went an' legged it on ya, like?'

'With a long marriage, Jenni, one needs to make the effort.'

'Fair dues t'ya, H. Guts o' thirty year on, like, an' still fleadhin' the same aul' bint . . . Not get samey?'

Logan squinted through the smoke and tightened his lips. Nobody else but Girly could talk to him like this. Hot night rippled in the salon's dense air. A slow moment passed – it had somehow a memorial taste. He sighed for Fucker. He slipped a little deeper into his dream, and he felt the seep of the Bohane lost-time, and he softened.

'Know how the Fancy got started, Jenni?'

Eyes-to-heaven from the Chinkee gal.

'Here he goes,' she said. 'D'ya remember when and d'ya remember how – stall a halt, 'bino, till I goes an' fetches me knittin'.'

'Was on account of the gee-gees, going way back,' he said. 'When we had the horses running.'

She gave in to him.

'Fancy was the lads what did the follyin' o' the hoss business, check?'

'The only money in this town was horse money, Jenni. And that's a fact, girl. In the Back Trace, out on the stoops? The boys would trade horse-talk all day. If we knew anything at all out here, we knew our horses. We had the best horses, the best track, best jockeys . . .'

'Spooky, jockeys,' said Jenni, 'when you see 'em in the ol' pix, like? Weird eyes.'

'Fancy opened out from the horse business. Went into herb and dream and hoors.'

Jenni lit the flame again.

'Always nice to hear about the olden days, H.'

He drew deep and held it a count against the nausea and then slowly exhaled. He ascended. She leaned in and kissed him. The kiss was slow and deep and not quickly to be recovered from.

'The fuck is that comin' from, Jenni?'

'Jus' a taste for ya, 'bino.'

'Don't ever do that again.'

'Won't so.'

'You'd have the melt out on a fucking statue,' he said. 'How'll the Gant get over you at all?'

A freeze ran through her sure enough.

'Fuck y'sayin' to me?'

'He'll get lonesome, girl. These long old spring evenings . . .'

Gathered herself quickly.

'Am I lookin' impressed, H?'

221

'Oh I don't blame you, girl. You need to keep the eye out on all sides in a small town. I'd almost have been disappointed if you hadn't.'

Jenni's breath came evenly. She looked hard at him. She said:

'I didn't give him nothin' about the Fancy's dealings.'

'I know that, Jenni. He told me.'

For a moment she had no comeback, and looked scared. But she never let go the eye-lock. She said:

'I ain't no gommie lackeen, Logan.'

'No, Jenni,' he said. 'If there's one thing you ain't it's no gommie lackeen.'

38

Baba-love

Let it be said that the Hartnett magic still worked a drag across the city. Their reach yet was sinuous. It crabbed out across the rooftops, and each action they played in due course begot its reaction, and sure enough, before the month of April was done, there was an outbreak of Sweet Baba Jay mania on the Northside Rises.

In defeat, of course, they very often turned up there to religion. An SBJ revival needed no more than a little prompting. And within days of the faked stigmata appearing on the palms of the Cusack girl, there were holler-meetings being staged in the shebeen basements of the flatblocks. The meetings were writhing with fainters, swooners, hot-foot shriekers. There was a quare amount of roaring going on. One-time Norrie aggravators packed away the tyre-chains and the dirk-belts and the sweat was dripping off them as they swayed in the shebeens and roared tearful thanks to His Indescribable Sweetness. Great tremblings took hold of these boys and their knees buckled and oftentimes gave way altogether as Word was delivered from Messengers Unseen. Next thing, miracle gave onto miracle – as is the way – and there were reports that an SBJ icon atop the fountain outside Croppy Boy Heights had shed tears of blood. Sure the same wee stigmatic girl-chil' of the Cusacks saw it with her own fervent eyes. And thus a congregation was on its knees around the icon, night and day, praying for more signs. The Norries were hugging each other and whispering blessings on the bleak avenues. It became a season of midnight visitations. In no time at all, the Sweet Baba Jay was showing up all over. Was said His Likeness had smiled down from the gable wall of an avenue grogpit. Was said His Likeness had appeared in the shape of a cloud over Louis MacNiece Towers. Was said His Likeness had formed, and shimmered, though briefly, in a puddle by the top of the 98 Steps. Norries were waking in the night and sitting bolt upright in their cots and crying out the Word of Love. Norrie sound systems had packed away their dub plates and their Trojan 45s and were playing for the shebeen gatherings a sacramental music of harpsong and hymnal chant. Women of the Northside were sporting a more modest cleavage line. They walked primly their Patterns of Devotion in the sweltering spring afternoons. They muttered half-remembered novenas as they paraded. Many found that their hair had taken on a fresh shine. There was great colour in everybody's cheeks. Nobody went downtown much. They prayed for and pitied the doomed sinners down there. They forgave their recent losses. They forgave their fallen and their dead . . .

See the dream-fed twist of the 'bino's crooked smile.

. . . and tiny yellow flags were cut out from great screeds of fabric choo-chooed in specifically for the purpose, and the flags were initialled 'SBJ' in an ornate hand soon mastered by lads henceforth to be known as flag-stylers, and the flags were tied onto lengths of rope at measured intervals and were strung from rooftop to rooftop of the flatblocks – dozens of them, then hundreds, then the sky was filled – and the effect was at once festive and pious.

Swearing all but disappeared. Beards were trimmed.

Fornication – previously on the Northside an activity as common as sucking air and to be found, at all angles of the clock, on stairwells, in turf-bunkers, behind avenue wind-shelters, generally everywhere, and in broad daylight – was confined now to marital beds, and was soberly practised, missionary-style, and swiftly, wordlessly concluded. It became the habit of the Norrie gentleman to bite the pillow at the end-moment so as not to embarrass the air with expressions of bodily joy.

The yellow flags spun, the yellow flags turned, the yellow flags shimmered.

And though they were tied securely enough to withstand even the harshest assaults of Big Nothin' hardwind, the flags were found when the wind got up to create a many-voiced cacophony – they rattled and groaned and sang in the wind, and if one listened to the flags for long enough, the effect was mesmeric, haunting, and it became the common understanding this spring that messages were being transmitted by Sweet Baba Jay through the medium of the flags.

Oh indeed.

And there were those on the Northside this particular spring we're talking about who became acknowledged experts in flag-listening. These were generally older gents who had known a share of life. You would see them crouched on their haunches, there on the avenues, in the hot April afternoons, beneath the flags, listening, and betimes approaching each other to compare notes. Quiet, interested faces on them. Faces full of . . . Significance. And it became the practice that by teatime each day the listeners (as they were quickly named) would convene in the shebeen basement of a Croppy Boy Heights flatblock and come to agreement about the gist of the day's message. The message would then be written in block letters a foot tall upon banners that were carried along the Northside avenues, for a period of one hour precisely, by local sluts. The sluts were given the punishment of banner-bearing for their attempted seductions of decent Baba-devoted young Norrie men. At holler-meetings nightly, it was argued that banner-bearing was hardly punishment enough for these Baba-denying harlot bitches, and that their private parts should by force be rendered useless, with the aid of knitting needles and hot knives, but this was controversial. An editorial comment in the *Vindicator*, while acknowledging and declaring joy at what it called 'The Miracle of the Flags' – a souvenir supplement was issued – had quietly suggested that genital mutilation might, at this stage, be a step too far, even by the standards of the Bohane uptown. And so for now the sluts merely marched with their heavy banners, and they wept under the strain of the weight, and upon the banners were such flag-whispered messages from the Sweet Baba Jay as:

Grog Is The Devil's Spit!
Dogs Have Souls Too!
Polacks Can Never Be Clean!

Sweet Baba Jay was telling them which side was buttered, sure enough, and the people of the Northside were eternally grateful for His Direction. Each night, devout Norrie families would line the avenues for the slut parade. They would kneel and babble in tongues and they gave lusty voice to their Baba-love as the banners were carried past. If the sluts were treated cruelly and occasionally bottled as they stumbled along, it was felt that it was no more than those painted-up little trollops deserved. Certain sluts could take it no more, however, and they banded together, and they fled the Northside Rises under cover of dark.

Yes and so it was this springtime we are talking about that near-feral Norrie sluts hit the downtown, and began to roam the Back Trace, and they took up with the bands of wilding girls who had lately come together there in devotion to the killer-bint Ching, and their shrieks of solidarity were heard across the city – the Northside and the Trace united – and most surely these would mark the summer to come.

I could hear them from the back room of the Ancient & Historical Bohane Film Society as I sat late and drank exquisite Portuguese wine direct from the neck of the bottle, and you may trust, as ever, that I made careful notes.

Beyond the shrieks, the river carried as ever from Big Nothin' its black throbbing.

Oh and heed this, my fiends, my tushies, my gullible children:

There was nothing good coming in off that river.

39

Logan's Letter to Macu

Macu, I miss you so badly. Especially at night. I lie there half raving without you beside me. It's as though you've been years gone from me. I can't even hear your voice. I close my eyes and I picture you but I can't hear you. I tell you, Macu, I feel barely human without you. I can't be on Beauvista without you. I think about you all the time. I am ashamed of how jealous I've been. All I can say is my love for you has maddened me. I see that clearly now I'm alone. I asked the Gant to do his worst. I asked him to test you and I knew he would try. Please don't blame him, Macu. The game was mine, he saw it only as a chance to win you back. And I pity the man now his lonely years. I would not have had the strength for them. I'm sorry, Macu. And it's hideous, I know, but my game has proven your faithfulness. I want you back so badly. Remember once when we were young and we walked in the Trace one night and we found a bottle of moscato, perfectly chilled, just waiting for us on a stoop? With nobody anywhere to be seen. Just you and me in the Back Trace, Macu, and we drank the wine. I ask you to forgive me. I know you will need time. You'll need these months to understand the pain that was in me. But I know your love is there still. If you want me to pull back from the Fancy, I will. Mr Mannion will deliver this – where are you, Macu? I think maybe I sense you in the Trace. I expect no letter in return. All I ask is that you think about the years ahead. Apart we are nothing. If you choose to come back to me and give me life, Macu, you will meet me at the Café Aliados. At 12 midnight. On the night of August Fair.

Logan

40

Late Nite at Tommie's

It was the eve of May at the Supper Room, and Tommie the Keep had the ceiling fans set to their highest ratchet, and they whirred noirishly against the night, and were stoical, somehow, like the old uncles of the place, all raspy and emphysemic. Tommie's eyes scanned the room and read a hard scare in each and every one of the Bohane merchants, the Bohane faces. Everybody's nerves were shot, and the sweet, seductive voice of the girl singer as it wafted from the corner stage seemed only to amplify the tension.

'*As looooong as dat yella moon riiiise . . .*'

She sang a slow, blue-beat calypso – old love songs of the lost-time – and she clicked her fingers lazily with the melody born into her, the tips of her fingers opening and coming to rest between beats against the gleaming length of her silver, sequinned dress. She had for percussion a lone, sleepy-eyed drummer seated at an ancient snare, his hair quiffed high with pomade. She sang in the proper, carefully modu-lated Bohane calypso style – we are stern about such things – and she had a good charge of huskiness in the delivery, and certainly she was beautiful.

'*As loooong as dat black river flow . . .*'

But even such a girl was poor distraction for the jowly merchants in the banquette booths. Those old boys quiv-ered, almost – they could barely lift the tankards to their lips. Their eyes were drawn to a pair of men seated on high stools at the far end of the Supper Room's bar. One was broad and densely packed, the other tall and slender.

Double-take:

It was Logan Hartnett and the Gant Broderick.

A tight huddle they had settled to, and they were whispering there. And in a hoarse whisper also the girl's song came through.

'As long as dem stars still shiiine / As long as our twined love grow . . .'

Tommie the Keep occupied himself with chipping ice from a ten-pound block into splinters for the cooler buckets. Almost lost a pair of fingers to the chisel, Tommie, as his scared glance shot along the counter to the men. Hartnett with a raised hand signalled now for another bottle of moscato, and Tommie fetched one and brought it. The men paused in their talk as he nestled the bottle among the ice chips in their cooler. Each wistfully smiled for him.

'Mr Hartnett,' said Tommie. 'Mr Broderick.'

Tommie was not brave enough to linger and he scuttled again down the length of the bar. The girl singer finger-clicked still as her drummer whittled a high thin beat on the snare. In the booths, the heavy lads nervously swayed. Temperatures were yet in the thirties, even after midnight, and the city's mood was edgy.

Logan Hartnett and the Gant Broderick both rested their forearms on the bar counter, and they both stared straight ahead, and they both rotated their glasses slowly with the tips of their fingers – each unconsciously mimicked the other.

The Gant lifted his glass then and sipped at his moscato. 'Fuckin' breakfast wine,' he said.

'Have a Jameson so.'

'Swore off the whiskey over.'

Like a kid, Logan thought, like a surly little kid.

'Wasn't agreeing with you, G?'

The Gant shrugged, drained off the glass, and poured another. Held the bottle for Logan, raised an eyebrow; Logan demurely placed a hand to cover his glass. Like an old bint, the Gant thought.

'Like an ol' bint,' he said.

'Don't be bitter, Martin,' Logan said.

The girl singer held a slow note to its fade; it brought up the blue veins of her slender neck, and she let the note die, and she stepped from the stage then for an interval break, pinching carefully at the thighs of the silver dress so as not to trip.

Barely a scatter of applause came for the room was preoccupied: Dominick Gleeson, the fat newsman, slithered an oyster into his gob from the half-shell but barely registered the shiver of its sea tang as he worried about the Hartnett–Broderick clinch. Big Dom scowled tubbily in puzzlement, and it was a puzzlement shared, two booths over, by Edmund 'The Gypo' Lenihan, the old-school S'town hoor-master. Ed sipped sourly at a measure of moscato and laid a hand on his belly, the wine interfering lately with his ulcers. At a booth adjacent was a gentleman of the Bohane Authority, poured into a thin flannel suit and licking the salt off a pretzel, and he tried as best as he could to secrete himself in the Supper Room's shadows.

All watched the two men at the bar.

A great rip of trembling took hold of the Gant just then – he was *laughing*? – and Logan placed a brotherly hand on his back, as though to steady him.

232

Shudders in the booths, and nervous tabs were lit in a rolling relay around the room – the sparking of one inclined the sparking of the next.

Logan Hartnett took a handkerchief from an inside pocket to wipe away a morbid, a dream-sent tear.

'That day in August,' he said, 'I wasn't sure I'd know you right off.'

'You're actually weepin'?' the Gant said.

'Something in my eye,' he said. 'Twenty-five years, you know . . .'

'You're one strange animal, Hartnett.'

'As people never seem to tire of telling me.'

Again they mimicked without knowing it each the other's posture – each of them was a little slumped now, and they sat bluesily, sad-eyed; it was past midnite at Tommie's.

'If you were askin' me to place a bet,' the Gant said, 'I'd say she'll come back to you.'

'If she doesn't, I'm done for.'

'I wouldn't worry too much. A nice berth you made for her atop the hill, ain't it? And she always was a shallow bitch.'

'Did you really think she'd choose you, Gant?'

On a morning in August, in the grey dim of a deserted bar room, in the village of Ten Light, in the foothills of the Nothin' massif, they had sat with each other. The rendezvous was discreet and polite. Logan carefully laid out his terms. To test Macu's loyalty, and to test the Fancy's – this was the Gant's role, and in return for playing it, he was allowed safe passage again to Bohane, to his home and to his lost-time. He could return and he could stay – it was what he had pleaded for in the letters that he had sent to Logan. They spat and shook on it in the grey room. Even to shake hands had caused a wince of pain in the Gant – he'd returned with a last wound from the world beyond; his shoulder reefed in Whitechapel.

'When you told her about the arrangement,' Logan said, admiringly, at the barside in Tommie's, 'I thought, that's sly . . . to turn it back at me like so. Put me in an evil light in my own house, didn't it? Of course it did for your chances an' all.'

'Didn't want her,' the Gant said. 'Soon's as I saw her close up, y'check?'

'Tell yourself that often enough, Martin, and you might start to believe it.'

Maybe there was a want in the Gant to hurt him yet but was he capable of it? Brave as the dream he each night blew, Logan believed not – the Gant was sold to the past; the Gant was done for. But if the dream-smoke brought courage, it brought a harsh truth, also: Logan knew that he may not himself be far behind.

The girl singer downed a fast whiskey and returned to the stage, and she finger-snapped a double-quick beat, and she swung out her hips, she tried to get things moving at a jauntier pace, she tried to lift the tension, but the hot old boys in the booths shifted uncomfortably and dropped their piggy little eyes, and she sighed, and she let it slow again to ballad pace, began to croon one, and the merchants again sulkily swayed.

Logan and the Gant sat for a time in the selfsame brood; both rejected, it was an odd bond they shared, and sweetly painful.

'S'pose you done for the galoot lad?'

'Poor Fucker,' Logan sighed.

'Couldn't have let him go the High Boreen, nah? A boy o' what, fifteen?'

234

'He was seventeen.'

'Didn't look it.'

Anxiety spun a web across the room. Those who had passed word and information to the Gant Broderick over the winter and springtime feared now the consequences. They knew they had been tested.

'You're all shoulders, ain't you, Gant?' Logan smiled as he turned on his stool, a half-swivel, and took a slow reck of his old acquaintance. 'A big ham-faced lunk off the bog plain. Of course even as a kid you were a fucking unit. Even when you were in off the rez first, Martin Broderick, eight years of age, and putting the fear of the SB into grown men. Of course a brain would have been useful also.'

'A brain not so hot if it got maggots wrigglin' about it.'

'Ah what did she ever see in you?'

Logan sipped delicately at his moscato. Made a face – the wine had warmed in the night's humidity. Snapped fingers and pointed, simultaneously, at the optics, and Tommie the Keep scuttled for the John Jameson. One measure was brought, a second offered, but the Gant again refused it.

'Tell me more about your days over, G. Fun times?'

He joined his long thin hands, the fingers interlocking, about his middle. The Gant ignored the question, and presented his own.

'What do you really want, Logan?'

An intake of breath, and there was no front to the 'bino here.

'I want to go on for a while yet.'

'Then go an' hold a pillow over yer mother's face.'

'Leave my mother out of this.'

The Gant smiled at the advantage he'd found, and he knew it would niggle all the more if he did not play it.

And the girl singer swayed, and she sang, with a smokiness to her voice, and she ran her fingers along her slim hips, and the room went with her to a lost-time melody, the air rearranging as the night tensely progressed.

'S'the Ching gal I'd watch,' the Gant teased.

'You been whispering to her, Gant. You been encouraging her. You been saying pretty things in the paper about the young gals comin' through.'

'Hardly needs my word, that gal.'

'And what about Wolfie?'

'Well, the Wolfie-boy's got a prob, don't he? Wolfie's in love.'

'That is a problem.'

The coolers full, the shaved ice glistening, Tommie the Keep took them around to the booths, and he replaced the used ones, and he shared heavy glances with the merchants; who knew what strange course Bohane might be set to now?

The girl singer called her sweet laments, and the fat merchants went soppy in the booths, and the sleepy-eyed drummer teased a sad, slow rhythm with the brushes.

'Who's allowin' who to live?' the Gant said, and they both laughed at that.

Tommie the Keep ducked under his bar hatch again and took his cloth and hurried a shine into the counter. He strained to hear but he could not hear.

'When you told me that she talked about me still,' the Gant said. 'That she called out my name at night . . . Do you know I near enough believed it?'

'Poor fool,' Logan said.

It was early a.m. at the Supper Room, in the humid soup of a Trace night, and the high-quiffed drummer rode a bushweed drift, and he gazed at the hindquarters of the

236

svelte girl singer, and he floated a while on the rivers of the moon.

Dom Gleeson, in his booth, was defeated by the situation, could not by glance alone untangle its nuance, its news, and he thought, fuck it anyway, I'm away to S'town for the slap of a hairbrush.

The Authority man tried to get straight in his noggin the report that needed making for the members.

'The Gypo' Lenihan thought he had seen quareness in his time but nowt so quare as the pairing at the bar.

Tommie the Keep polished madly still the bar counter.

The Gant drained what was left of his moscato.

'That's me for the road,' he said.

He rose from his stool – yes, a big unit still – and politely Logan rose with him. They spoke just a few words more. The Gant turned to leave the Supper Room then but he hesitated, and he turned back again to Logan.

Briefly, oddly, they embraced.

IV
ON THE NIGHT OF
AUGUST FAIR

We came through the green hollows of June, and through slow lascivious July, and then the August Murk descended: it was late summer in the city, and our world was so densely made and intricate about us.

The Murk is a thick seafog that settles each year on the creation and just about smothers us alive. It is a curiously localised event that affects this peninsula alone of the western seaboard. The meteorologists, long puzzled, term it 'The Murk of Bohane', and leave it at that. The Murk comes down as a greyish, impenetrable mist and it lays a great torridness on the city, a swamp heat.

This is the weather of August Fair.

*

This is by tradition the time of betrothal in Bohane, and for the week leading up to Fair Day, all the young tush paraded the Murky streets in their glitter and swank.

Oh and the tushies worked it like only the Bohane tush can – their hair was pineappled and freshly streaked, the warpaint was laid on with shovels, and their navels gleamed with tuppenny jewels that shone as their eyes shone with badness and delight. All the young fiends followed at close quarters, with their tongues hanging out for the sheer want of it – sheer, the cliff face of adolescent desire – and festive mode for a fiend was to be barechested beneath a straw hat with a rash of sunburn and freckles across the nose and jaws. They fell into love as though to a precipice.

As the Fair's build-up progressed, Bohane Free Radio broadcast from the back of a herring boat and blasted righteous samba cuts across the dockside, and the young things danced on the cobbles with fervent desperation:

They did the Grind, and the Three-B (Bohane-Bum-Buster), and the S'town Shuffle.

Mothers and fathers sat nervously in the tenements and rotated slowly their thumbs one around the other – this was also, by tradition, a time of mass impregnation in Bohane.

Sure how many of us are mid-May babies, born of a Fair Day grapple down a Back Trace wynd? How many of us sucked at life for the first time beneath a taurine moon?

Indeed a quare shake of us.

★

Big Nothin' for weeks in advance worked itself up for the Fair's great release.

The seasonal lakes of the hillsides filled with Murky precipitation and the young lay about by these swimming holes, and they rolled into one another's arms, and they whispered of Fair Day on the soon-come.

Of course, many a stout-hipped daughter or big-arsed son of the plain would lose the run of themselves at the Fair. Was common enough for a Nothin' child to hit down the High Boreen for the Fair, innocent as a three-legged lamb, and be discovered, weeks later, haggard and dream-addicted down the wrong end of a Smoketown salon, and all set to be signed for a trick-pony ranch or hauled off to a lurcher cage.

But if there wasn't such danger, there'd be no such spice.

Expectation travelled the hill-country smallholdings, and along the poppy fields that extend east of Ten Light village – see the dream fields undulate in the tropic heat of August – and through the pikey rez, and the day at last came, and every stony acre of the plain tossed out a choice of spud-aters, and legions of them were led on the morning of August 13th by their livestock through the dawn gloom along the length of the High Boreen. They had calves for the slaughter and piebalds for to sell.

'Name t'me a price for yon palomino, kid?'

Fair Day of '54 had a grey and ominous sky: the usual Murksky.

Rain came in bad-minded spats.

An eerie wind taunted.

And the city of Bohane spread itself for all comers.

★

Smoketown geared up for the busiest day of its calendar. Half the creation would be over the footbridge for the suck of a dream-pipe, a hand shandy and a bowl of noodles.

Hoors waxed themselves.

Mortars of dream-bulb paste were expertly grinded.

Chillis were chopped, seeds and all, and fecked into vast tureens of mackerel chowder that were hauled around S'town and gave fine nutrition for the sweaty labours ahead.

Nervous hoors were adrift in the rustle of nylons and the fixing of garter-belts and lost in the misty valleys of their own cheap scent.

Oh the loneliness of it all.

★

It was the city's habit to drink hard for the week leading up to August Fair, and De Valera Street, by the morning of the 13th, looked as if a riot had already passed through.

Emptied wine sacks filled every gutter and diamonds of broken glass – Bohane gemstones – sparkled on the sidewalks. There was hardly a set of eyes in the town that weren't already at the far end of their stalks. Fair Day was a time of massive hilarity, and sentimental music, and it was a most useful pressure valve, for these were hard times in the city, in this hard town by the sea.

Along the dockside, the Merries were set up: the swing-bucket whirligigs were tested, the dog-fight rings marked out with hay bales, the test-your-strength meter raised on its platform. Impromptu stages made of ale barrels, ship's rope and lengths of four-be-two were erected for the bare-knuckle fistfights. Tiered seating was arranged around a rodeo ring and sawdust was thickly strewn. The dark-eyed carnies who set up these attractions were from the same families as always brought the Merries to Bohane. Powerful smokers, the carnies. And of course many a carnie was sprung from the peninsula originally. We would be the sort, outside in Bohane, who'd run away with the Merries as quick as you'd look at us.

Hoss polis were a heavy presence. Even at daybreak, they were at every Back Trace entry that led off from the docks. The brethren of the St John's Ambulance Brigade – Here come the good guys! In their little jackets! – were preparing to stretcher the wounded towards the medicine tents. Back Trace old dears threw back their shutters and from the high windows hung out their bosoms and were wistful for their own remembered Fair Days.

Fair Day, as we always say in Bohane, is a day for the youth.

And they lace into it like pagans.

August Fair . . .

August the 13th . . .

We whisper of it for months in advance, and we are as long again recovering.

*

Logan Hartnett stepped over stuporous bodies on the Bohane front. He heard the cry of the auction down the yards: all the old taunts and threats of the horse trading, which was the main business of Fair Day. He swivelled a reck along De Valera and the 'bino's glance was clear-eyed and sharp this weather as he reckoned the polis numbers. He moved for the Trace. He was barechested. He wore three-quarter-length black strides in a narrow-leg cut over a pair of Spanish Harlem arsekickers. The scars on his chest were faded and wattled, like folds of chickenskin, and were reminders of the reefings he'd walked away from in his day. He had a dress-shkelp in his belt, ivory-handled.

As he turned into the Trace, the air changed, as it always did, and he asked how many times in his life he had swung into these dank, narrow streets for some whispering rendezvous.

Herb and sick and tawny wine were on the air.

Each turn of the Trace that he took signified – there he'd had a knee-trembler, there he'd bled a foe. He took a particular turn and the broken glass on an alleyway's surface amped his footfall to a noirish crunch. The yellow light of an early-doors caff gleamed from the back of the alley.

There was a handful of customers already at the caff: lads who had been late at the bottle, and were now haggardly hunched over Bohane Specials, and wondering how long it would be before their lungs could chance the first tab of the day.

At a rear table, nursing a short black joe and puffing a stogie, was Jenni Ching.

Logan took the seat opposite.

'You wouldn't chance a fry, Jenni, no?'

The girl laid a hand on her ribcage.

'Me body's a fuckin' temple, like.'

'I suppose if you can't look out for yourself, Jen?'

'Then there ain't nobody gonna do it for you, Mr Hartnett.'

The serving girl came, and Logan asked for coffee only, and he winked at Jenni, who nodded sombrely, as if that was the best decision a grown man could make. The shocking yellow of the egg-yolk stains on the Special plates would not anyway betray a man to gluttony.

'Polis is bought,' Jenni said.

'The price?'

'Fuckin' savage.'

'I'd imagine.'

'But at least they's gonna face off the sand-pikes.'

'Saves us doing it, Jen-gal.'

'O' course Prince T is born canny. He's gonna be keepin' to the rear end o' things when the polis fucks arrive.'

'A leader's prerogative,' Logan said.

'If you say so, H.'

'Maybe time you learned such things?'

Jenni scowled.

'Way it's pannin',' she said. 'Ed Lenihan reckons it's the night to clear Wolfie a path to the Far-Eye.'

'Tremendous.'

They drank joe; they smoked tabs. They were wary of

each other but fond, too. He knew she had watched out on all sides – the swivelling glance an S'town apprenticeship will teach – but she had betrayed no Fancy confidence; she had given nothing to the Gant.

'Ain't been seein' ya at the Ho Pee these nights,' she said.

'Keeping my snout clean, Jenni,' he said. 'Got to stay on top of things.'

'Plenty happenin' 'bout the place awrigh', H.'

'Speaking of, Jenni. I'm to understand you've got these Trace girls at your beck lately?'

'It's said.'

She bopped in high innocence a smoke ring.

'And you got the Gant naming you to all and sundry as the soon-come kid.'

'A sloppy aul' dude wanna spout bollick-talk an' he down the boozer, it ain't my lookout to stop him.'

'Of course my darling mother is lending the weight an' all, ain't she, Jen?'

'Girly and me is close.'

'Oh, more than that, I think. Not a hand to be laid on the Jen-chick ever, is there? That's my instruction.'

'You wanna try a hand, 'bino?'

He smiled.

'It's hard not to love you, Jenni.'

She pulled down her coldest glaze, gave him a blast of it, briefly, and then let her eyes scan the morning wynd beyond.

'Those Fancy boys don't stand a chance against you, do they, Jenni?'

Logan raised the joe to his lips and savoured its bitterness. Old photographs on the cafe walls were of Bohane faces – hard-set stares in hard-chaw faces – and he looked at them a moment.

'See this gang?' he said.

Jennie surveyed the faces.

'You'd notice a type. Their noses in the air, watch? Haughty! Even if they ain't got the arse of their kecks. What we are in this town is an arrogant fucking breed. We think it's all been thrown down to our particular design.'

All the old faces were in their own time fabled in the Back Trace universe, he said. The Trace was a world within a world, he said, and each of these dead souls had a power in the world once, was known for his swiftness with the shkelp, or his knack with the tush, or his canniness with a buck. Each was in the boneyard now, he said; Logan Hartnett, reality instructor.

'You have to remember, Jenni, that all we're trying to do is keep the place someways fucking civilised.'

'Y'spoutin' me own creed, H.'

'We get a stretch of Calm in place and we get the S'town trade flowing in the right direction again and then we can decide on what comes next, yes?'

'I'm listenin'.'

'Oh I know you are, Jenni. I know it too well.'

★

The Alsatian cur Angelina sloped low to the ground across the Big Nothin' plain. She aimed contrary to the Bohane river as it surged through the August Murk. Great swathes of rhododendron along the bank filled and shimmied with gusts of a hardwind and the knotweed swayed on its copper-red canes all along the malevolent river. Angelina shivered her bones to loose the 'skeetos that fed hungrily on her blood and she keened; the sharp of the yellow fangs showed.

Angelina went upriver.

And she passed along the way a mute child bound for the city as he steered with the tip of a whitethorn switch to its rump a feral mountain goat.

The puck goat's hard grey eyes pierced the Murk.

Angelina threw a hungry glance at the pair but she walked on, and she kept low to the ground, and she searched everywhere with snout and hooded eye.

Mute child and the puck goat moved west, and away; they went with the river's flow.

By 'n' by the rooftops of the high bluffs loomed through the Murk.

River followed its drag through the backswathe of the city, its hinterland – that vague terrain.

Mute's busy snout rose to snag on the salt tang:

And the wash of the ocean air on this morning of August 13th brought all the colours of the North Atlantic drift.

Bohane was green and grey and brown:

The bluish green of wrack and lichen.

The grey of flint and rockpool.

The moist brown of dulse and intertidal sand.

*

A slouch of old lads hunkered in the late morning over breakfast pints at the Capricorn Bar on the Bohane front. Weather-bleached skulls of Big Nothin' goats were mounted behind the bar atop the optics and stacks of tin tankards. Beyond the dusty windows, August Fair shrieked and writhed into rude life; the horse trading busied, the Merries sparked. The old lads wistfully watched it all as they met the day with Wrassler stout, sausage sandwiches, and wistful memories.

The Gant was among them, and having been gone so

long, he was himself a relic of the lost-time, and they prompted him, and he succumbed.

'Do you not remember, G?'

'Oh, I do, I suppose. I do.'

'You'd have come out of that place one arm longer than the other.'

'It was roughish. It sure was. An' was it Thursday nights it was on there?'

'Tuesdays and Thursdays but the Tuesdays were quiet. Tuesdays only if you were stuck with a fairly severe lack of it.'

'Ah yeah, Tuesdays was for plain girls . . .'

Laughs.

'And of course it was a place you'd want a twist of black-currant in the stout to ease the taste?'

'Ferocious taps. Though nothing at all to what they were serving below in Filthy Dick's.'

'Stop!'

'Do you remember, Gant, the way all the pony-and-traps would be lined up outside Dick's?'

'Of a Sunday. Every fuckin' latchiko in the town would be out there.'

'If you came home out of it with the two eyes still in your head, you'd be thinking: result.'

'Was it Dick had the daughter married the fella of the Delaceys?'

'Indeed. The daughter married up. Delaceys the bakers.'

'Where was it they were again, Gant? Top end of Dev?'

'Just so – opening onto Eamonn Ceannt Street off the New Town side.'

'Ah . . . yeah . . . there was a sideway in?'

'Of course there was – you'd be knocking in for an apple slice. Through the hatch.'

'Oh Sweet Baba they were something!'

'Stop the lights. The finest apple slice that was ever slid across a counter in this town.'

The apples stewed since early morning in the ten-gallon pot. The apples all stirred about by the big, sweating, ignorant-looking Delacey father. The crumble for a topping that was made always with prime Big Nothin' butter, and the crumble baked till it was golden, and the way the sour note of the cooking apples hung in the air for two blocks at least.

'Delaceys, yes . . . Would have been alongside . . . Alo Finnerty the jeweller?'

'Alo. A lightin' crook.'

'Was said. Then what would you come to, Gant?'

'Jerry Kycek the weeping Polack butcher.'

'Of course you would. Poor Jerry!'

'That man went through the fucking wringer.'

'Always, with the wife he had. Of course, he was known for his black pudding?'

'He was. Wrapped in the pages of a *Vindicator* you'd get it, with the blood still dripping.'

'Drippin'!'

★

So happened that not all of our knocking shops in Bohane were on the S'town side of the footbridge. The infamous Blind Nora's, for example, drew its clientele down a hard-to-find sideway of the Back Trace, and Ol' Boy Mannion, as Fair Day built to a noontime roar, turned a dainty toe towards the place.

By midday an air of happy derangement had settled on the Trace. You could barely walk the wynds for the large and ragged crew that bounced off the tenement walls. There were big lunks of hill-country sluggers, and pipe-mad pikeys on the loose from the rez, and syphilitic freaks with lost-time dreams in their eyes, and washed-up auld hoors, and one-legged trick-ponies (the gout often a danger to the lads of that trade), and sand-pikey watches roved the city with a strange, unnameable fear about them, and the Fancy boys blithely prowled, and the polis beaks, and scar-faced Norrie mendicants with wooden bowls for alms, and wilding packs of feral teenage sluts, and tormented preachers hollering the wages of sin from the tops of stoops, and any one of this crowd could turn a shkelp in your lung as quick as they'd look at you, but as he walked through it all, with his snout held high and a wryness even in his carriage, even in his footfall, Ol' Boy Mannion was notably immune to the madness, and he felt no fear.

Ol' Boy wore:

A three-piece skinny-dude suit in the classic mottled-green shade, a pair of silver-painted jackboots (square-toed) on the dancers, and a dove-grey stovepipe hat up top, leaning westerly, with a delicate length of crimson scarf tied around it.

Snazzy, no?

Slugged from a hip flask of the Beast, did Ol' Boy, and took the occasional draw on a herb-pipe.

Wasn't high so much as maintaining.

The wynds of the Trace were mud and shite and puke underfoot and he placed the step carefully, with an eye to his boots, because they hadn't cost him tuppence ha'penny, no, sir.

He went down a sideway, and then another, and took the twist of a turn once more, and the Trace quietened some as he went deeper into it, and he came at last to Blind Nora's.

It was a low joint. It was patronised only by the very desperate. If you were turfed out of every place else in the city, there'd be a roost for you yet at Nora's. They even let the Haitians in. And the Tipperary men. Ol' Boy entered past the doorkeep, a big simian brute smoking the butt of a stogie – 'Howya, Dimitri?' – and he could not but wince against the smell of the place.

Troubled ladies in tragic fishnets were slung down on ancient couches. They clutched pipes and drinks and SBJ medals. A mulatto inebriate put an old rocksteady seven-incher on a wind-up turntable and danced uncertainly as the tune grainily kicked in.

Stumbled against Ol' Boy.

'Watch yerself, kid,' said Ol' Boy, gently.

A wretched hoor laughed and showed her toothless maw. Now there was a dangerous-looking tunnel for you. The bordello shades were drawn against even the Murky daylight and the place was lit by table lamps on upturned crates and coloured silks were drawn over these – for *mood*, no less – and the silks were singed by the heat of the lamps and the burning smell met with others in the air: pipe, Beast, baccy and seed.

Ol' Boy smiled for each of the ladies in turn but he was not here to have his needs satisfied. It wouldn't be Nora's he'd be hitting if that was the cause. Ol' Boy was here to see the woman herself.

'Is it you?' she said.

'You know it is,' he said.

Nora was an enormous cheese-coloured old blind lady with ringlets of black curls, like a doll's. She was perched on a divan down back of the room. She drank psychoactive mushroom tea, delicately, from a Chinkee pot. She was magnificently fat. She beamed for Ol' Boy and shuffled along the divan, haunch by ample haunch, and he moved in beside her, crossed his legs, laid a hand on her knee.

'Another one 'round to us, Nora?'

'Fair Day come 'round so quick, Mr Mannion.'

Together they smiled, and they were comfortably silent for a time. Savoured the day and their moment together. Then Ol' Boy said:

'You've that lady well hid for me yet?'

'I have, sir.'

'You're to keep her well hid today, Nora, if you can at all.'

'Oh?'

'It's just sometimes I get a black feeling . . .'

'She's well hid, sir.'

'Where have you her, Nora?'

'I wouldn't even tell you that, Mr Mannion.'

'Trace-side anyway, I s'pose?'

'She's well hid, sir.'

They sat a while. And then he turned to her again, and squeezed her hand, and he said:

'Will you sing one for me, Nora?'

She loosed a hard laugh that rippled her fleshy shoulders. She took a nip of the Beast from the flask he offered. She leaned back, and a lovely gentleness spread over her features, and it was from the heart that she sang:

'I was thinking to-day of that beauti-ful laaand . . .
That we'll see when the sun go-eth down . . .'

★

Jenni Ching had the polis palm crossed with Judas coin and them polis fucks they was hard-prepped for a swipe at the sand-pikey ranks, y'sketchin'?

Jenni Ching had her lovelorn beau Wolfie-boy Stanners hard-prepped to wield a shkelp in the direction of the Far-Eye maniac Prince Tubby, y'heed?

Jenni Ching had a pack of feral teenage sluts at her beck 'n' call in the Bohane Trace, y'check me?

★

Every time Logan closed his eyes he saw Fucker again. He saw the pain, the way it twisted as the shkelp was moved neatly from side to side, and then the quick deadening of the features. He felt over and again the moment, the way he had leaned in, sadly, and the feeling of the dead boy's brow as it fell onto his.

It was the first of his killings that had lingered so. He knew it now for a mistake. He'd seen only the need for vengeance. He hadn't played the long game. He hadn't reckoned on the loyalty a reprieve might have bred in the Fancy's ranks. Gant had been right – he should have just sent the galoot out the High Boreen.

Logan Hartnett was the most sober man on De Valera Street. He walked a tread of memory and regret. The street in the hot afternoon roiled, thrashed, simmered; August Fair was remorseless.

★

From her divan, at the sad bordello, Blind Nora yet sang:

'That bri-ight stars may be mine in the glor-ious day,
When His praise like the sea billow ro-olls . . .'

★

At the Capricorn Bar, as the crowds thronged outside on the Bohane front, as the Merries got into swing, the old-timers worked a whiskey-fed reminiscence, and the Gant was its conductor:

255

'Of course the *Vindicator* itself was at that time on De Valera Street?'

'It was. This would have been before Big Dom Gleeson's time. Before Dom came in and got notions about the New Town.'

'Notions in Bohane'd be nothin' new.'

'No, Gant.'

'What was the bar the *Vindicator* lads would drink in? The printers?'

'You mean the place . . .'

'Down off . . .'

'Off . . .'

'Half Moon Street?'

'Precisely so . . . You're talking about the Llama, aren't you?'

'No I am not. I remember the Llama. A filthy place.'

'Filthy. A honk out of it.'

'A honk that'd knock you. But that wasn't the printers' bar . . . Was it Corbett's I'm thinkin' of?'

'Corbett's was polis always . . . The polis frats all drank there, goin' way, waaay back . . .'

Yes. A dim-lit saloon with pictures of old sergeants on the walls. Touts sneaking out of it late on – looking left, then right, a swivel of their Judas eyes. A jukebox loaded with sentimental Irish ballads ('Mother McCree', 'Four Green Fields', 'The Goat Broke Loose') and in the lounge section a few sanctioned hoors peddling herb and dream up top of their tricks.

'Corbett's was polis, you're right.'

'Polis had more to them at that time.'

'They did. And were rotten on account o' the heft they had.'

'Rotten . . . And do you remember at all Silly Herbert the loolah?'

'Ah poor Silly! I do.'

The Gant all but weeping then.

'A desperate masturbator!'

'Will anyone ever forgot the time he hauled it out in the middle of the 98er Square?'

'Of a Christmas Eve?'

'An' he chokin' the squirrel?'

Christmas Eve, and poor Silly, the lunatic, smashed on sherry given as a present by the Devotional Brigade, with his hideously long member in his hand, and he lying in the middle of the square, with his kecks around his ankles, and the old Trace crones blessing themselves as they passed by, with fresh-plucked fowl and bags of Brussels sprouts under their oxters, and trying to keep straight faces on them, and failing.

'Silly came to a bad end. Of course they do, up in that place they had him.'

'And there was Candy, do you remember Candy?'

'Candy Stanners!'

'I dunno if there was ever a finer dip-pocket on Dev.'

'Not a one then or since fit to lace her boots.'

'Of course she'd a bad end as well.'

'That's the Back Trace for you.'

'Oh that's the Trace.'

★

Wolfie for a share of quiet travelled the Back Trace roof-tops. He scaled the Trace by the rickety Zs of its rusting fire escapes. He turned at the landing of each flight, and climbed again with a jolting grab on the handrail, and the packed wynds faded to a grey-voiced murmuring

257

below – his stomper boots bamped the oxide-red steps.

Tenements were so densely packed you could make it across the Trace without ever once setting foot on the ground. It just took a leap here and there, that was all, above the green voids of the wynds.

He looked out into the Murk, and he remembered Candy, the softness of her touch. He felt the fear reach deep into his bones now – he no longer had the galoot beside him.

Wolfie riffed on a double-tip:

He would take the Far-Eye – he had shamed his clutch, and Jenni came first. And then he would take vengeance for Fucker – the 'bino would suffer.

Wolfie on the rooftops felt for the shkelp, and he wielded it for heft and balance in his palm, and he twirled it, and flicked it, and he caught it.

Night would come quickly.

⋆

And Blind Nora in the bordello sang:

> 'Will there be any stars, an-y stars in my crown,
> When at evenin' the sun go-eth down . . .'

⋆

Ol' Boy Mannion left Blind Nora's, and he skulked through the wynds, and he watched the revel thicken in the Trace, and he bought a falafel from a cart in the 98er Square.

Spat the first bite and tossed the deep-fried mulch back at the cart's keeper.

'Wouldn't feed it to a fuckin' cat,' he said.

Hit for the dockside, and he had a particular heaviness on him – an odd feeling. Name it fear. Checked his timepiece, and he made for the livestock yards, as the Fair Day's late bidding rose to a great and rhythmical chant in the near distance. It was out back of the yards that Ol' Boy rendezvoused with the mute child.

Child was a scruffy wee thing off the far reaches of Nothin', about knee-high to a grasshopper, with a snotty face on, and that strange, impenetrable glaze you'd get always on a bog-plain no-speak.

Of course, Big Nothin' has always been known for its high incidence of mutes. You would so often see those word-less children out there, roaming the wastes, forming abstract shapes on their lips, and squealing mournfully into the hard-wind.

Now the mute eyed Mannion and he was brazen and wilful.

'Bin the hardchaw gimmick,' said Ol' Boy. 'Where's the cratur?'

Mute child flapped an arm and directed Ol' Boy towards a dark corner of the stock sheds. There the most regal puck was tethered.

'How we now?' said Ol' Boy.

The goat acknowledged him with a brief lowering of its gaze. The most important thing for an August Fair puck was that it had a gnarled, ancient look to it. It needed that whiskery Nothin' gravitas.

'You've picked a good 'un here, child,' said Ol' Boy.

A squeal from the mute sounded and dogs barked distant in the Bohane Trace. Ol' Boy reached for the inside pocket of his jacket and he took out a brick of compressed herb and he passed it to the child and the mute hungrily sniffed it and again squealed.

'Ah but hush, would you?' said Ol' Boy.

259

The mute child grinned. Ol' Boy raised the back of his hand as though for a smack but the mute brazened him and spat on the ground. Child knelt by the puck then and put his wordless lips to its ear and moaned softly – very odd, a type of keening – and the puck flickered its gaze in response, and turned its head to regard Ol' Boy with a most intelligent disdain.

'Don' mind that auld Nothin' bollocks,' said Ol' Boy but he was unnerved.

Was said always on Nothin' our mutes had the gift o' goatspeak.

The mute rose then and he went out through the yards and on the lightest of feet vaulted the steel gates. These mutes could have a very superior air to them betimes. Ol' Boy took the goat's tether and the animal tensed against his touch.

'Hup now,' said Ol' Boy.

He dragged the puck through the sheds and made for the dockside where the Fair's revels were by degrees supplanting the business of the day.

Samba blasted; the Merries roiled.

The puck goat would tonight be raised on a platform mounted on tall stilts and carried through the city. The puck was symbol and spirit of the place and as the Bohanians marked the goat's passing, they would, as per tradition, beat slowly at the air with switches of hazel to make a whooshed and haunting music.

No argument: it is a thin enough layer of civilisation we have laid over us out in Bohane.

★

As Fair descended into evening, a pathway opened for Logan through the manic throng. The pasted faces of the drunks briefly sobered as they made a reck on the pale tall figure passing by:

Long Fella's abroad.

Albino's abroad.

Hartnett . . . Ye sketchin'?

Screams and chants pierced the Trace-deep night. Fornication was not entirely kept to the shadows – fiends and tushies were wearing the gobs off each other in every doorway of the wynds. They dry-humped in a slow, rhythmical grind to the Trojan dub plates that blasted from the rooftop sound systems. The Murk of Bohane sat in unexcitable billows of fallen cloud that obscured the entries and closes, and the city's many-coloured mobs passed this way and that; the motion on the streets was as a single, great rolling, and bottles were smashed, and go-boy taunts were hollered, and dream tents were hucstered by bearded touts with crackly loudhailers, and hysterically devout Norries screamed the Word of the SBJ, and the Ten-Light Ebonettes did the Three-B with skipropes, and the wilding girls snogged each other viciously, and the whole great raucous night of the 13th drew in around us.

Drumbeats sounded everywhere in the city – timpanis and tom-toms, snares and tenors, lambegs, bodhrans, dustbin lids.

Logan Hartnett took a turn onto De Valera Street. He smiled like a wry old bishop as he passed along, as though humorously outraged by all that he saw. He was not a man, however, to let a carnival spirit take hold inside – he was too gaunt and graceful for that.

And Fair night made him wistful always – would he see another one?

★

At the Capricorn Bar:

'And of course there was the dunes you'd saunter off to of a fine evening? Summer.'

261

'If you had a girleen in tow, a kite to fly.'

'A roll in the dunes takes the badness out of a young fella.'

'What puts it there, Gant?'

'Well now . . .'

'Wasn't even pikey on the dunes in those days.'

'Pikeys there now sure enough.'

'Those days a pikey knew his place. Made pegs out on the reservation. Raised a dozen bairn or so. Played a bit o' fiddle music and had a scrap at a weddin'. Strange now to see a shake of 'em in S'town?'

'You remember, of course, when Atta "The Turk" Foley had the poolhall down the dune end?'

'Turk's . . . I do.'

'All the young crowd.'

'All the girls, all the boys. Summer evenings and the blinds drawn against the sun. An' remember you'd get the holy marchers coming down through Smoketown? All the old dears with their tongues hanging out for Baba-love?'

'Patterns o' Devotion being made . . .'

White-face preachers in ankle-length soutanes swinging incense on the wharfside cobbles. The women shaking out holy water from Jay-shaped plastic bottles as their headscarves were whipped about by random assaults of hardwind, as though it was the devil himself sprang it from Nothin'.

'I remember,' said the Gant, 'the way on the night of August Fair we'd burn whitethorn branches at the bonnas all along the Rises . . .'

'. . . and the way we'd be collecting a month for the bonnas and stashing the wood.'

'You'd have gangs of young fellas going around stealing

from each other's woodpiles. Got good and vicious now, recall?'

'Oh I do.'

'Rucks bustin' out on the 98 Steps.'

'Heavenly times, Gant.'

'Was it Sergeant Taafe had the polis that time?'

'One of the greatest fucking maggots that ever crawled into this town off the Big Nothin' plain. Where was it Taafes were from outside, G?'

'Taafes were this near side o' Nothin' Mountain. Skinned goats for a trade his people.'

'Was a price paid for goat pelt that time.'

'A fine price. But that's all gone now.'

'All gone.'

'Lots of it gone.'

'Lots of it.'

'Oh we're all getting old now.'

'Old, yes.'

'Oh, old.'

'Old!'

'Oh.'

The Gant slid from his stool at the Capricorn Bar and stumbled to a corner and vomited.

★

A twist and a turn and a feint, then a twist and a left turn, and the wynds gave onto wynds, and deep in the heart of the Bohane Trace, at its still calm centre, as the Fair roistered distantly about the edges, a set of high tenement doors opened – heavy wooden doors carved with renditions of hares, sprites, rooks – and Macu emerged.

Macu wore:

A fitted knee-length dress of lynxskin, a fox stole, a ritual

263

eyepaint that drew flames of crimson from the corners of her eyes, and a slash of purple lippy.

Macu set to walking.

A twist and a turn, a feint. A twist and a turn, and the pathways of her thoughts were intricate as the Trace, and as indeterminate. He would be waiting at midnight in the Café Aliados. She did not yet know if she would go to him there.

★

The notables of Bohane congregated on the plaza outside the Yella Hall. It was the moment for the crowning of the puck – the most famous moment of the Bohane year – and all the usual faces were in evidence: the draper de Bromhead, the sawbones Fitzsimmons, the Protestant Alderton. All were growing old and hideous together. A movement, then, from the dockside, and all heads turned, and cheers were raised as Ol' Boy Mannion led his regal puck onto the plaza, and the hunchback, Balthazar Mary Grimes, captured the moment for the *Vindicator* with a shriek of blue flash.

The gulls squalled – *mmwwaaoorrk!* – and rain came in warm drifts from the August sea, and a fat merchant of the city stood on a crate to drone the night's courtesies.

'An' as always on this happy occasion we remember our fallen and our dead and aren't we so lucky and Baba-blessed to be suckin' yet at the air o' Bohane city and didn't the likes a us . . .'

There was more interest in the goat. The crowd gathered around Ol' Boy, the puck was expertly inspected, and compliments were passed on the fine bearing of the creature.

'. . . an' this majestic beast afore us now has in the great tradition of August Fair been taken from the gorsey wilds o' Big Nothin' by a member o' the Mannion family and here beneath this glorious Murk that is our curse and favour let it be said that . . .'

Four stout sons of the city – slaughterhouse boys – stepped forward as the puck was tethered to its platform on the tall stilts. The creature was raised slowly into the night sky, and great applause broke out, and whoops and hollers and roars, and the procession set off, in medieval splendour, towards the snakebend roll of De Valera Street.

Puck didn't bat an eyelid.

★

Wolfie Stanners crossed into the S'town night and he met with the Gypo Lenihan and he was led by a tangled course down past the dune end's pikey watches.

They ghosted through the night, the pair, and went unseen.

Came at length to a particular alleyway and the Gypo arranged the boy carefully in its shadows.

'Wait here, Wolf. It's where he come up for air from the grindbar yonder, y'heed?'

'You're sure?'

'I'm sure.'

Wolfie was left alone, and waited, and he was bare-chested against the hot Murk as it came down freely now as a weird, greenish rain.

Felt for the bone handle of his shkelp, its heft.

★

Long Fella threw a sconce along the dockside. The judder of the hook-up generators was a memory jolt from adolescence. Diesel tang was sharp memory of the lost-time. The youth of Bohane balled through the Merries. The youth were in rut heat; for Logan, it was a careful parade through the fun.

He smiled for the old familiars of the town. The smiles he took back were as scared and respectful as always but they were weighted with emotion, too. Smiles were as though to say . . .

We've made it, 'bino, we've made it to August Fair again.

Since he was a child, Logan Hartnett had not missed a turn around the Merries on the night of Bohane Fair. The sights of it never changed:

Sweatin' lunks of spud-ater lads in off Nothin' took turns to slap the hammer at the test-your-strength meter.

Chinkee old-timers threw five-bob notes in each other's faces at the dog fight.

Face-offs erupted between fiends for the affections of particular tushies, the shrieked challenges as old as time in Bohane:

'Said c'mon!'

'Mon way out of it so!'

'Said c'mon so!'

'Mon!'

Dreary-voiced yodellers up on Tangier orange crates howled death ballads. Knots of SBJ devotees from the Norrie towers knelt on the stones and joined hands to pray against the evil of the Bohane frolics but they were as much a part of them as everyone else. The lights of the Merries were a gaiety against the darkness that had descended over the Bohane front. The whirligigs turned young lovers through the air, and the screams of the girls spiralled, wrapped around, twisted.

A strolling brass band played lost-time waltzes.

A pikey rez sound system set up on the back of a horse cart spun rocksteady plates.

A transex diva hollered Milano arias from atop a bollard.

At the rodeo an eight-year-old Nothin' child stayed the course and rode an epileptic Connemara pony into the dirt and great hollers of approval rose – the kid had a future.

And the girls' screams twisted, turned in the air.

Bets were hollered, notes counted, palms spat on. There were fire-eaters from Faro, sword-swallowers from Samoa, jugglers from Galway. Pikey grannies read palms, stars, windsong.

Shots of primo Beast were offered at a fair price by the infamous retard brothers from the Nothin' massif and the polis turned a blind eye having made off with a couple of crates theyselves.

There were stabbings, molestings, stompings.

Bohane city rose up on the spiral of the girls' screams as they twisted in the air.

And Logan came upon the boy Cantillon then. He sat alone on the harbour wall – the fishmonger's orphan, his glands swollen with quiet rage. He was lit gaudily by the lights of the revel and he looked at Logan as if he knew him from somewhere but could not quite place him.

The smile the boy gave was faint and murderous.

Logan raised an eyebrow in soft questioning but it was not answered. He approached but the boy hopped from the wall, and walked a little ways ahead, through the Merries' crowd, and he took the same stride as Logan, precisely, with his hands clasped behind his back – this was a mockery.

He turned once and winked, the boy Cantillon, and then he disappeared into the throng.

'Mon so!'

'Said c'mon way out of it so!'

'Said c'mon!'

★

And Blind Nora gave voice again to her old song:

'That bright stars may be mine in the glorious day
When His praise like the sea billow rolls . . .'

★

The Gant walked off his nausea but not his bitterness. He settled into a circuit of the Trace and De Valera Street, a ritual circling of the old city, and all the while he watched for her. He saw her slip into the face of every young tush he passed by, and the drums of Bohane city carried a rhythm and a message both.

Maybe he would never walk himself clear of . . . Macu . . . Macu . . . Immaculata.

★

Girly Hartnett, on the occasion of her nintieth Fair, stood before a full-length mirror in her suite at the Bohane Arms Hotel. She wore stockings, a suspender belt, a bodice and a scowl. Mysterious injections from a whizz-kid Chinkee sawbones were keeping her upright. She laid a frail hand across her belly and sucked in deeply. She eyed herself dispassionately. She made a plain and honest read of the situation, and it was this:

She wasn't in bad fuckin' nick at all.

A particular knock sounded. She cried an answer to it. Jenni Ching entered. She wore a white leather catsuit up top of silver bovvers, and this outfit Girly now considered.

'Choice,' she said.

Jenni raised a moscato bottle, found it empty, and instead poured herself a slug of John Jameson from the bottle on the bedside table.

Downed it in one, and lit a cigar.

'Who breaks the news to him?' Jenni said.

'That ain't your worry, child. Now c'mon an' get me dressed.'

Jenni went and slid the door of the mirrored wardrobe and flicked through the frocks that were piled there – many of them dated back as far as the lost-time.

'You decided, Girly?'

Girly sighed.

'I'm wondering if I shouldn't go with a class of an ankle-length?' she said. 'Maybe the ermine trim? Kinda, like . . . Lana Turner-style?'

Jenni fetched it and unzipped it. As she offered it, she asked of her mentor quietly:

'What do I do later, Girly?'

'You jus' got to show yerself.'

Girly took the old frock and sniffed it. She passed it back. She raised her feeble arms above her head.

'Now strap me in,' she said, 'and alert the authorities.'

★

A line of hoss polis came along the cobbles towards the S'town footbridge.

Sand-pikey taunts sounded cross-river.

From the Merries, dockside, Logan watched and listened.

He lingered a while by the dog fights.

Winked at the old bookmaker there – an Afghan off the Rises.

A pair of bull terriers went at it, their great muscled necks hunched, their hackles heaped and muzzles locked, the blood coming in spurts.

'Who'd ya fancy, Mr H?'

Logan carefully regarded the dogs – he let a cupped palm take the weight of his chin.

'I'd put tuppence on meself yet,' he said.

*

The alleyway of the Smoketown dune end:

Clicker'd heels on smooth cobbles.

Two young men circled but slowly.

Each handled a shkelp and moved warily, slowly.

Tip-tap, the heelclicks . . . tip . . . tap . . . tip . . . but slowly.

Seeping of bile and poison.

Jealousy's bile.

Fear's poison.

They circled.

Then a lunge . . .

A feint . . .

A stumbling . . .

A righting.

They circled.

A lunge.

A feint.

Shkelp blades gleamed as moonlight pierced the Murk.

They circled.

Wolfie kid and the Far-Eye.

They circled.

No taunts, no foulspeak, no curses.

Just a lunge.

A feint.

A stumbling.

A righting.

They circled.

They lunged.

Their blades ripped the air.

*

There came a time always on the night of August Fair when the badness took over.

Clock outside the Yella Hall sounded nine bells, and then ten, and then eleven, and nastiness cut the air – it was as high-pitched and mean as the homicide cry of the gulls.

The surfeit of moscato soured in the belly.

The herb took on a darker waft.

The dream-pipe twisted more than it mellowed.

And the fists of all the young fiends balled into hard tight knots, and the tushies egged 'em on . . .

'Said y'takin' that, like?'

. . . and scraps broke out all over the wynds, on the front, along the snakebend roll of De Valera Street, and on either side of the footbridge.

The decent and the cowardly fled along the escape routes offered by the New Town streets.

Rest of us piled in like savages.

And this year the badness was set to follow a particular design – an S'town riot was orchestrated.

It took quickly.

Big Dom Gleeson and Ol' Boy Mannion had a vantage view of the riot from the hot tub on the roof of Ed 'The Gypo' Lenihan's joint.

They had bottles of the Beast to hand, their herb-pipes also, and an amount of hoors on stand-by.

It was quickly a general bloodbath and the two men sighed in despair and happiness both.

On the main drag a line of sand-pikeys faced up to a massed assault of hoss polis.

Hoss polis were straining to make it to the S'town dune end to raid the premises there but the pikeys were keeping a firm line.

Smoketown revellers traded their frolics for violence, and the polis/sand-pikey face-off as the night progressed took in random participators. Eyes were being taken out down there, and ears were bitten off, and gobs were twisted open.

'Is it any wonder, really,' said Ol' Boy, 'that this place has the bad name it has?'

Yes and the hardwind was making speeches agin the August night and fresh hordes of sand-pikey back-up came in off the dunes and fell in by their brethren and wore hare-skin pelts and had branded themselves with hot irons from the forge – abstract symbols of the sand-pikey cult were engraved on every chest – and they waved dirks and tyre-irons and then a quare shake of polis back-up trudged over the Smoketown footbridge and it was noted that they were guzzling whiskey and moscato from carry-sacks as they came, and taking nips of the Beast, and howling the ritual chants of the polis frats, and they aimed headlong for the sand-pikeys who were about an equal to them in number and certainly in terms of derangement.

'Tell you one thing,' said Ol' Boy, 'this shower will keep goin' a while yet.'

Big Dom, meantime, had arranged a tushie on his lap and he was gently brushing her hair with a pearl-encrusted brush and the girl's eyes glazed with dream-sent romance.

'They'll take quare damage on both sides, Mr Mannion.'

'Much,' said Ol' Boy, 'to the Hartnett plan.'

★

272

The Gant saw her pass through the 98er Square.

He followed.

She took the turn of a wynd, and then another, and she looked back, and she saw that it was him, but she did not stop.

'Macu!'

He watched her go. He allowed her to disappear into the darkness of a sudden turn. He said beneath his breath:

'Don't ever go back to him.'

★

*'It would sweeten my bliss in this ci-ty of gold,
Should there be any stars in my-yy crooown . . .'*

★

Prince Tubby the Far-Eye's death journey was a beautiful voyage. He sailed over the clouds and across his dune-side terrain and the great spectacle once more was enacted for him.

Here was a place of wind and rain and violent starburst, where the throw of light is ever-changing, is constantly shifting, and he saw the great expanse of the bog plain, and the lamps of Bohane city, too, as they burned against the night of August Fair.

★

Wolfie Stanners sat on the stone steps cut into the river wall and he held both hands tightly against a gut wound and he closed his eyes and a fever sweat broke on his forehead as the S'town riot raged nearby.

Heard the black surge of the Bohane as it called to him.

★

Big Dom topped a fresh bottle of Beast and torched a whackload of primo Big Nothin' bushweed sourced from the pikey rez.

He squinted to bring into focus the progress of the riot:

The beak of the law was blunted by the sand-pikey assault; the pikey ferocity was dulled by polis resolve.

And lives went under, it has to be said, but as quickly as their vitals dimmed they came to again, out beneath the Nothin' plain, in the ruts and tunnels of the Bohane underworld, where the strange ferns rustle and the black dogs roam.

Meantime:

Ol' Boy Mannion nodded in the direction of the Smoketown footbridge.

'Y'watchin'?' he said.

Big Dom clocked it.

'The killer gal,' he said.

Jenni Ching surveyed the riot serenely from the high arch of the footbridge – bopped smoke rings from her pouted lips.

*

Logan knew that the boy had circled to follow him.

He could sense movement behind on the wharf.

He sighed in long-suffering.

He turned into the stockyards and slipped into the shadows to wait.

The boy Cantillon appeared.

Logan stepped out, noiselessly, and he was quick as a stoat as he took the boy's throat in a forearm lock, and he took from the boy's belt his shkelp and he drove it into his heart, and whispered to him – unrepeatable words – as the young life began to drain.

Felt the tip of that life as it tilted towards the dark but he took no savour from the moment.

He let the Cantillon boy fall and he considered for an

incredulous moment, there in the foul stockyards, the advanced stupidity of the dead kid's frozen features.

The Long Fella would not stain his dress-shkelp with such frivolous blood.

He walked on. There was a tiredness now on Logan. He knew his own line would end soon enough and, with it, his renown. The succession had been decided beyond him when he was lost to an April dream. All that was left, maybe, was the consolation of Macu's touch.

He aimed his boots for the Café Aliados.

★

'How would you imagine all this might play out, Mr Mannion?'

'Not prettily, Dom.'

★

At Blind Nora's low-rent bordello the Gant cued an old seven-incher on the turntable, and as the tune came through he felt it in the balls of his feet, and he skanked alone on the floor, and the toothless hoors on the ratty old couches grinned and hoarsely sang along, and Nora handclapped the beat, and the Gant danced slowly, and his bearing was quiet, and proud, and sane.

★

The Café Aliados was deserted but for the bar girl as Logan waited on a high stool there.

He sipped at a John Jameson.

On the cusp of midnight he slipped off the stool and went to the jukebox and he selected a slow-burner of an old calypso tune from the lost-time.

She'd know this one.

He sat again by the barside as the old music played and with an unsure hand he fixed his hair.

And at midnight precisely, on this the night of August Fair, the cut yellow flowers in a vase on the Aliados countertop trembled as the sideway door opened, and stilled again as it closed, and he turned a quiet swivel on his stool.

'Well,' she said.

A set of ninety Bohane Fairs were graven in the hard sketch lines of her face, and already he was resigned.

'Girly,' he said.

*

The night aged, and the city quietened along its length, and the young were drawn by the hard pull of their blood to the river. We throbbed with the pulse of August in Bohane.

At intervals along the wharf, on the stone steps of the river wall, the young lazed in pairs and held each other. Their lips made words – promises, devotions – and the words carried on the river's air and mingled with the words of its murmurous dead. A single voice was made in the mingling, and this voice had in mysterious ways the quality of silence, for it blocked out all else; it mesmerised.

The taint came off the water as a delicious mist.

A green lizard crept between a crack in a fall of steps and climbed across a mound of flesh and fed on the blood that caked around the gut wound of a dead boy with a black-bird's stare.

The hardwind rose and shifted the cloudbank and the rooftops emerged from the Murk – the city's shape reasserting – and now the lamplight of the city was fleet on the water. The water played its motion on the green wrack and stone of the river wall. We listened – rapt – as it carried through the city of Bohane, as it ran to the hidden sea, as the sea dragged on its cables.

Summer's reach was shortening; we would face soon

what the autumn might bring, and what the winter. But the city was content on this one night for time to slow, for a while at least, and it sent its young down to the river.

★

First ache of light was inaugural:

Jenni Ching rode bareback a Big Nothin' palomino along the Bohane front.

On either side of her mount – as its flanks worked smoothly, slowly in the ochre dawn – a half-dozen wilding girls marched in ceremonial guard – they wore cross-slung dirk-belts, groin-kicker boots, white vinyl zip-ups, black satin gym shorts – and the native gulls in the early morning were raucous above the river.

A mad-eyed black-back dived at the killer-gal Ching but she raised a glance and eyed it as madly for an answer and the gull swerved and turned and wheeled away downriver.

Jenni cried a taunt after it:

'Mmwwaaoork!'

And all the girls laughed.

The procession moved, and the chained dogs in the merchant yards along the front cowered in the cold shadows of morning, their own thin flanks rippling with fright.

Hung upon the livid air a sequence of whinnies and pleadings, the dogs, and the first taste of the new life came to Jenni

as she rode out the measured beat of her ascension and a bump of fear, too, y'check me

as she searched already the eyes of her own ranks for that yellow light, ambition's pale gleam

as she saw in the brightening sky at a slow fade the lost-time's shimmer pass.